CHERISHED
ENOUGH

OTHER BOOKS BY KELLY ELLIOTT

COMING SOON
Love in Montana (Meet Me in Montana Spin Off)
Fearless Enough
Cherished Enough
Brave Enough – August 29, 2023
Daring Enough - November 21, 2023
Loved Enough - February 6, 2024
Forever Enough - April 30, 2024
Enchanted Enough - July 23, 2024
Perfect Enough - October 15, 2024
Devoted Enough - January 7, 2025

Holidaze in Salem
A Bit of Hocus Pocus
A Bit of Holly Jolly
A Bit of Wee Luck
A Bit of Razzle Dazzle – Summer 2023

The Seaside Chronicles
Returning Home
Part of Me
Lost to You
Someone to Love
Series available on audiobook

Stand Alones
*The Journey Home**
*Who We Were**
*The Playbook**
*Made for You**
*Available on audiobook

Boggy Creek Valley Series

The Butterfly Effect*
Playing with Words*
She's the One*
Surrender to Me*
Hearts in Motion*
Looking for You*
Surprise Novella TBD
*Available on audiobook

Meet Me in Montana Series

Never Enough
Always Enough
Good Enough
Strong Enough
*Series available on audiobook

Southern Bride Series

Love at First Sight
Delicate Promises
Divided Interests
Lucky in Love
Feels Like Home
Take Me Away
Fool for You
Fated Hearts
*Series vailable on audiobook

Cowboys and Angels Series

Lost Love
Love Profound
Tempting Love
Love Again
Blind Love

This Love
Reckless Love
*Series available on audiobook

Boston Love Series
Searching for Harmony (New Edition Coming 2023)
Fighting for Love (New Edition Coming 2023)
*Series available on audiobook

Austin Singles Series
Seduce Me
Entice Me
Adore Me
*Series available on audiobook

Wanted Series
*Wanted**
*Saved**
*Faithful**
Believe
*Cherished**
*A Forever Love**
The Wanted Short Stories
All They Wanted
*Available on audiobook

Love Wanted in Texas Series
Spin-off series to the WANTED Series
Without You
Saving You
Holding You
Finding You
Chasing You
Loving You
Entire series available on audiobook
*Please note *Loving You* combines the last book of the Broken and
Love Wanted in Texas series.

Broken Series
*Broken**
*Broken Dreams**
*Broken Promises**
Broken Love
*Available on audiobook

The Journey of Love Series
Unconditional Love
Undeniable Love
Unforgettable Love
*Entire series available on audiobook

With Me Series
Stay With Me
Only With Me
*Series available on audiobook

Speed Series
Ignite
Adrenaline
*Series available on audiobook

COLLABORATIONS
Predestined Hearts (co-written with Kristin Mayer)*
Play Me (co-written with Kristin Mayer)*
*Dangerous Temptations (*co-written with Kristin Mayer*
*Available on audiobook

CHERISHED ENOUGH

KELLY ELLIOTT

Joshua Ty
Hunter Mason
Nathan Christopher
Rose Marie
Morgan Elizabeth
Lily Hope
Blayze Lucas
Tanner & Timberlynn Shaw
Ty Jr & Kaylee Shaw
Brock & Lincoln Shaw
Beck Shaw
Bradley Michael
Stella Shaw & Ty Sr Shaw
Avery Grace
Dirk & Merit Littlewood

Shaw Ranch

Shaw Ranch
HAMILTON, MONTANA

DIRK & MERIT

Hunters Cabin

Tanner & Timberlynn

Barn

Ty Sr & Stella

Brock & Lincoln

Ty Jr & Kaylee

Prologue

MORGAN

"This Halloween party sucks. We should have stayed at our dorm and studied like I suggested," Krista said as she glanced around the room.

We were at one of the frat houses for what everyone said was the most epic Halloween party on campus. So far we'd been hit on by nearly every male in the room. I watched more guys take girls up those stairs than I cared to count.

"We need to find Heather, and then we can leave."

Krista rolled her eyes. "She's probably in some room with her dress up to her waist and some guy in her—"

"Krista!" I squealed.

She gave me a befuddled look. "What? You know I'm right."

I laughed, then stood on my toes in an attempt to look over everyone.

"Would you like to dance?" a voice said from behind me. Turning to look over my shoulder, I couldn't help but smile at the guy's costume.

"A skeleton ringmaster. I love it."

He smiled back.

"Whoever did your face makeup should be given some kind of award," Krista stated.

"Thank you," he said, his voice sounding a bit muffled. "Dance?"

He held his hand out to me, and I looked over at Krista. "For fuck's sake, go dance," she said. "At least one of us needs to have some fun. I'll go find the whore."

"Krista!" I said with a pleading look.

"Fine." She rolled her eyes. "I'll go find the tramp."

I let out an exasperated sigh as my best friend turned on her heels and headed up the steps in search of the third person in our trio of friends.

Turning back to the stranger, I placed my hand in his. We weaved our way through the crowd of people on the makeshift dance floor. The frat house was in a historical home right off campus, and it looked like we were in the old ballroom.

The skeleton drew me to him, and I cleared my throat and took a step back. It was a little bit too close for my comfort.

"Sorry," he said with a wicked gleam in his eyes. "What's your name?"

"Morgan," I answered. "You?"

"Rich."

"Nice to meet you, Rich," I said as we moved to the slow song that was playing. His hand drifted a little more down my back, but I wasn't sure if I was imagining it or not.

"Are you in the frat?" I asked.

"No, my best friend is, though."

I nodded.

"Are you in a sorority?"

"God, no!" I blurted out. "Not that there's anything wrong with them. That's just not my scene."

It was his turn to nod.

"You look familiar to me," he said. "I wonder if we're in any classes together."

Looking up at him with a bit of a flirtatious grin, I replied, "I couldn't tell you since I can't see what you look like."

"Tell me you don't like the mystery of it."

"It is pretty neat," I said, laughing somewhat nervously. He was for sure moving his hand down.

"Can I kiss you, Morgan?"

Okay, that was a first. Guys didn't usually ask—they just dove in.

"Um…"

"Do you have a boyfriend?"

I shook my head as a memory of Ryan holding me while we danced resurfaced in my mind.

"Then what harm is one little kiss?"

I licked my bottom lip and noticed how he reacted to it. Pressing my mouth into a tight line, I looked around. The place was packed with people. What would the harm be? If I thought about it, I freaking deserved a kiss for staying at this stupid party for as long as I had. If a guy pinched my ass one more time, I was going to scream.

"I guess one kiss would be harmless."

He smiled, and I couldn't help but notice his perfectly straight teeth. I suddenly wanted to know what Rich looked like.

I reached up onto my toes, and he leaned down. The kiss was soft at first. Nice. He licked my bottom lip, and I opened to him. When his tongue touched mine, I could taste beer and peppermint. Gum, maybe?

He moaned and deepened the kiss. At least one of us was getting something from it because I felt nothing. He was a good kisser, but still…nothing.

When he grabbed my ass with both hands and pulled me against his body, I gasped at the feel of his hard erection. I put my hands on his chest and pushed as hard as I could.

"Stop!"

A few people turned and looked at us, and he stepped back and ran his hand through his hair. "I'm sorry."

Wiping my mouth, I exhaled. "Listen, I'm not interested in anything."

"You kissed me, though."

Frowning, I said, "That doesn't mean I want to go any further with you."

Taking a step closer, he leaned down. "Are you sure, Morgan? Because I really, really want to f—"

"Found her!" Krista said as she pushed between me and Rich. My eyes were wide with horror because I was pretty sure he'd been about to say that he wanted to fuck me.

"Great, let's go," I said as I grabbed Krista and Heather's hands and practically ran from the party.

"What was that about?" Krista asked when we got outside.

I dragged in a few deep breaths. "Christ," I said. "I hate men. The guy asked me to kiss him. I thought it would be harmless, but I swear he wanted to take me right there on the dance floor."

Krista rolled her eyes. "Men are pigs, especially when they've been drinking."

I looked at Heather. "Where were you?"

She blushed and looked away.

Krista scoffed. "About to have a threesome with two guys."

My mouth fell open. "What?"

Heather laughed. "Just because some of us are saving ourselves doesn't mean the rest of us can't play and have fun."

"You're either going to end up pregnant, or with some STD," Krista said as we hooked arms and started to walk down the street toward my car.

"There's something called a condom, Krista. You should try one," Heather said. "You need a good pounding to jolt you out of your virtue."

A strange feeling crept up my neck as I glanced over my shoulder and back at the party. My eyes scanned the outside and porch, but thankfully, I didn't see the skeleton ringmaster guy.

Facing forward again, I shook off the feeling and counted down the days until I got to go home and see my family.

And Ryan.

Ringmaster

I watched her walk away with her two friends. My mouth still tasted of her. It wasn't enough. I wanted more. The sting of her rejection burned, but I needed to remind myself that she wasn't like her whore of a friend, Heather. Morgan was a good girl.

And good girls were always worth the wait.

Chapter One

Morgan

Christmas Eve Night - Present Day

I stood and stared at the building in front of me. The Coming Soon sign was the first thing I'd seen when my older brother Blayze removed his hand from my eyes. My gaze went to the store name, and I was pretty sure my breathing stopped.

A La Chic Boutique – Owners, Georgiana Crenshaw and Morgan Shaw.

I'd told Georgiana, Blayze's girlfriend, that if I ever opened my own boutique, I wanted to call it something with the word "chic" in the name. We'd been in England at the time because Georgiana was writing a fashion piece for *Vogue* and had invited me to come over with her for a week. I had jumped at the chance since she was interviewing one of the top up-and-coming designers, Lady Mary Douglas.

Georgiana had replied with, "How about A La Chic Boutique?"

"I love it!" I'd squealed, writing the name in my dream journal. It was something I'd started when I was only ten. My mother's idea. She had given it to me on my tenth birthday while we were out riding. It was a place to record all my dreams, she'd said. And I had written down a *lot* of dreams over the years, but becoming a designer had always been the most enduring one.

Of course, there'd also been the dream of having Ryan Marshall, my brother's best friend, fall madly and deeply in love with me. But I learned how to push that dream away.

The feeling of warm tears on my cheeks pulled me back to the present.

"Morgan? Are you going to say anything?" Georgiana asked.

As I wiped the tears away, my brother wrapped his arm around me and said softly, "Not to rush you and this experience, but the snow is coming down harder and I can't feel the tip of my nose anymore."

Leave it to Blayze to lighten the mood. I looked at Georgiana with what I was sure was a dumbfounded expression. "A *boutique*? You really want to open a boutique and have me be your partner?"

Georgiana nodded and let out a soft chuckle. "Not only my partner. I want you to design a line of clothing that's exclusive to the store. Morgan, you're crazy talented and your work needs to be featured. Mary agrees."

Oh. My. Gosh. I pressed my hand to my mouth as a sob slipped free, along with more tears. I looked back at the building in shock. Was this even possible? Could all my dreams literally be coming true right now? Well, almost all of them. There was still the Ryan dream. I was still secretly head over heels for him. That thought was for another time though.

"If you need time to think about it, I completely understand," Georgiana said. "I know you have a semester of school left and—"

"Yes!" I screamed out. A group of people walking by all turned to stare.

"She's just excited about a new clothing store coming soon," Blayze stated with a bemused expression that said he was sorry for my crazy outburst.

I wanted to throw myself at Georgiana. "Oh my God, yes! Georgiana, this is my dream. I never imagined it would come true so soon. I don't know what to say. I mean, I'm broke, and I'm not sure how I'm supposed to help pay for this."

Blayze and Georgiana both laughed, then she replied, "You'll more than make up for that with your clothing line. Besides, your father and mine are helping us both reach this dream by backing us financially until we can start turning a profit."

I wiped my tears away and then threw myself at Georgiana, causing her to nearly stumble back. I couldn't control my emotions as I cried into her coat, repeatedly saying "thank you" and telling her how much I adored her and couldn't wait for her to be my sister-in-law.

Pushing me back to arm's length, Georgiana said, "Sweetie, I can't understand a word you're saying."

"I don't know how to thank you!" Turning to my brother, I blurted out, "You have to thank her for me with some amazing sex or…or…like a trip somewhere!"

Blayze's face went red and he blinked at me a few times. "You couldn't have just suggested taking her on an amazing trip?"

I waved off his comment. "Really, Georgiana, thank you so much for this opportunity. I love you!"

"Oh Lord, here come more tears," Blayze mumbled as Georgiana started to cry, which made me cry all over again.

He rolled his eyes. "Okay, let's take this back to the truck where there's heat and at least your tears won't freeze on your faces."

Blayze and Georgiana dropped me off at my grandparents' place, and I discovered that some family and friends were still there. I rushed into the house and ran to my father first, throwing myself into his arms.

"Daddy, thank you so much! Thank you!"

He laughed as he wrapped his arms around me. "I'm so proud of you, Morgan.

Looking up at him, I smiled. "I couldn't have done this without you and Mom."

He winked. "I like to think we might have had some small part in it, but it's all you, pumpkin. You're the one with the talent."

I buried my face against his chest, then felt the warmth of another person behind me. I knew instantly it was my mother. Turning, I fell into her embrace.

"Mom," was all I could manage to get out before I started to cry again.

Kissing my temple, she whispered, "You're going to do amazing things, baby girl."

When I drew back, I caught sight of Ryan watching the exchange. My heart did that familiar flutter it always did when it came to my brother's best friend. He was a few years older than me, twenty-six, and the only man I'd ever truly had a crush on.

Okay, maybe you could call it a crush when I was ten. Now it was more like I lay in bed at night and pictured him as I slipped my hands between my legs. And there were times when he looked at me, and I swore he felt the same way.

He smiled, and I returned it before quickly looking away. It was easier for me to pretend like I wasn't secretly in love with the guy. Easy enough, since most of the time I was angry with him, which caused us to bicker. I knew he probably had no idea why I was so bitter. But the hurt he'd caused me two years ago felt as fresh now as it had back then. He'd flirted with me at a charity dance, causing me to think he might feel the same way, only to shatter my heart the next morning.

I had decided to bite the bullet and go to his house to tell him how I felt about him. What I hadn't expected was to see him standing on his front porch, kissing Emma Myers, right before she told him she'd had a wonderful night. When Ryan had glanced up and saw me, I'd quickly turned and rushed away. Even now, I still prayed he hadn't seen the tear rolling down my cheek that morning.

After that, I decided I needed to forget about Ryan Marshall and move on. Easier said than done.

Thoughts are much easier than action. I was still hung up on the bastard—though "hung up" might not be a strong enough description for how I felt about him.

Rose and Avery, two of my many cousins, rushed over and demanded I tell them everything about the boutique. I was soon surrounded by family who wanted to know what was happening.

My father had two brothers—Uncle Ty and Uncle Tanner. They lived on our family ranch with their respective wives, Aunt Kaylee and Aunt Timberlynn, and each had two kids. Ty and Kaylee were the parents of Rose Marie and Joshua. Tanner and Timberlynn had Lily and Nathan. We'd all grown up together on the ranch as one huge, happy family, and my cousins felt more like siblings to me and my brothers, Blayze and Hunter.

Then, of course, you had Uncle Dirk and Aunt Merit. They weren't really blood related, but it felt like they were. Bradly and Avery Grace were their kids. They lived on a ranch not far from ours. Needless to say, when we had family gatherings, there was a lot of chaos. I knew my grams and grandpa loved it. Even Bradly and Avery Grace called them that, instead of Stella and Ty Senior.

And Ryan...well, he'd always been part of the family, since he was Blayze's ride-or-die best friend.

Only a few minutes later, I felt my entire body tingle when Ryan walked up behind me.

"Were you surprised?" he asked softly, his breath only inches from the skin under my ear.

Turning, I forced myself to breathe normally and act as if his presence wasn't playing havoc with my body. "Very surprised! I'm in shock, and I'm not really sure I deserve this opportunity that Georgiana and my parents are giving me."

"Nonsense," Ryan said. "You're talented, Morgan, and you're going to do wonderful things. Not only for Hamilton, but for yourself as well."

How did Ryan know I was talented? "Well, you can say that, but have you ever seen anything I've designed?" I asked with a nervous chuckle.

"Of course, I have," he retorted—then looked as if he regretted the words the moment he'd said them.

My heart picked up, pounding in my ears. "When?"

He gave me a one-shoulder shrug. "I think Blayze showed me a few of your designs before."

I raised a brow. "Really? And you thought they were good?"

Ryan's expression softened. "Yes. I mean, I have no idea about fashion, but they were...um...really nice. Very pretty. For a girl. I guess."

Feeling my cheeks heat at his compliment, I looked away for a moment before I focused back on him. "Thank you, Ryan. That means a lot coming from you."

He smiled, and my stomach flipped. "You're welcome, Morgan. I really am happy for you."

There it was. That look he gave me. It made my insides melt and my heart feel as if it would beat right out of my chest. When his eyes drifted down to my mouth, I instinctively licked my lips, and I swore his eyes sparked with desire.

My grandmother, Stella, walked up and handed Ryan a bag. "Ryan, I packed you some leftovers and made sure to put a piece of Timberlynn's cheesecake in there, along with pieces of apple, pumpkin, and cherry pie."

Ryan's eyes went wide with surprise, and I covered my smile with my hand. "Three pieces of pie and a piece of cheesecake? You do realize it's only me eating this, Stella."

Grams winked. "You never know when someone might stop by and want a bite to eat."

I couldn't ignore the twinge of jealousy that zipped through me at my grandmother's statement.

He smiled. "Considering I live alone, and my best friend is currently falling all over Georgiana, I'm going to assume it'll only be me eating all of this."

Patting Ryan on the chest, Grams smiled back at him. "You're a hardworking young man, you could use the energy." And with that, she walked back toward the kitchen.

Ryan looked at me, his brows raised. "Does she really think I can eat all of this food alone?"

I nodded. "I'm afraid so. You, um…you aren't seeing anyone?"

He let out a gruff laugh as he raked a hand through his brown hair. "No. I don't have time to date."

Okay, why does that totally sound like a lie?

When his caramel-brown eyes met my blue gaze, he asked, "Are you? Seeing anyone?"

I shook my head. "Senior year is pretty packed, and I'm busy focusing on my classes."

"That's good. I mean, it's smart of you to focus on school."

Nodding, I let my gaze fall to his mouth, wondering what a kiss from him would feel like.

"Well," Ryan said, causing me to jerk my gaze back up to his. "I'm sure I'll see you before you head back to school."

"Probably. I'll be with Dad when he picks up Starlight from you guys."

His eyes lit up when I mentioned the cutting horse his father had been training for my dad. Ryan's parents, Tina and Bobby, owned a horse ranch called High Meadows Stables, where they trained and raised performance horses. Ryan's love of horses was one of the things that first caused me to fall in—

Nope, you're not going there anymore, Morgan. Remember?

"Great. She was a sweet girl to work with. I think your dad will be really happy with her."

"I'm sure he will be," I said as I smiled.

"Okay, well…see you around, Morgan."

With a quick nod, I replied, "See you around, Ryan."

After he turned and walked away, I watched him make his rounds as he said goodbye to everyone. He saved Grams and Grandpa for last. He hugged my grandmother and most likely said something flirty, because she blushed like a schoolgirl. He shook Granddad's hand, then headed out through the house.

I stood there, debating if I should follow him or stay where I was.

Turning, I looked around the room. It was clearing out and most everyone was gone. Deciding I wasn't ready to say good-night to Ryan yet, I hurried in the same direction. By the time I got to the foyer, he was gone.

I opened the door to see snow still falling. Ryan was at his truck, slipping inside the cab. I opened my mouth to call out, but then clamped it shut and quickly stepped back into the house, shutting the door before he saw me standing there like a silly girl.

Turning, I dropped back against the door and let out a long sigh as I closed my eyes and rubbed at the slight ache in my chest.

"Damn you, Ryan Marshall. Damn you."

Chapter Two

Ryan

Six Months Later - Early June

"How can one person have so much stuff?" Hunter asked as he pulled another box of his sister's belongings from the back of his truck. "I thought you lived in a dorm."

I took a smaller box out and handed it to Morgan while she glared at her younger brother. She looked beautiful today. But then, I thought she looked beautiful every day. Her light brown hair was pulled up into a ponytail, and her blue eyes seemed to match the color of the clear sky above.

"For your information, Hunter, I lived in a two-bedroom house for the past three years."

Hunter paused for a moment, then grinned. "That's right, with your hot roommate. What was her name again? Heather! That's it."

Morgan rolled her eyes and headed over to the stairs that led up to her apartment on the third floor above her boutique. Construction was nearly done on the store and the second floor, which housed storage, an office, and a design studio for Morgan. The third floor was a two-bedroom flat where Morgan would be living. Her dad, Brock, had started the construction pretty much the day after Christmas to get everything ready to open by summer. Right now, opening day was set for June 30th.

"And the security system is in?" I heard Brock ask Blayze.

"Yes, Dad. I told you I'd make sure that was set and ready to go when she moved in," Blayze said, catching my eye right before they both walked by to grab more boxes.

"My dad is driving Blayze crazy," Morgan said conspiratorially as she bounced up the three flights of stairs ahead of me. I wasn't sure where in the hell the girl got her energy. We'd been up and down these steps what felt like a hundred times already. I was tired, and I'd only been unloading stuff into her second-floor studio.

"You're going to have the best-looking legs in Hamilton with all these stairs," Avery, Morgan's younger cousin, said as she passed us going back down to grab another box.

"I know!" Morgan said and I heard the excitement in her voice. I was happy her dreams were coming true, and even happier she was going to be staying in Hamilton. One of my biggest fears had been that she'd move to Paris or New York City to pursue her fashion design career. Lucky for me, her future sister-in-law had gotten her to stay in town by partnering with her on the boutique.

I walked into the flat and let out a whistle. "This is nice."

Morgan beamed. "Right? You haven't seen it yet, so let me show you around."

Letting Morgan grab my hand, I attempted to ignore the zip of energy that raced from the contact between our fingers.

She looked at me and grinned. "I love the open feel it has up here."

I nodded as I looked around the large room. I already knew that when you took the stairs at the back of the building, you passed through a small laundry area off Morgan's bedroom. When you walked in from the street-level entrance, as we had, there was a stairwell that took you to a third-floor door leading straight into her living room. The sofa was to the left, with a coffee table and two chairs opposite it. On the wall across from the sitting area was a large TV with built-in bookcases on either side.

The opposite side of the room had a galley-style kitchen, and a table with four chairs separated the living and kitchen areas.

"It's bigger than I thought it would be," I said as Morgan walked straight ahead and into what I guessed was her bedroom. It was pretty big, with a king-size bed and a large dresser. My gaze wandered over to her bed, and I tried hard not to picture her naked on the soft bedding.

She opened the door to her bathroom. "Look at that shower and the huge tub!"

I instantly pictured Morgan pressed against the wall of the walk-in shower while I pushed inside her…or us soaking in the tub, Morgan resting back against me while I gently rubbed my hands over her body.

"Are you okay?" she asked, shaking me from the erotic movie playing in my head.

"Ah…yeah. It's beautiful."

She stared at me for a moment, and I swore she could feel the crackle of electricity between us.

"Are you a shower kind of guy or a bath kind of guy?"

I glanced over at the tub, then back to Morgan. "If I had *that* tub, I suppose I'd be a bath kind of guy."

Morgan bit down on her lower lip for a moment before she let out a breathy, "Oh."

"You said it was two bedrooms?" I asked, just to get us the fuck out of the bathroom.

"Yes! The other bedroom is this way."

Once again, she grabbed my hand and led me back through her room and down a short hall off the living room. "There's a bathroom there, then the guest bedroom is right here."

I looked inside to find a queen-size bed and a smaller dresser. "It's nice."

"It's great to have two bedrooms in case anyone wants to stay."

I looked at her and nodded.

"I mean, like Rose or Lily or Avery. One of the girls."

Smiling, I replied, "That'll be fun."

"Wait! I didn't show you the best part of my room!"

I followed her back toward her room, missing the contact of her hand in mine. When we walked back inside, I noticed more built-in bookshelves. I'd been so focused on the goddamn bed, I'd missed half the room.

"I like the built-ins," I said.

"That's my favorite part. Well, except for the balcony that my dad had added on. There's a small one off the kitchen and living room that looks out onto Main, but this one is more private and looks out over the small courtyard in the back. I mean, you can see the parking lot as well, but that's okay."

We both stepped outside, and I drew in a deep breath. Summer was here, and the air was crisp and smelled like flowers. In a few short months it might be filled with smoke if we got any wildfires. But we'd had a wetter than normal winter and spring, so I was hoping that wouldn't be the case.

"I bet it'll be great out here at night."

Morgan nodded as she leaned over the rail. "I can't wait to decorate it for fall and Christmas."

I laughed again, and she turned to face me. "I'm actually not far from your place," I said.

Right out of college, when I'd thought I needed to be on my own, I'd bought a small house close to downtown Hamilton. Slipping my hands into my pockets, I blew out a breath. "Or, I used to be. I sold my house."

Her eyes went wide. "What? Why?"

With a half shrug, I replied, "I think I was going through a rebellion phase when I bought it straight out of college. I'm back at my parents' ranch now. I've been looking for something with a bit of land to build on someday."

"I see," she said with a smile. "Are you living with your parents then?"

I shook my head. "Above the barn on the ranch."

"Oh, wow. Easy commute."

"Roll right out of bed and head to work." I winked, noticing how her eyes seemed to flare at the action.

"Morgan! Morgan!" Avery called out.

She pushed away from the railing and headed back into her bedroom, with me following behind.

"I'm in here," Morgan shouted.

Avery burst into the room, a bouquet of flowers in her hand. "These were delivered for you!"

I watched Morgan's face light up. "From who?" she asked, taking the flowers and walking back into the living area. She set the bouquet on the kitchen counter, opened the card, and started reading it out loud. "Congratulations on your new adventure, Morgan. I cannot wait to see you thrive."

She jerked her head up and looked at the now-full room. Brock, Blayze, Lincoln, and Hunter all stood there as well, smiles on their faces.

"Who's it from?" Avery asked.

Morgan glanced back down at the card and slowly shook her head. "It's not signed."

"What's not signed?" Georgiana asked as she stepped next to Blayze and set down a box.

"The card," Morgan answered. "Did you send me flowers?"

Georgiana pointed to herself. "Me? No."

"Did you get flowers too?" Avery asked.

With a shake of her head, Georgiana smiled at Morgan. "Secret admirer?"

When Morgan glanced my way, it actually pissed me off that I had to say the flowers weren't from me. One, because I hadn't thought of sending her flowers, and two, it meant someone *else* had—and that someone probably had a crush on Morgan.

"You didn't send them either?" Morgan asked with what I swore was a hint of disappointment in her voice.

Sheepishly looking at the flowers and then at her, I replied, "No, I'm sorry. I wish I'd thought of it, though."

That seemed to make her brighten up a bit.

"You have a secret admirer, Morgan!" Avery enthused. "I wonder who it is?"

Glancing back down at the card, Morgan grinned. "I guess I do."

Annoyed, I watched Avery and Morgan start to name off potential people who could have sent them.

With a loud clap, Brock got everyone's attention. "Let's go, folks! The rest of those boxes won't carry themselves up here."

Hunter groaned while Blayze laughed. The latter fell in step next to me and bumped my shoulder. "Be careful, Ryan."

"Of?" I asked, a note of frustration in my voice.

"From the way you were glaring at those flowers and clenching your fists, people might think you've got a thing for my sister."

I stopped walking and watched Blayze continue on, a slight chuckle slipping free as he descended the steps.

Georgiana walked past me and squeezed my arm, giving me a sympathetic smile. "Maybe next time you'll beat whoever it is to the punch."

"Wait—what?" I asked as she skipped down the steps... whistling what I was almost positive was "So This is Love" from *Cinderella*.

Chapter Three

Morgan

Opening my eyes, I couldn't help but smile when it slowly sank in where I was. In my very own apartment, above a store I co-owned with my future sister-in-law. Not to mention my very own design studio was directly beneath me, where I would soon get back to work on a line of clothing exclusive to our boutique. The first few designs had already arrived from the company we'd hired here in Montana to make them. To say I was over the moon was an understatement.

But despite so many exciting things happening, I still felt like something was missing.

I stretched my arms and legs before I sat up. With one look to my right, I smiled once again.

The flowers.

Who in the world could have sent them to me? And was Ryan's reaction just my imagination, or had he seemed bothered by them? Avery and Georgiana also thought Ryan seemed peeved about the flowers.

I swung my legs over the bed and stood. One more stretch, and then I was off to shower before heading to the gym to get in a workout. I had a ton of things to do today, but I wasn't about to start blowing off my exercise routine. Most days, it was the only thing that kept me grounded.

An hour later, I walked into the gym that was only a few blocks down from my new place. I'd been a member since I was a senior in high school, and I was glad to finally be back in town and able to go regularly.

"Morning, Morgan!" Sylvia said from behind the front desk.

Holding my card out for her to scan, I replied, "Good morning!"

"Here for the spin or yoga class?"

I snarled my lip and groaned as I answered, "Spin."

Laughing, she replied, "Be careful, your excitement's almost too much."

"Have a good one," I called out, smiling over my shoulder. As I turned to face forward again, I slammed into something hard.

Instantly, I knew who it was from the way my body seemed to come alive.

"Ryan," I gasped as he took hold of my upper arms to steady me.

"Are you okay?"

I nodded. He was the last person I thought I'd see at the gym at seven in the morning. "What are you doing here?" I asked.

The corner of his mouth twitched before he answered, "Working out."

I let out an awkward laugh. "Right. Sorry. I guess I assumed that since you're living out at the ranch you wouldn't be driving to the gym so early."

"It wasn't a big deal this morning. I spent the night right off Cherry Street and Fifth."

I felt my brows draw down. Was Ryan dating someone? Had he stayed at her house last night?

"Oh. Girlfriend?" I asked before I could stop myself.

He smiled at me, and my stomach did a little flip. "No, no girlfriend. Buddy of mine I went to high school with recently got married. I was at his and his new wife's house pet sitting for them last night. Her mother's taking over today. She should be getting here sometime this morning from Billings."

"Pet sitting?" I asked with a teasing smile. "What kind of dog?"

He blushed, and I felt my smile turn into a full-on grin. This was going to be good.

Ryan cleared his throat and mumbled something as he looked away.

"I'm sorry, I didn't quite get that. What kind of dog is it?"

He looked back at me, clearly frustrated, and tilted his head in the most adorable way. "It's not a dog."

"Cat?" I asked.

Ryan rolled his eyes. "It's a rabbit."

"A rabbit? You're pet sitting a *rabbit*?"

"In my defense, they do have an outdoor cat that presented me with breakfast this morning by dropping a dead mouse at my feet."

I wrinkled my nose. "Gross!"

He nodded. "I thought so too."

Laughing, I took a step away from him, instantly missing the heat from his body. "I better get to class."

"Spin?"

"Yep. See you around."

He didn't say anything, following me as I started to walk toward the room where spin class took place. I glanced over my shoulder and gave him a questioning look.

"I'm not following you. I'm heading to spin class too."

"Really? Cool."

He nodded. Once we stepped into the room, two women about Ryan's age quickly rushed toward us.

"Ryan! I was hoping you'd make it today."

The other woman, her brown hair pulled up into a pony, put a hand on his arm possessively. "I saved you a bike."

"Thanks, Katie."

She flashed him a smile and directed him over to a couple of bikes across the room. I scowled and looked away.

"You new in town?" a male voice asked from behind me. Turning, I glanced over my shoulder to see a guy maybe a couple years older than me—twenty-four or so—sitting on his bike, ready to work out.

"Good morning," I said, putting my drink in the holder and draping my towel over the handlebars. "Born and raised in Hamilton."

He lifted his brow. "Really?"

"Yep. You?"

"Moved here about six months ago when my then-fiancée decided she wanted to live in the mountains."

"Then-fiancée? What happened?"

He laughed. "She hated it, I loved it. She moved back to New York, and I stayed here."

"Wow. I'm sorry things didn't work out with you guys."

Flashing me a dead-sexy grin, he winked. "I'm not."

The smile and the wink were nice, but they didn't make my insides want to melt like butter on a hot roll. I politely offered my hand. "Morgan Shaw."

His handshake was firm yet not tight to the point where he was trying to prove he was the more dominant one. "Pete Bennet."

"Nice to meet you, Pete Bennet."

"The same goes for you, Morgan Shaw."

I smiled at him before I turned to climb onto my bike. I glanced over at Ryan, and he looked away when our eyes met. Katie was going on and on about something, but it didn't appear Ryan was paying attention to a damn thing she said.

"Okay, class! Let's get ready to move those bodies! And if you're new, I don't do well with complainers!" the animated instructor announced.

An hour later, I slid off my bike and nearly fell to the ground. Good ol' Pete was right there to lend a helping hand.

"Wow, I take it you haven't been to a spin class in a while."

"What gave it away? Me in dead last on the board, or my wobbly legs?"

Pete laughed. "Both."

"Thanks, I'm good now," I said as I looked down at where his hand was still on my arm.

He quickly pulled away. "Right, sorry."

"No worries."

Pete was about to say something else when Ryan walked up. "How'd you like the class?"

Turning my attention to the handsome man I'd been lusting over for years, I grinned. "It was great. But I'm afraid I haven't got my bike legs steady just yet."

Ryan laughed, and I wanted to close my eyes and memorize the sound. "Need help?"

Pete, nice guy that he was, stepped between me and Ryan. "I've got this."

When Ryan raised a single brow, I almost started to laugh. "You've got what?" he asked.

Pete looked confused.

"Thank you, Pete," I said, "but I actually know him, so you don't have to hang around."

Pete looked surprised that I'd told him to leave. "You... know him?"

I nodded.

Looking back at Ryan, Pete scowled before focusing back on me and smiling. "Okay, well...if you're sure you're alright."

Crossing my heart, I held up two fingers. "Swear, I'm fine. Thank you, though."

He smiled again and gave me a bob of his head before he turned and headed out of the room.

Ryan watched him leave, then looked back at me. "Do you need help?"

Rolling my eyes, I felt my cheeks burn with embarrassment. "I think I'm fine now. I'm sure your friend Katie never has this problem."

Oh. My. God. Where had that come from?

"Katie?" Ryan asked, seeming confused.

"Did you forget her name already?" I said with a smirk. He stared at me for a moment, and I hated that I sounded like a jealous idiot.

"She's been coming here as long as I have."

"Well, don't let me hold you up from...um...from...anything."

"Did you walk here?"

An obvious change of subject. "I did."

"How about you let me give you a ride back to your place, and maybe next time you don't come to the advanced class."

My mouth fell open. "Is that why it was so freaking hard?"

Ryan laughed once again, and goodness, did it do things to my lady parts.

"Were you going to take a shower?" I asked.

"Nah," he said, motioning for me to walk ahead of him.

With a shaky start, I soon got my legs working. "I think I'm okay now. Note to self: check the classes."

"Offer's still on the table if you'd like a ride back."

I chewed on my lower lip for a moment before I shrugged. "Yeah, I think I'll take you up on it."

The corners of his mouth rose slightly, and we walked out of the spin classroom and through the gym. I wasn't sure if it was my imagination, but it felt like people were watching us leave together.

Shaking off the weird vibe, I waved goodbye to Sylvia with a promise that I'd be back tomorrow.

Ryan walked to the passenger side of his truck and opened the door. He held out his hand, and for a moment I wanted to ignore it—girl power and all—but knowing my legs were about to cramp up, I took his offer of help. Nothing wrong with accepting a little chivalry.

After he shut the door, I watched him walk around the front and jump in. The second his truck started, the radio blared—and I jumped and let out a scream.

"Jesus H, Ryan! Are you freaking deaf?"

He quickly turned it off and gave me a look of apology. "Sorry, I was listening to a podcast and I always need to turn them up."

Hmmm, intriguing that he would listen to a podcast. "What kind of podcast?"

"I listen to all sorts of them, but my mother got me hooked on this one. I don't advise listening to it, especially if you live alone."

"Why?"

"It's a crime podcast called *The Dark Night*."

"Oh, maybe I *should* listen to it."

Ryan shook his head. "I don't think that's a good idea, Morgan."

Folding my arms over my chest, I asked, "And why not?"

"You live alone. You'll be terrified."

I glared at him. "Because I'm a girl?"

Ryan nodded. "Yes. *And* you live alone."

"You mentioned that."

He shrugged. "Suit yourself. But don't complain to me when it creeps you out."

Huffing, I stared out the front window. The first thing I'd do when I got the chance was download an episode of that stupid podcast.

The drive to my place from the gym was a quick one. "Do you mind parking out front?" I asked. "I want to see how things are going with the store."

"Sure thing." He parked directly in front of the boutique, and we both got out.

"Wow, they're moving along fast," he said as we stepped into the store.

I couldn't help but smile. "I know. They said they should be finished right in time for the opening."

"Blayze says Georgiana is beside herself with nerves and excitement."

"I feel the same."

"It's going to be great, Morgan."

Turning to look at him, my breath caught in my chest. He was so damn handsome, and that smile of his would surely be my downfall one day when I finally fell to my knees and confessed that I wanted him.

"Morgan? How are you?"

I spun around to see David Keller, an old high school friend of mine, entering the shop behind us. His father owned the construction company in charge of the renovations.

"David! It's so great to see you!"

After a quick hug, I motioned between him and Ryan. "Do you guys know each other?"

"Afraid not," David said as he reached out to shake Ryan's hand.

"Ryan Marshall, it's a pleasure to meet you."

"David Keller, pleasure's all mine. Your father owns High Meadows Stables, the horse ranch right outside of town, right?"

A wide smile erupted across Ryan's face. "He does."

"My girlfriend, Jenn, brought her horse in to be trained for barrel riding. She's been winning left and right."

"That's good to hear. I'll be sure to let my mother know."

David nodded. "Please do. Listen, I better get to work. Great meeting you, Ryan, and I'll talk to you soon, Morgan."

"Bye, David," I said.

After taking a quick tour of the store to see the progress on the renovation, I stepped out the back door and into the courtyard. Ryan was still inside, talking to someone he knew on the crew. I lifted my face and let the bright sun shine down on me. It felt so good to have warm weather after the freezing-cold winter and spring.

A sudden shiver swept over me, and I quickly straightened and looked around. I had the strong feeling someone was watching me, but there was no one else in the courtyard.

"Sun feel good?"

Ryan's voice instantly put me at ease. I wanted to ask him how long he'd been standing there. Maybe it was his gaze that I'd felt. Instead, I just said, "Feels amazing."

He smiled. "I'm going to take off. I hope your legs get to feeling better."

I felt my cheeks heat. "That's what I get for not paying attention to the class level."

Ryan drew in a breath, and I assumed he was going to say goodbye. Instead, he asked, "Did you ever find out who sent you the flowers?"

I was so caught off guard by the question, I stared at him for a long moment. Finally snapping myself to attention, I shook my head. "No. No clue who it was."

He gave me a single nod and then pushed off the door he'd been leaning against. He opened his mouth to say something else, and I found myself holding my breath.

He simply smiled and said, "I'll see you around, Morgan."

My heart felt like it dropped to my stomach. I didn't know what I expected. Maybe an invite to dinner?

Oh, stop it, Morgan. He clearly doesn't see you that way.

Forcing a smile, I replied, "Sure. See you."

I watched Ryan walk around the corner to the small alley that separated the building I lived in from the bakery next door.

After exhaling a long breath as soon as he was gone, I slowly turned and made my way up the back stairs to my apartment, ignoring the way I suddenly felt very alone.

Chapter Four

RYAN

My phone buzzed on the nightstand, and I sat up in bed and looked at the clock. It was two in the morning. No one would be calling me in the middle of the night unless it was an emergency.

Reaching for my phone, I saw Morgan's name. My gut clenched as I quickly answered.

"Morgan? What's wrong?"

"Hey, Ryan!" she said in a voice that was far too chipper for the middle of the night.

"Is everything okay?" I asked, scrubbing a hand over my face.

She paused for so long, I started to panic. "Morgan? Are you okay?!"

"I am! Sorry. And everyone else is fine."

"Okay," I slowly said. "Then why are you calling me at two in the morning?"

I heard a nervous laugh come through the phone. "It's... well...I've got this problem. It's not a *big* problem, just a little one."

I threw the covers off me and swung my legs over the side of my bed. "Tell me what's going on."

"Well...you see...I was trying to prove you wrong."

"Prove me wrong about what?"

"Um...the podcast..."

Closing my eyes, I attempted not to sound frustrated. "You started listening to *The Dark Night,* didn't you?"

"In my defense, I thought you were being a little over the top with the whole 'you live alone and you'll get scared' bullshit!"

"But?" I asked, now smiling because I simply couldn't help myself.

"Their damn tagline is 'danger lurks beneath the covers.' I'm scared to death to get out of bed and I have to pee! *Really* badly!"

I laughed. "So you want to pee with me on the phone?"

She paused for a moment before she spoke. "I'd like to pee, but...mostly I don't want to be here alone. I'm so creeped out!"

Frowning, I asked, "What do you want me to do?"

"I was thinking you might be able to come over and, you know...check around the apartment and make sure no one's here? I called Hunter, but he didn't answer."

My mouth fell open.

"Ryan?"

I pushed a hand through my hair. "You want me to drive into town, so I can check your apartment for murderers?"

"Also so I can pee!"

"Morgan...have you been drinking?"

"What? No!"

I sighed. "I'm not driving over there in the middle of the night. You have an alarm; you'd know if someone had gotten into the house."

"But this is all your fault!"

"How is this *my* fault?" I asked with a disbelieving laugh.

"You all but dared me to listen to the podcast!"

"What?" I huffed. "I told you *not* to listen to it. I told you it would scare you."

Morgan made some kind of growling sound. "You said it was because I was a woman, and you eluded to women being scaredy cats!"

"And I was right."

A muted crash sounded from the other end of the line and Morgan let out an ear-piercing scream.

"What was that?" I asked when I heard the sound of an alarm. I got up and started pulling on sweatpants and a T-shirt so fast, I was positive I did it in record time. "*Morgan*?"

"The alarm for the shop is going off! I think someone threw something through the glass down there."

"Is your alarm on?"

"Yes," she said, her voice riddled with fear.

"Do *not* move. Lock your bedroom door and stay in that room, do you hear me?"

"Y-yes. Ryan?"

I grabbed my keys and raced down the steps to the barn and out to my truck. "Yes?"

"I'm *really* scared now!"

"I'm in the truck, sweetheart. I'll be there as fast as I can. Call the police."

"I hear sirens. I think the police are already coming."

"I don't care, Morgan. Call nine-one-one. I'm on my way."

"O-okay. Be careful."

"Hang up, sweetheart, and call right now."

There were a few beats of silence before she replied, "'Kay. Bye."

The moment she hung up, I called Blayze.

"Ryan?" he mumbled sleepily. "What's wrong?"

"The alarm at the store is going off. Morgan said it sounded like the glass was broken. She's calling the police now."

I could hear Blayze already moving on the other end of the line. "Hold on. Georgiana got a call from the alarm company a couple minutes ago, but her phone was on silent."

Fuck! "I'm already on my way there," I said as I blew past stop signs and pushed harder on the gas.

"Wait—Morgan called you first?"

I wasn't sure how this was going to sound, but at the moment, I could care less. "I was already on the phone with her when it happened."

"And she's okay?"

"When I last talked to her, she was. I told her to lock herself in her bedroom, then I made her hang up and call the police. Wait, she's calling me back now."

"The alarm company just notified Georgiana that the police have arrived. We're on our way."

"Okay, see you there in a few."

I hit End and picked up the other call. "Morgan?"

"The police are here. I mean, they're down in the store *and* here in my apartment. One officer said it looks like someone threw a big rock through the window."

"I'm almost there." The moment I heard her start crying, my entire world flipped upside down. I was going to kill whoever did this. "Don't cry, sweetheart."

A few sobs slipped free before she managed to say, "Of all the nights I picked to listen to a damn true crime podcast!"

◆ ◆ ◆

Morgan sat on her sofa with her legs drawn up and her arms wrapped around them. I could see she was still shaking, even though she was trying hard to act like she was okay. I sat next to her and held out the hot tea Georgiana had made.

"Here's the tea," I said quietly, waiting for her to take it. Blayze sat on her other side, and Lincoln was in the chair opposite the sofa.

"Thank you," Morgan replied softly as she reached for the mug. Her hands shook, and I had to hold back the rage I felt for the person who'd scared her.

Brock walked into the apartment, a scowl on his face. "The police seem to think it was teenagers messing around. There were a couple other businesses hit as well."

Morgan took a shaky breath, and I thought I saw her shoulders relax a little.

"Why don't you come on back to the ranch tonight, Morgan?" Brock suggested.

"No," she replied. "I was a bit rattled, that's all."

Lincoln stood, walked over, and sat on the coffee table in front of her daughter. Taking her hand, she said, "Of course you were. Anyone would be. I think your father is right, though. You should come home. Just for tonight."

Morgan shook her head, giving her mother a soft smile. "Honestly, Mom, I'm fine. I don't want to leave. Besides, Ryan is staying the night in the guest room."

My gaze whipped to Morgan, then around the room. All eyes were on me—and I found myself focusing on Brock more than anyone else.

"Is he?" Brock asked at the same time I said, "I am?"

Before I could even utter another word, Blayze stood. "Okay, then it's settled. Ryan's going to stay. I'll be sure to follow up with the police tomorrow. It's late; I think we should all head on home." He looked down at Morgan. "If you're okay with that?"

She nodded. "I'm exhausted and ready for some sleep."

Lincoln stood and kissed Morgan on the forehead. "You're sure you want to stay here?"

Morgan dropped her legs and stood. "I am. And like I said, Ryan will be here."

I forced myself to nod when Lincoln gave me a smile.

"Thank you, darling, for staying with her."

"Um…of course."

Lincoln stepped around the table and Morgan followed. Brock walked up to her. "You call us if you need anything, pumpkin. Got it?"

Morgan kissed her father on the cheek. "I will, Daddy."

Brock turned to face me—and I readied myself for whatever was about to come.

"Thank you for staying with her tonight, Ryan. I feel better knowing you're here…that she's not alone."

Okay, not what I'd expected. But he wouldn't be saying that if he knew the dreams I'd had about his daughter. Clearing my throat, I shook his hand. "Of course, Brock. I don't mind at all."

He slapped me on the arm and started for the front door. Georgiana hugged Morgan, followed by Blayze. I stood back while Morgan walked to the door and said goodbye to her family. Blayze paused in front of me, and I saw the smile he was attempting to hide as the corners of his mouth twitched madly.

"We'll talk tomorrow?" he asked. I wasn't sure if it was a question or a command. I decided to take it as a question.

"For sure."

He kissed his sister on the cheek and then shut the door. Morgan locked it behind him and turned to face me. I was ready for her to make some kind of joke about me staying so many feet away from her or something about lines that couldn't be crossed.

Instead, tears spilled from her eyes, and she threw herself at me. I instantly wrapped my arms around her, holding her tight. After a moment, I lifted a hand and smoothed the back of her hair, noting how fucking soft it was. "Shh, it's okay. I've got you."

She buried her face in my chest while we stood there. Hell, I'd stand there all night if she needed me to. When she finally got herself calm, she stepped back. Using the back of her hand, she wiped it under her eyes, then across her nose, and I fought the urge to grin.

"I'm sorry I broke down. It's just…that stupid podcast and those dumb teenagers!"

"Hey." I reached for her hand, ignoring the fact that she probably had snot on it. "It's okay. It would have scared the hell out of me too."

She sniffled. "It would have?"

I nodded. "Yes! Especially if I'd been listening to that damn podcast. My mom's cat jumped onto the kitchen counter once while I was listening to it, and I screamed like a little girl."

Morgan blinked at me a few times before she started to laugh.

"Come on, let's walk you to your room. You look exhausted."

"If you told me that story any other time, I'd have some smartass thing to say. But I don't have it in me tonight." She sniffled again. "God, I must look like a mess."

I shook my head. "Morgan, you look beautiful, just tired." The words slipped out so freely, I couldn't have stopped them if I tried. Morgan didn't seem the least bit fazed by them, though.

I pulled her covers back, and she crawled into bed. She had soft blue sheets and a comforter with blue and yellow stripes.

"There you go." I pulled the covers up and took a step back, ready to head to the guest room.

"Where are you going?" she asked, suddenly sounding panicked.

"Ahh...to the guest room?"

Morgan slid over, shaking her head. "Will you sleep in here with me?"

I stared down at her like she'd lost her damn mind. I rubbed at the back of my neck. "You want me to sleep in the bed with you?"

She nodded. "Please, Ryan? I really don't want to be alone, and even knowing you're in the other room won't be enough. I'll sleep better with you here."

Holy shit. This is like a dream and a nightmare all in one.

Morgan looked up at me, those blue eyes of hers silently pleading. What reason could I give for saying no? *Oh hey, sorry, Morgan, but if I lie next to you, I won't be able to sleep because I'll only be thinking about kissing you. Touching you.*

It was like my mouth had lost communication with my brain. "Slide over more."

Morgan sighed in relief and did exactly that. I sat on the edge of her bed and took off my shoes and socks, moving them off to the side. Thank God I'd put on sweats and wasn't forced to wear my jeans to bed.

I lifted the covers and slid in, staying as close to the edge of the bed as possible.

The sound of Morgan's breathing played havoc with my body. After a minute or two, I heard her sleepy voice.

"Thank you for not leaving me, Ryan."

Closing my eyes, I fought the urge to tell her there wasn't *anything* I wouldn't do for her. Instead, I simply replied, "Get some sleep, Morgan."

She sighed softly, and within five minutes, her breathing slowed and I could tell she was asleep. I rolled over to look at her in the moonlight—and felt like someone had hit me dead in the chest with a sledgehammer.

Morgan was also on her side, facing me with her hand tucked under her cheek as she slept. She looked like an angel, and as I studied her, I swore I forgot how to breathe. I lifted my hand, but stopped when it was inches from her face before drawing away. What was it about her that pulled me to her like a moth to a flame? Of course, she was beautiful, but her heart was even more so. I'd spent countless nights lying in bed and dreaming about what it would be like to have her in my arms. There had been so many times I'd wanted to ask her out, but with her in college and me being older, it never felt like the right thing to do. Of course, then there was Blayze. He'd seen it, though, my attraction to Morgan, and he'd given me his blessings. So what in the hell was I afraid of? Maybe it was knowing if I gave Morgan my heart, she would have the power to destroy it. But wouldn't it be worth the risk? Yes…she would totally be worth the risk.

"Goodnight, Morgan," I whispered. Then I watched her sleep until I could no longer keep my own eyes open.

Chapter Five

MORGAN

I slowly opened my eyes and instantly knew I wasn't alone. Everything from last night came rushing back to me. Including how I'd asked Ryan to stay with me—and to sleep in my bed.

He was still sleeping next to me. And when I say 'next to me', I mean his arm was draped over my side, firmly around my stomach, and he was spooning me. And was that…? Was he…?

Oh. My. God.

Squeezing my eyes shut, I fought to keep my breathing even. It was kind of hard to do when the guy I'd been secretly crushing on for the past six years had his morning wood pressed into my ass. And goodness he felt…big.

It's okay, Morgan. All men get it. It's not you, it's simply biological.

Frowning, I decided I wasn't a fan of that line of thinking.

Ryan moved, and I held my breath. He must have realized where he was—and who he was with—because he immediately froze.

We could either make this awkward or act like it was no big deal. The last thing I wanted was for things to be weird between me and Ryan. It was the first time in ages that we weren't exchanging barbs every other second.

Okay, no big deal it is.

Stretching, I said, "Oh man!"

Ryan instantly moved as if he'd been burned. I rolled over before he had time to get fully away from me. He was on his back now, with a look of what I could only describe as terror on his face.

Smiling sleepily, I said, "I slept so good knowing you were here. Thank you for staying."

He blinked a few times. "Sure. It wasn't a problem. Um, sorry, I must have rolled over in the middle of the night."

I gave him a confused look. "That's okay. I didn't think you would sleep in one spot, stiff as a board."

His cheeks turned red, and I almost started to laugh. I hadn't meant to say it that way, but seeing him nearly jump out of his own skin was kind of fun.

Rolling onto my back, I stretched again, then tossed the covers off me and jumped out of bed. "You're more than welcome to take a shower or anything you need to do. I'm going to make coffee."

Ryan was getting out of bed, and I had to force myself not to look below his waist, instead staying focused on his face.

"Thanks, but I better get back to the ranch. I mean, if you're okay with me leaving?"

I waved off his concern. "I'm totally fine now that it's daylight. I never plan on listening to another podcast for as long as I live. Well, not a crime one, at least."

Ryan chuckled, and I felt my breath catch. I loved his laugh.

"Coffee to go then?" I asked.

"That would be amazing."

"Meet you in the kitchen."

A few minutes later, Ryan walked into the kitchen...and a strange tingling sensation came over me. I could totally get used to having him here. Waking up every day with him in my bed, maybe enjoying a little morning sex...

"Everything okay? You look flushed."

"Yep! Everything's fine. It's just a bit hot in here, I think," I muttered as I handed him the tumbler filled with coffee.

He held it up and said, "Thanks. I'll be sure to give this back."

"I'm not worried about it. Thank you again for staying last night."

His eyes met mine before they drifted down to my mouth, then jerked back up. I swore for a hot second he was thinking about kissing me. Instead, he cleared his throat and took a few steps back.

"Anytime, Morgan. If I'm being honest, it wasn't a hardship sleeping next to you. Or waking up with you in my arms."

Did he really say that?

"That *was* nice," I said softly.

His eyes moved to the right—and he frowned. Following his gaze, I saw the flowers that I'd moved to the dining table yesterday. "I still have no idea who sent them."

Ryan made a grunting sound before he looked back at me. "I better take off. You're sure you're okay?"

"Positive. I'm going to head down to the studio to do some work."

"Let me know what you find out about the broken window in the shop."

Shit. I'd already forgotten about that. My dad and brother had boarded it up for me last night. "I will, for sure."

Walking behind him to my front door, I couldn't help but notice how nice his ass looked in those sweats. When he suddenly stopped and turned, I shot my eyes up and plastered on a casual smile.

"Talk soon?" he asked.

My heart tripped over itself at those two simple words. "Yes."

He leaned in and kissed me on the cheek. "Have a good day, Morgan."

"You too, Ryan."

He opened the door, and I watched it slowly close behind him until the soft click of the door latching caused me to jump. I pressed my fingers to my cheek, where I swore my skin was still tingling. Turning, I leaned against the door and sighed as I felt a wide smile erupt on my face.

"I've got to tell Krista!" I said to no one before rushing back into my bedroom and grabbing my cell phone. After finding her name, I tapped my phone to call her.

Krista's groggy voice came through the line. "Do you have any idea what time it is?"

Glancing over at the clock on my nightstand, I said, "It's eight-thirty."

"Yeah, and I'm still on vacation. It should be a sin to call me before eleven in the morning."

I rolled my eyes. "Ryan kissed me."

She gasped. "Shut the hell up!"

"Yes! Well, it was on the cheek, but I'm pretty sure he wanted to kiss me on the mouth. At least his eyes said he did… and the way he looked at my mouth."

"When was this?"

"Five minutes ago!"

"Wait, where are you?"

It took everything I had not to giggle with excitement. I was still creeped out about last night, but waking up with Ryan's dick pressed against my ass had put me in a pretty amazing mood.

"I'm in my apartment."

She paused for a moment, then I heard her moving around. "Why was he at your apartment so early? I thought you said he was living on his parents' ranch?"

"Oh, he is. But he spent the night here last night."

I heard a loud noise, then Krista cussed. "Fuck! I stubbed my toe. Hold on a second. Ryan stayed at *your place* last night? Did you guys…? Oh my God, did you finally pop your cherry?"

"No! We didn't have sex, although I'm thinking he would have been down for it from the feel of his hard-on against my ass when I woke up."

"Okay, I need to sit down. Start at the goddamn beginning. My head is swimming!"

After I explained everything to Krista, starting with me listening to the stupid podcast and ending with him kissing me goodbye—including the fact that he seemed to be pissed about the mysterious flowers—she was silent for a good minute.

"Are you still there?" I asked.

"I'm processing."

"I know, it's a lot."

"Who sent the flowers?"

I pulled my head back in surprise. "After all of that, you're wondering who sent the flowers?"

"Yeah. You don't find it strange that someone sent you flowers?"

Shrugging even though she couldn't see me, I replied, "Maybe they forgot to sign the card."

"Maybe, but it sounds kind of odd to me."

"Have *you* been listening to a crime podcast?"

Krista laughed. "No. Did you think about calling the florist?"

"Actually, no, I hadn't thought of that," I said as I slipped on a pair of jeans. "That's a good idea."

"That's what I'm here for. Then, I think you need to invite Ryan over for dinner."

"Dinner?" I repeated. "Are you serious?"

"Yes! Girl, it's clear the guy has feelings for you. He raced to your place last night, he stayed the night with you, no questions asked, and what did you say he said to you before leaving?"

The memory of his words came rushing back to me, and I felt a warm sensation float through my body. Clearing my throat, I repeated, "He said it wasn't hard waking up next to me."

"He's all but telling you how he feels about you."

Laughing, I put the phone on speaker and set it down while I pulled a shirt over my head. "Krista, no one wants to believe that more than I do, but I'm tired of waiting for something to happen between us."

"Exactly. That's why you need to pull your grown-up panties on, go buy a hotter-than-hell dress, and ask him to dinner. It's the modern world now, Morgan. Women ask men out all the time. Hell, I asked a guy out last night—and he's still in my bed right now."

I closed my eyes and shook my head. "You mean you swiped right?"

"I'm sorry, you have me confused with Heather. I didn't meet him online. We met at…well, it doesn't matter where I met him."

Grabbing my mascara, I swiped some on then pinched my cheeks to bring some color into them. I didn't have time to do my full makeup routine this morning. "You *have* to tell me where you met him now!" I giggled as I did a quick walk around the apartment to make sure nothing was on before I left.

"It's not important."

"It is if you refuse to tell me."

Krista let out a long sigh. "Fine. I met him at a singles church group dinner thing. My mother forced me to go, and apparently his mother forced him as well. We only hooked up out of spite for them. But the guy did this one thing with his tongue…and holy hell."

I groaned. "Ugh! No! Don't say another word or I'll gag. The last thing I need is to hear you describe your sex life. Especially when I don't have one."

"I'm simply saying, you could if you took the leap," Krista said with a hint of teasing in her voice.

I knew she was right. And I had a feeling if I *did* ask Ryan out, he'd say yes.

"A hotter-than-hell dress, you say?" I mused, setting my alarm before I slipped out the door of my apartment and down the steps. Suddenly, my plans for today had changed. After working on designs for a bit and checking on the progress of the store, I was going shopping…for a new dress.

◆ ◆ ◆

I watched the workers put a new window in with Georgiana right next to me.

"I'm surprised they were able to get it replaced so fast," I said, shaking my head a bit.

"I think that had something to do with your father."

Glancing at her, I asked, "What do you mean?"

"When they told me it would take a week to replace the window, he made one phone call and…well—" she motioned to the men working—"we have a window."

My brows shot up, and I exhaled. "I guess it pays to have a well-known dad."

Georgiana chuckled, but then her expression turned serious.

"What's the matter?" I asked.

She shook her head. "I don't know. I just hope it doesn't happen again."

"It won't." I hoped I sounded convincing.

The sound of Blayze's voice calling out caused us both to turn and watch him approach. "The bank on the corner has security cameras, and they were able to pull the license plate off the truck that stopped out front last night. Turns out the police were right. It was a group of teenage boys. Guess they thought they'd get their kicks by driving around destroying property. They got some residential homes a few streets over too. Someone's Ring camera captured their truck."

"What little brats!" I seethed as I looked back at the window. "And of all the nights to do it."

"You said that last night," Georgiana reminded me. "What did you mean?"

Rolling my eyes, I answered, "I was listening to a stupid crime podcast right before it happened. Ryan had mentioned the damn thing earlier in the day, and he'd all but challenged me to listen to it. Never again. It scared the hell out of me."

My brother and Georgiana both laughed.

"Go ahead and laugh, but it scared the living daylights out of me."

My phone buzzed, and I pulled it out of my back pocket to see a text from Ryan.

Any news on who broke the window?

I thought about texting him back, but I decided to take Krista's advice and ask him out to dinner. I couldn't let the new dress I'd bought go to waste, after all.

"Excuse me, guys, I need to make a call."

"I'm going to take off; I have to get back to the ranch," Blayze said as he kissed my cheek. "No crime podcasts tonight, okay?"

Gently pushing him on the shoulder, I said, "Trust me, I learned my lesson. I love you, be careful."

He winked, then turned to Georgiana. "Are you ready to head out?"

She nodded before gesturing to me. "I was thinking tomorrow we could go through some inventory? With the opening in a few weeks, I want to make sure we're ready."

"Okay. I spoke with Gene as well. He has a few more items from the line ready to go and will be sending them next week."

Georgiana took my hand in hers, a wide smile on her face. "Are you excited?"

I pulled in a deep breath and nodded. "I am. But I'm also scared. What if people hate my designs?"

"They won't!" she said, squeezing my hand. "Trust me, okay?"

"I trust you."

She gave me a quick hug. "I'll see you in the morning."

"See ya then," I said before calling out my goodbyes to them both. I rushed through the store, then raced up the steps to my apartment and shut the door. I pulled up Ryan's contact info and hit his name to call him. I put it on speaker and headed to my bedroom, where my new dress was hanging up.

"Hey, is everything okay?" he asked.

"It is. I thought it'd be easier to call instead of trying to type it all out in a text. Can you talk right now?"

I heard the sound of a horse in the background, and I instantly missed my own horse, Titan, who was back at my family's ranch. I hadn't gone riding in so long. I made a mental note to go as soon as possible.

Slipping out of my clothes, I picked up the phone I'd set down and headed to my bathroom.

"Yeah," Ryan said, "I'm finishing up in the barn and then heading over to my place to clean up."

An image of Ryan in the shower flashed through my brain, but I quickly pushed it away. I wrapped myself up in my robe and concentrated on staying focused.

Don't think of Ryan naked. Don't think of Ryan naked.

"They found out who did it. It was some teenagers. They were able to get their truck on a couple of cameras around town. I guess they hit some residential homes too."

"Little bastards."

I chuckled. "I said the same thing."

"I'm glad they found out who did it."

"Me too," I said as I sat down on the little bench in my bathroom. I pressed my hands together, gathering my courage. "Are you free tonight for dinner? I wanted to say thank you for staying with me last night…"

"I *am* free, but you don't have to thank me, Morgan. And I don't need an excuse to spend the evening with you."

My heart jumped in my chest at his words. "I was thinking maybe a nice dinner at the country club. I haven't been in forever."

"So," he chuckled, "you want me to dress up?"

Laughing, I replied, "Would it be so bad?"

"Not at all."

"Besides, you know how to rock a suit, if I remember."

"You think?" he asked, a hint of teasing and amusement in his voice. "I'm glad someone thinks so. I feel out of place in them."

"I can see that, since your work attire is jeans, boots, and T-shirts. A suit *would* feel weird."

Ryan laughed, and I pressed my hand to my chest. God, the way he made my heart flutter should be a sin. I closed my eyes and thought back to last night when he'd called me sweetheart. The last few years, I'd wasted so much energy being angry at Ryan, and I was tired of holding a grudge for a slight he wasn't even aware of. Krista was right. I needed to admit to myself, and Ryan, how I felt about him…and simply hope he felt the same way.

"What time should I pick you up?" he asked.

I bit down on my lip, suddenly a bit nervous by how bold I was being. I quickly pushed the nerves away. "Let me make reservations, and I'll text you. Is that okay?"

"Sounds good. I'll see you later on then."

"See you later."

After hitting End, I clutched the phone to my chest and drew in a deep breath, closed my eyes and exhaled. "Please don't destroy my heart, Ryan."

Chapter Six

RYAN

Staring at myself in the mirror, I debated if what I was about to do was a good idea. It wasn't like I was worried about what Blayze would think. Hell, he'd already given me his blessings months ago when I'd admitted I had feelings for Morgan. I wasn't worried about Brock. He knew me well—and that I would never do anything to hurt his daughter.

No, the reason I was terrified was because I knew Morgan Shaw had the power to crush my heart. When I'd woken up earlier that morning with her in my arms, it had felt so goddamn right. She'd fit against me perfectly. And those blue eyes staring back into mine nearly had me confessing how I felt about her. A man could get lost in them if he wasn't careful.

"Slow. You need to take things slowly," I said as I looked at my unshaven jaw. Shit. I should have shaved. I'd run out of time, though, and I would be late picking up Morgan if I didn't get a move on.

"It's dinner, Ryan. That's all. Dinner."

I adjusted my tie and turned on my heels. Grabbing my truck keys, I headed out of my temporary home and down the steps to my truck.

I heard a whistle from the barn area and turned to see my father walking toward me, his hat in his hand while he wiped the sweat from his forehead.

"Where in the heck are you going all dressed up?"

I smiled. "Dinner at the country club with Morgan."

His brow rose. "Little Morgan Shaw?"

"Dad, she's not little anymore."

He rubbed at the back of his neck with the rag. "No, I guess she isn't. How does Blayze feel about it?"

"It's only dinner," I said as I opened the door of my truck.

"And the fact that you stayed the night with her last night...?" His words trailed off.

I paused and looked back at him. "Means nothing. She was scared and asked me to stay, so I did. She wants to take me to dinner to say thanks for being a good friend."

My father smiled and looked off in the distance for a moment before he focused back on me. "Son, I don't often give advice."

I groaned.

"I almost let your mother go because I was afraid to admit my true feelings for her."

My brows pulled down. "Dad, it's complicated."

He chuckled. "Love is complicated, Ryan."

"Love?" I asked.

"I'm only saying my best piece of advice for you is to follow your heart. It's just like with horses."

Now I was confused. "You're comparing Morgan to a horse?"

Dad rolled his eyes. "There's a *reason* I don't ever give advice."

Laughing, I walked over to my father and pulled him in for a quick hug. I slapped his back and said, "Thanks for the advice, Dad. I think."

As I headed back to my truck, he called out, "You should have shaved! Your mother would be pissed if she saw you unshaven for a date!"

Ignoring him, I lifted my hand and waved as I started the truck and headed down the road toward the gate.

I parked in the back of the store next to Morgan's car. I wasn't sure why in the hell I was so nervous. Taking in a calming breath, I got out of the truck and made my way up the outdoor steps to Morgan's door.

With one more internal reminder to keep it cool, I knocked on the door. When Morgan answered it a few moments later, my eyes nearly popped out of my head. And from the way my mouth opened and closed a dozen or so times, it was clear I had forgotten how to talk.

Morgan smiled brilliantly and motioned for me to come in. I slowly shook my head as I scanned her entire body. She wore a black dress that hugged her to perfection. A slit in the front showed her bare leg up to the middle of her thigh. The bodice was sleeveless and wrapped around her neck like a halter top. A belt cinched her waist, showing off her curvy figure. Her hair was pulled back into a ponytail, and she wore the lightest amount of makeup.

"You look…um…" I cleared my throat. "You look beautiful, Morgan. You take my breath away."

A blush moved up her neck and into her cheeks, giving her an even more stunning glow. "Thank you. And you're looking very handsome," she said with a grin, her eyes moving up my body and landing on my mouth before she jerked her gaze up to meet mine.

I rubbed my slightly stubbled jaw. "Sorry, I didn't have time to shave."

She shook her head. "I like the day-old stubble. It adds to your ruggedly handsome looks."

"Tell my father that. He about bit my head off when he saw me."

Morgan chuckled. "Let me grab my clutch and phone, then we can head out."

When she turned, I couldn't stop my eyes from wandering down to her ass. Fucking hell, that dress was going to have me fighting a hard-on all damn evening. I nearly moaned when she bent to grab her clutch from the coffee table.

Deciding I needed to look somewhere else, I took in all the boxes that Morgan still needed to get to. "Do you need help unpacking sometime?"

She glanced around before she looked at me, a brilliant smile on her face. "Are you offering to help?"

"I am," I replied with a smile of my own. "I just figured with you moving and trying to get things ready for the opening of the store, you could use some help."

"That's sweet of you, but Rose and Avery are going to be stopping by this weekend to help me out. Rose has such an artistic eye, I was hoping she'd help me decorate."

I nodded. "Well, the offer stands if you need any help with anything."

Her eyes seemed to twinkle as she whispered, "Thank you."

"Ready?" I asked, holding my arm out for her to take. She nodded.

The drive to the country club was filled with Morgan talking about the new store, her designs, and how shocked she still was that Georgiana was taking such a leap of faith with her. She said she prayed she wouldn't let anyone down.

"Morgan, you are incredibly talented, and Georgiana sees that in you. She wouldn't have asked you to do this if she didn't believe you could."

I felt her eyes on me. "You really think I'm talented? I mean, I know I've asked you that before."

Taking a quick glance in her direction, I said, "Of course I do. I've seen how you've gone from cutting up your Barbie clothes to make new ones all the way to the outfits you've made for yourself through the years. Did you make the dress you're wearing?" I asked.

"First, thank you for that sweet compliment, Ryan. It really means a lot to me. And no, I bought this dress, but it's super cute."

I let out a humorless laugh. "*Cute* is not the word I would use to describe that dress."

"Really?" she said, a bit of teasing in her voice. "What word *would* you use?"

Turning down the drive that led to the country club, I looked at her. "Sexy. Sexy as fuck."

Morgan blushed. "That's three words."

She looked away from me and stared out the window. I'd have given anything to know what she was thinking. But we both remained silent until we pulled up to valet parking.

"Are you staying with us, sir?" the younger man asked as I handed him my keys.

"No, just dinner."

He filled out the valet ticket and handed it to me. "Text this number when you're ready to leave, and we'll have your vehicle here and waiting for you."

"Great," I said as I handed him some cash. "I appreciate it."

"Thank you, sir."

After rounding the front of my truck, I held out my arm once again for Morgan. She took it and we walked through the club to the restaurant. It had a beautiful view of the Bitterroot Mountain range, and we were right on time to watch the sunset.

"Someday I want a log home," Morgan said, looking around as if she'd never set foot in the country club before. Hell, her parents were part owners—even though they hardly ever used their membership.

"I'll have to show you the plans for my future house… or the drawing, I should say. Rose sat down with me one day when she was in town and drew them out. It's only a dream right now."

She looked over at me. "You want to build a log home?"

"At the moment, I'm trying to find some land to build it on. I'd like to be close to the ranch but also close to downtown, especially if I open up a brewery."

Morgan looked like she was about to ask a question when we were interrupted by a woman about my age. "Good evening," she greeted as she glanced between me and Morgan. "Do you have reservations?"

Morgan answered, "Yes. Morgan Shaw, for two."

The woman's eyes lit up as she recognized Morgan's last name. "Oh! Yes, we have your table ready, Ms. Shaw. Please, follow me."

We followed her through the restaurant to a corner table right next to the huge picture windows. We would definitely have a great view of the sunset from this spot.

"Is this okay?" the hostess asked.

Morgan gave her a warm smile. "It's perfect, thank you."

Pulling out Morgan's chair for her, I nodded and thanked the hostess as she put our menus on the table.

I pulled out my chair and slid into it. "Looks like we've got the best seats in the house."

Morgan nodded as she looked out the window and then exhaled. "I love watching the sun setting over the mountains. It's one of my favorite things. I missed the mountains when I went to visit Georgiana last December in England."

Placing my napkin over my leg, I asked, "You didn't like England?"

She quickly swiveled her head from the sunset to me. "I loved it. It was beautiful in its own way, but it wasn't home. Montana has this special place in my heart. It always will."

The waiter approached and nodded at me—then did a double take when he saw Morgan. "Hello, how are you both this evening?" he asked, pouring Morgan a glass of water, then one for me.

"We're doing well," Morgan replied as she opened her menu.

The server gave me a brief look, then focused back on Morgan. "May I get you a drink from the bar?"

"Not for me; I'll stick with water," Morgan said. "Ryan?"

"Not tonight. I'll have a Coke."

The waiter nodded. "Appetizer?"

Morgan scanned the menu before glancing up at me. "Do you want anything?"

"Not unless you do."

Facing the waiter, she said, "I think we'll pass."

"Good enough. I'll be back with your drink and a larger water for you, miss."

We both thanked him and focused back on the menu.

"What are you thinking about ordering?" Morgan asked.

I couldn't help but smile. It drove Blayze crazy that Morgan had to know what everyone else was getting before she made up her mind about what she wanted.

"I'm thinking the salmon with veggies."

"Ohh, that sounds good."

I lifted my menu a bit higher to cover my grin. "You?" I managed to get out without laughing before I closed my menu and watched her peruse her own.

"The salmon does sound really good, but I'm in the mood for pork chops. They have the best ones here, and the garlic mashed potatoes are to die for."

"I'll let you have some of mine if you let me have some of yours."

She lowered her menu and looked at me. "You want to share?"

I shrugged. "Why not?"

"I love that idea."

The waiter came back and took our orders. When he left, Morgan and I fell into an easy conversation about how it felt for her to finally be out of school. Then the conversation moved onto High Meadows Stables, and finally, she asked about the brewery I'd always wanted to open.

"So...the brewery. Are you finally going for it?"

"I'm thinking about it," I hedged. "I love working on the ranch with my father, and horses will always be a big part of my life. But I also love brewing beer. I met a guy about a year ago—his name is Bradford. He's a fan of home brews, and he also has a culinary degree. We've been discussing the idea of opening a brewery and restaurant together."

"Ryan, that's amazing! You should do it."

Laughing, I narrowed my eyes at her. "I believe last fall you said you didn't care for my beer."

"No, I said I've had better."

"Isn't that the same thing?"

Her cheeks turned pink. "I might have been lying. It was actually really good."

I gave her a questioning look. "Why would you lie about that?"

Morgan started to chew on her lower lip, and I couldn't help the way my eyes drifted down to where she was abusing it. I wanted to reach across and make her stop.

"I was mad at you."

Leaning back in my chair, I nodded. "You seem to have been mad at me for the last couple of years…"

She exhaled. "Well, let's just say I grew up and realized I was acting like a child."

"Want to tell me why you were mad?"

Morgan reached for her water, smiled, then took a sip before she set it back down. "No."

I grinned. "But you're not mad at me now?"

Her eyes searched my face intently, and I noticed how she lingered on my mouth before her gaze met mine again. "No, I'm not mad. I want to be friends, like we were before."

That felt like a gut punch. "Friends?"

She nodded. "I'm guessing since you helped me last night and you're here with me now, you're down for being friends as well."

Reaching across the table, I placed my hand over hers. "I've always *been* your friend and always will be."

Morgan looked down at our hands, then met my gaze. A slow, sexier-than-hell smile spread across her face. "What types of benefits come with your friendship?"

Shocked by the question, I stared at her for a moment. I was about to answer when the fucking waiter showed up with our food.

Chapter Seven

MORGAN

The heat in Ryan's eyes was unmistakable. He opened his mouth to reply to my very sexual question when the stupid waiter appeared. Ryan moved his hand and leaned back in his chair, looking as frustrated as I felt.

After setting our food down, the waiter looked from Ryan to me. "What else can I get you?"

A private room so I can jump the man sitting across from me, because if he keeps looking at me like he wants me for dessert, I'm going to explode.

Clearing my throat and pushing all naughty thoughts of dessert and Ryan from my head, I answered, "Nothing for me."

"I'm good, thanks," Ryan stated, his voice seeming a little strained. I smiled.

As we ate, Ryan started to talk about my father, the store, the ranch, Blayze...everything I'm sure he could think of to forget about the conversation we'd been having.

After finishing our meals and skipping dessert, Ryan picked up the check despite my insistence that I'd been the one to ask him to dinner.

"Thank you for dinner," I said when Ryan placed his hand on my lower back and guided us through the restaurant. I'd seen my father do that to my mother countless times, as well as Blayze with Georgiana. And now I knew why it was written about in romance books. There was something about a man's hand at the small of your back, gently guiding you through a room, that seemed so intimate. My insides were on fire from the simple gesture.

This must have been what it felt like when Mr. Darcy took Elizabeth's hand and helped her into the carriage.

Ryan opened the passenger side of his truck, and when he took my hand to help me up, I gasped and froze. My gaze shot down to our hands, then back up to his eyes.

This man was my Darcy.

"What's wrong?" he asked.

"I, um...I...I remembered something, that's all."

His brows drew down a bit. "Is everything okay?"

Blinking a few times, I saw the concern not only etched on his face, but in his eyes as well. "Everything's amazing."

He smiled, looking relieved, and my bones felt like they'd turned to liquid. Oh dear God. I wasn't simply crushing on Ryan Marshall. I was falling in love with him.

Gently pulling my hand from his, I got into the truck and focused on my breathing.

Ryan shut the door, then made his way to the driver's side. He climbed up into his truck and said, "Home? Or is there any-where else you'd like to go?"

"I'd say we should go play pool, but I'm afraid I'm a bit overdressed."

Ryan gave me a look. "And I'm afraid I'd be put in jail for kicking everyone's ass who dared to look at you in that dress."

My heart jumped and my stomach fluttered all at once as I let out a nervous laugh and focused on the road ahead of us.

Make small talk, Morgan! Make small talk!

"Tell me more about the brewery," I nearly shouted.

He cleared his throat. "Not really much else to tell. Right now, it's a dream that I'm not sure I should pursue."

"Why not?" I asked.

He shrugged. "I really love the ranch. When I was younger and my father made it clear he expected me to join the family business, it was something I wasn't passionate about. But I think that's because I didn't want anyone to tell me what I had to do. Does that makes sense?"

I nodded. "It does. How did you meet…what was his name again?"

"Bradford. We met at a bar. He happened to sit down next to me and Blayze and made a comment about the beer on tap. We got to talking, and it turned out he enjoyed home-brewed beer. We all started to hang out, and he's become pretty good friends with me and Blayze."

"Is he from Hamilton?" I asked.

"Missoula. His parents moved here to be closer to his grandparents, since they're getting older. Bradford came to visit, loved Hamilton, and thought it might be a great place to open a restaurant."

"That's kind of cool. What does he do now?"

"He's a chef at Le Vacher."

"Oh, the French restaurant in town? I called them to see about reservations, but they were booked for tonight."

Ryan laughed. "If you'd told me, I would have called him. I bet he could've gotten a table for us."

"My mom and Aunt Kaylee were talking about it the other day. They've been, and they said the food is amazing."

"We can go to dinner again if you want. I'll talk to Bradford about getting us a reservation."

The idea of going out again with Ryan nearly made me as giddy as a damn schoolgirl. "I'd love that. Do you think maybe Blayze and Georgiana would want to join us?"

Ryan grinned. "A double date?"

I felt my cheeks heat. "I guess so."

"See what day works for them, and I'll talk to Bradford about it."

Once we got back to my place, Ryan parked and said he'd walk me up to my apartment.

"Did you want to stay for a glass of wine or a beer before you head back?" I asked as he helped me out of the truck.

"That sounds great. The beer, not the wine."

I chuckled and started up the steps. For some reason, I knew Ryan's eyes were on my ass. I might have swayed up those steps a little more than was called for. When I got to the top, I stepped onto the balcony and froze.

"Is that—" I pointed toward my front door—"a bird?"

Ryan stepped around me. "Yeah. Oh man, looks like it's dead. It's a blue jay."

"What?" I gasped. "I love blue jays! Oh, I hope it's not the one that's been coming to my feeder on the balcony. I only put it up a couple of days ago."

"It might not be. Let's get inside, and I'll get something to pick it up and throw it out."

Handing Ryan my keys, I said, "I'll wait out here. The dustpan is right inside the laundry room."

Ryan stepped over the bird, and I put my hand to my stomach, feeling sick that the poor thing had died on my doorstep. Coming back out, Ryan used the dustpan to gently scoop up the bird.

"Do you think it flew into the door?" I asked.

"I'm not sure. Maybe. Or…maybe he killed it and left it for you."

"Who?" I asked.

Ryan pointed to the orange and white cat that was sitting on the bench behind me.

"Oh my gosh, where did you come from?" I said as I rushed over to the cat. It stood and pushed against my hand. "You're so sweet! Why are you taking out poor innocent birds, huh?"

The cat meowed, and I scooped him up into my arms. "Do you have a home, sweetie?"

"Bird's taken care of. I'll wash off your dustpan."

Glancing over my shoulder, I thanked Ryan and then set the cat back down. "I'll pick up some kitty food tomorrow, little guy, and ask if anyone in the neighborhood is missing a handsome orange and white bird killer."

The cat meowed again and jumped off the bench. He casually made his way to the steps before racing down them.

I shook my head and headed into my apartment, shutting the door behind me. "Do you think he belongs to anyone? He didn't have a collar on," I asked when I joined Ryan in the kitchen.

He was drying off the dustpan with a paper towel. "Who can say? He sure was friendly for a stray cat, if no one owns him."

"I've always wanted my own cat."

Ryan leaned against the counter and looked at me thoughtfully. "You had a ton of cats growing up, didn't you?"

"Barn cats," I said as I slipped one shoe off and then the other. I could feel Ryan's eyes watching me while I moved about. Heading to the refrigerator, I grabbed two beers, opening them before handing one to Ryan. "Here you go."

He took the beer and held it up. "To...friends."

My face heated instantly as I hit the neck of his beer bottle with mine. After Ryan took a drink, he set the beer down and pushed off the counter.

His gaze locked on mine.

I took a step toward him and could practically feel the heat building between us. Ryan closed the distance and lifted his hand to my face—but before he could make contact, his cell phone rang.

He closed his eyes and cursed. "Shit. That's my dad's ringtone."

"You should answer it."

Nodding, he replied, "Yeah." He pulled his phone out of his pocket and swiped across the screen. "Hey, Dad." He listened for a minute, then turned away from me. "Is she okay?"

My heart tumbled, and I held my breath. I hoped nothing had happened to his mother.

"Okay, yeah. I'm on my way home now. Will do."

He tapped the phone and turned to me. "I'm sorry, Morgan. There's an issue with one of the mares, and my dad needs help."

I exhaled and put my hand to my chest. "Thank God."

Frowning, Ryan tilted his head and stared at me in confusion.

"No, I mean—I'm sorry to hear that, but I'm glad it wasn't your mom!"

"Oh, yeah," Ryan said as he headed toward the back door. "Thank you again for tonight. I had a really great time."

I held the door open for him and smiled up into those brown eyes of his. "I did too. Thank you for dinner and for getting rid of the bird."

He smiled and my heart skipped a beat. Ryan leaned down, and I held my breath as he kissed me on the cheek before moving his mouth to my ear. "Goodnight, Morgan. Sweet dreams, sweetheart."

It was a damn good thing I was holding onto the door because my legs suddenly felt like jelly.

"Goodnight, Ryan," I whispered, my voice sounding way too husky and deep.

He drew back and winked at me before he headed out the door. I let out a deep breath and locked it behind him, then set my alarm.

I headed toward my bedroom. That was twice in one day Ryan had left me feeling like I might melt into a puddle on the floor.

Stripping, I hung up my dress and slipped out of my bra and panties. My thoughts kept going back to Ryan. His smile. The heated looks he had given me tonight. The whispered goodbye that I swore hinted at something more.

After taking a shower and answering a few emails, I couldn't take it any longer. My thoughts kept moving back to Ryan. If his phone hadn't gone off, I was positive he'd been about to kiss me. The sexual tension between us earlier was so thick, you could have cut it with a knife.

"Ugh. Damn mare!" I said as I shut my laptop and crawled into bed, slipping under the covers.

I wasn't sure how long I stared up at the ceiling, willing myself to think of something other than Ryan. The throbbing between my legs only grew more intense until I finally gave in. With my hand between my legs—and naughty images in my head pretending it was Ryan's mouth instead—I soon cried out his name as an orgasm ripped through my body.

Panting, I rolled over and grabbed the pillow he'd slept on the night before, hugging it to my body.

Slowly drifting off to sleep, I wondered if Ryan was thinking of me too.

◆　◆　◆

My phone alarm sounded, and I reached over to turn it off. After stretching, I pushed the covers off me and got ready to head to the gym. I'd double-checked that the spin class this morning wasn't advanced.

I made a cup of coffee to go, grabbed my cell, and made sure my license, gym card, and a debit card were all tucked into the little pouch on the back of my phone. On a whim, I sent a text to Ryan.

Me: Spin class this morning?

It didn't take him long to reply.

Ryan: Slacker. I've already been at the gym for thirty minutes.

Grinning like a fool, I sent him another text saying I'd see him soon.

My phone buzzed again, and a text from Krista popped up, asking about dinner. I started to reply to her as I attempted to juggle my coffee, the phone, and unlocking my front door. When I stepped outside, I immediately tripped over something.

I looked down, then staggered back into my apartment as I let out a scream that I was sure my parents could hear all the way at our ranch. I slammed the door shut, tripped over my feet, and fell hard onto my ass. Scrambling away from the door, I started crying as I called the first person I could think of.

The second Ryan answered, I attempted to speak.

"What're you saying? Morgan! Sweetheart, I can't understand what you're saying. Take a breath for me."

"The cat! Ryan, the cat! Oh my God! It's dead! It's dead…" I cried harder as I pressed my back against the cabinets in the kitchen.

"The cat? From last night?"

"Someone killed the cat! They killed him and put him at my door!"

Ryan cursed. "I'm on my way."

The door to my apartment flew open less than five minutes later. The second Ryan saw me on the floor, he came rushing over and dropped to his knees. I threw myself against his body and cried hysterically.

I wasn't normally so freaking emotional, but the image of the dead cat, a knife sticking out of his fur, was more than enough to make me lose it.

"Shh, it's okay. It's okay."

I shook my head. It wasn't okay. I would *never* be able to get the image of that sweet orange and white cat with a knife in his chest out of my mind.

"Someone killed him!" I sobbed. "They killed him!"

Ryan held onto me as he pulled out his phone. "Blayze, I need you to get to Morgan's. She's okay, but I think we need to call the police. Someone killed a cat and left it at her door."

I buried my face deeper into Ryan's chest. My body shook with both anger and fear. Who would do something like that to an innocent cat?

Lifting my head slightly, I looked up at Ryan. "Do you… do you think…those teenagers did it again?"

He tightened his arms and pulled me back against his body. "I'm not sure, but we'll find out. I promise you, we'll find out."

Chapter Eight

Ryan

It turned out Blayze and Georgiana were already headed into town to meet with their wedding planner, so they got to Morgan's place before the police did. Georgiana rushed into the apartment and took Morgan into her bedroom while I joined Blayze outside. The police showed up a minute or so after that.

"There's a note," Blayze said, his eyes meeting mine.

Nodding, I rubbed at the back of my neck. "I saw it, but I wanted to get to Morgan first."

One of the police officers started to ask me questions, while the other took photos of the cat and the area around Morgan's back steps.

"Have you seen any teenagers hanging around back here?" the officer asked.

"No," I answered, watching as he put gloves on and carefully removed the paper from beneath the cat. "I haven't noticed anything odd, but I don't live here. Hell, Morgan's only been in the apartment for three days." I glanced at Blayze. He was so laser-focused on the paper that he hadn't heard a word I'd said.

"Anything else unusual besides the broken glass in the shop below?" the other cop asked.

"A dead bird was at her door last night, but we figured the cat had killed it."

Blayze looked at me, his brows pulled down tight with worry. "What?"

I shook my head as I watched the other officer read the note, a look of concern on his face. "When we got back from dinner last night, there was a dead bird by the door. The cat was sitting on the bench up here. I figured he'd killed it and left it by the door. Maybe the people who lived here before owned the cat," I said. "What does the note say?"

The other officer looked up at me. His gaze moved to his partner, who was climbing the steps, then back to me and Blayze. "Are you Ms. Shaw's boyfriend?"

I jerked my head back, confused.

"She doesn't have one. I mean, I don't *think* she does," Blayze said as he looked at me, one brow raised.

I shook my head but didn't say anything else.

The officer let out a long exhale. "Do you know if she has anyone who's giving her unwanted attention?"

I swallowed hard. "You mean like a stalker?"

The officer nodded.

"Not that I'm aware of," I said, looking at Blayze.

He shook his head. "She hasn't mentioned anything."

"We need to check for prints on this paper, but someone is clearly trying to get her attention—and that someone is angry."

"What does it say?!" I demanded. Blayze put his hand on my shoulder and gave it a squeeze.

The officer cleared his throat before he read the note.

"This is what you're doing to me every time I see you with him. You're mine, Morgan. Mine."

I heard a gasp behind me, and I turned to see Morgan standing in the doorway. All the color drained from her face, and I lunged past the police officer and caught her right before she fell to the ground.

◆ ◆ ◆

"There's no way you're staying here, Morgan," Brock said as he paced back and forth across Morgan's living room.

"Dad, I'm not going to let some crazy person scare me out of my own home. I haven't even been here a week! I have a life, and designs to work on, and the boutique is opening in less than two weeks."

Lincoln was sitting on the sofa next to Morgan. She took her daughter's hands and said, "You'll be safer at the ranch, darling."

Tears formed in Morgan's eyes, but she blinked them back. "Mom, I don't want to hide out."

"This person put a *knife* through a cat's heart, Morgan! He's fucking crazy, and you're not staying here," Blayze nearly shouted.

Morgan's gaze flew to her brother. "I'm not leaving."

"I can move in and stay in the guest room," Georgiana said.

"The hell you will!" Blayze retorted, glaring at his fiancée. "It's bad enough my sister's here. The last thing I want is for you to be here as well."

Brock cleared his throat. "Then it's settled. Morgan, you're coming back to the ranch."

She stood up, her hands clenched into fists as she started to argue with her father. Blayze joined in, followed by Hunter.

Morgan's younger brother had been standing off to the side, not saying anything until now. All three men clearly seemed to think they could tell Morgan what to do, which pissed her off more.

"Okay, everyone calm down." I walked into the middle of the room where they were all now standing and shouting over one another. "Calm down," I said louder.

When it was clear no one was paying any attention to me, I let out a whistle, then yelled, "Everyone calm the hell down!"

All eyes turned to me...but the only person I looked at was Morgan.

"Morgan won't be alone. I'll be here with her."

A look of relief crossed her face, and she closed her eyes for a brief moment.

"But you'll be at the ranch during the day. How do we know this person won't try to do something when she's alone?" Georgiana asked.

"My father can handle things at the ranch for a bit. Blayze and I already talked about beefing up the security system and putting in some cameras."

Morgan folded her arms over her chest and glared at Georgiana. "I don't need a babysitter twenty-four hours a day."

"For fuck's sake," Blayze hissed. "Do you *want* this guy to do something to you, Morgan?"

She snapped her head over to glower at her brother. "Of course not. Ryan will be here, but he doesn't have to be here constantly. There are a lot of people coming and going from the shop during the day."

"I'll be here during the day too," I assured Blayze. "If nothing else happens, I'll head back to the ranch when the store opens."

He studied me with worried eyes. "Ryan, I can't ask you to do that."

Smiling, I replied, "You're not asking."

Brock let out a weary sigh. "If you're able to stay here with her, Ryan, that would at least make me feel better."

"Me too," Lincoln said, standing up. She smiled at me and squeezed my hand.

"I'll be in town for a while, so I can stay if Ryan needs to head to the horse ranch occasionally," Hunter said.

Morgan shook her head at her younger brother. "You don't have to step away from the riding circuit, Hunter. I would never ask you to do that."

He nervously looked at Brock and Lincoln before he said, "I kind of broke my ankle."

"What?" we all said at the same time.

"You broke your ankle and you're walking on it?" Lincoln asked as she rushed over to her son.

With all the focus now on Hunter, Blayze made his way over to me. "You sure about this?" he asked.

"I'm positive. Dad will understand. You know how much my parents adore Morgan. If I need to go to the ranch for any reason, I'll make sure she's not alone."

Blayze glanced over at his sister then looked back at me. "Who in the hell could it be?" he asked, keeping his voice quiet. "She literally got home from college a couple weeks ago."

Lowering my voice as well, I asked, "Has she ever mentioned anyone doing anything like this to her at school?"

He shook his head. "Not to me. And I know for a fact that if she'd mentioned anything to Rose or Georgiana about this, they would have told me."

"Maybe since she's been back, she's caught the eye of some nutcase." I immediately thought of the guy in spin class the other day.

Blayze rubbed at the back of his neck. "Possible. She's been at the shop nearly every single day. Could it be someone working on the crew?"

I looked at Morgan before focusing on Blayze again. "I guess it's possible, but hell, Blayze. You and I know most of those guys."

"*Most*, but not all of them. I'm going to talk to Marcus, the contractor. I want to make sure he's done a background check on every single one of the guys working for him on this project."

All I could do was nod. Then my gaze caught on something. "The flowers."

"What?" he asked.

"The flowers that someone sent to Morgan when she first moved in. What if the same person who did this sent her the flowers?"

He pulled out his cell. "I'll call the florist right now."

As Blayze made his way into the guest bedroom for privacy, Morgan walked over to me. "What was all that whispering about?"

"Blayze is calling the florist to see if they have a record of who sent you the flowers."

"Don't bother, I already did. They said the person paid over the phone with a Visa gift card and didn't leave a name."

My stomach lurched. "They paid with a gift card?"

Morgan nodded, the fear returning to her eyes. "At the time, I didn't think anything of it, but now…Ryan, do you think it's the same person?"

Pulling her into my arms, I held her tightly. "I don't know, sweetheart. But don't worry. As God is my witness, no one is going to hurt you."

She fisted my shirt at the waist, then let go as she looked up at me. "Thank you for staying with me. I didn't really want to be here alone, but I also don't want whoever did this to think they have any control over my life."

Brock walked over, and Morgan stepped out of my arms. I instantly missed her warmth but tried not to let it show. "I got a call from the alarm company," Brock said. "They're on their way to add some cameras to the stairs."

Morgan chewed on her thumbnail. "Good. Good. That will be great."

Blayze walked back into the room and when our eyes met, he shook his head.

"Morgan already told me they paid with a gift card," I said.

Blayze cursed under his breath as Brock glanced between us. "What are you two talking about?"

Jerking my head toward the flowers, I answered, "The anonymous flowers that Morgan received. The person who sent them paid with a Visa gift card. Blayze and I were thinking it might be the same guy."

"Sick bastard," Brock mumbled as he drew Morgan to his side. "Don't worry, pumpkin, we'll find out who this is."

She gave him a tight smile. "You all don't have to stay here. I know you have things to do at the ranch."

Lincoln made her way over to Morgan. "I can make you some lunch or something."

I could see Morgan was starting to feel suffocated with everyone hovering around her. I was about to suggest pizza when she cleared her throat.

"Ryan's going to head to his place to pack up some stuff, and I'm going with him. I need to get out of here and get some fresh air. Plus, I haven't seen his folks in a while. And Ryan mentioned that we might go riding."

Lincoln smiled at me, and I returned the gesture before glancing over at Blayze with a *what the hell* expression. He simply shrugged.

"I think going for a ride will be a great distraction, and I'm positive Tina and Bobby will love to see you," Lincoln said as she put her arm around Brock's waist. "You'll call if you need anything?"

Morgan nodded.

Lincoln turned to me. "Ryan?"

"Yes, ma'am. I promise."

Brock reached his hand out to shake mine. "Thank you, Ryan. It means a lot to us that you'll be here, watching out for our girl."

I drew in a breath and shook his hand. "I swear to you, I'll keep her safe."

An expression passed over Brock's face, but it was gone before I could read it. "I know you will, son. I know you will."

"I spoke with a friend of mine who works at the police station, and he said they're going to keep an officer close by for the next few days," Hunter added.

"That's nice of them to do that," Morgan said as she walked over and gave her brother a hug. "Go home, get off your foot. If I need anything, I'll call you."

Hunter looked at his sister with so much concern and love, it made my chest squeeze. "Promise me, Morgan. I'm home for a couple of weeks, so I can stay here if Ryan can't."

She hugged him once again. "I promise. I love you."

He drew back and kissed her forehead. "I love you too."

"Are you still up for meeting with the interior decorator later?" Georgiana asked as she walked over to Morgan. "She wants to make sure we're good on a few last-minute things."

"Yes," Morgan stated firmly. "It's business as usual. This person doesn't get to keep me from living my life."

Georgiana grinned and took Morgan's hand. "Okay, we're meeting at four in the studio. I'll see you then?"

Morgan nodded. "See you then."

After walking everyone to the door and saying their good-byes again, Morgan shut the door, locked it, then leaned her forehead against the surface. She let out a long, exhausted sigh. I made my way over, turned her, and pulled her into my arms.

"I hate this, Ryan. I hate that someone can make me feel this way."

I ran my hand up and down her back. "I know, and I'm so sorry. We'll find him, Morgan. I swear."

Chapter Nine

Morgan

A feeling of utter peace washed over me as I dropped my head back and let the sun warm my face. The feel of the horse walking underneath me in a calming motion put my anxiety at ease.

"Penny for your thoughts," Ryan said from his horse, which was walking next to mine.

"Nothing makes me happier than being on a horse."

"Nothing? Not even designing?"

I turned my head to see him watching me. "That's different. Designing lets me be creative and it's a great outlet. But riding...I don't know. There's something about being near a horse that makes me so happy. I wish I could have Titan with me in town so I could ride him every day."

Ryan grinned. "Well, my parents' place is a lot closer to town than your family's ranch. You're more than welcome to keep him here if you want."

"Really? Your mom and dad won't mind?"

That time he laughed. "It's a horse farm, Morgan. They love horses."

"I'll take care of his feed and grooming and everything. They won't have to lift a finger."

Ryan waved me off. "Please, the more horses the merrier."

I looked down at the chestnut mare I was riding. "But you won't be here to help them."

"One more horse isn't going to break us. Besides, I think Titan would fit in well. He's so gentle that he might actually be good for some of the problem horses we work with. Would you mind if we partnered him up, if need be?"

"I don't mind at all. He always tends to favor the more timid horses. It's like he's trying to welcome them into the herd. He's a good boy."

We rode in silence for a bit until we came upon a creek and got off to let the horses take a break and get some water. I stood at the edge of the water and stared out over the rolling pastures of High Meadows Stables. Ryan's grandfather had started the ranch as a horse rescue years ago, then moved on to specializing in training barrel horses and team roping. Since Bobby took over the place, he'd taken on more troubled horses. Folks in town called him Hamilton's horse whisperer. Ryan had the same gift when it came to horses. It was like he knew what the animal was feeling. I was surprised he'd even consider walking away from it to brew beer.

Ryan had hung back with the horses, and I was guessing it was because he thought I wanted the alone time. What I really wanted was to be near him.

"If you do the brewing, will you leave your work with the horses altogether?" I asked as I sat down and leaned back against a large tree.

Ryan walked toward me, looking thoughtful. He sat and stretched his legs out, crossing them at the ankles. "I don't think

I could ever stop working with horses. They've been such a huge part of my life. Hell, I was a little over one year old when my father first put me up on a horse and walked me around. He said he saw my eyes light up the moment the horse started to walk. From that day on, I've been addicted to them."

"What do you mean by that? Addicted to them?"

Ryan shrugged. "I don't simply love riding or training. I love being near them. There's something about horses that I connect with. I don't know how else to explain it. It's like when I look into their eyes, they understand me and I understand them. Emotion-wise, I mean. Like earlier, when we walked into the barn and Tay whinnied and started to stomp when you stopped at her stall? I knew she was telling me that you needed her."

My chest felt tight.

"Tay is gentle, never in a hurry. If you want a lazy ride, she's your girl. You want to hug her neck and bury your face into her and cry, she'll pull you in with her head and hug you back."

Looking back at the horse, I saw she was watching us as if she knew Ryan was talking about her.

"She hugs?" I asked.

Ryan smiled. "She does, if you need it."

Standing, I made my way over to the mare. She took a few paces forward to meet me and stopped only inches away.

"Hi, beautiful," I whispered as I rubbed between her eyes. Moving to the side, I rested my forehead against her shoulder… and when I felt her head turn and press into me, I squeezed my eyes shut and took in the moment. It was one of the most beautiful experiences of my life.

"They're pretty good hugs, aren't they?"

"The best." I sniffled and fought to hold back my tears.

Tay lifted her head and whinnied when Ryan walked up. He stroked her neck and softly told her what a good girl she was. I watched the two of them interact—and I knew in that moment my heart was sealed. If I suspected I'd been falling in love with Ryan before, now I knew I was for sure.

"Ryan," I whispered as I moved my hand along Tay's neck. We both stopped moving when our hands touched.

Dipping his head down, Ryan met my gaze. "Yeah?"

Tell him how you feel, Morgan.

"Thank you for being here for me. I honestly don't know what I would have done without you. I feel so small and weak right now. That really pisses me off."

"Listen to me, Morgan. You're one of the strongest women I've ever met. The fact that you won't let this person cause you to run away is a testament to that. And letting me stay with you isn't a sign of weakness."

"It feels like it."

He shook his head. "It's not. It's you being smart and realizing this is something you can't take on alone, and that's okay."

I nodded because I knew he was right. But something had been nagging at me all morning long, and it was driving me insane. "Why *me*?" I asked.

Ryan searched my face. "I don't know."

Lifting my gaze, our eyes met, and I drew in a deep breath. My hand touched his as we both started to stroke Tay again. I was going to take the first step in admitting how I felt about him—and I was scared to death. But if he was going to move in with me—even temporarily—he had a right to know how I felt.

"I need to tell you something…and I'm honestly a little nervous."

He frowned. "What's wrong?"

Swallowing the lump in my throat, I drew in a lungful of air and then exhaled. *Here goes nothing.*

"I've had feelings for you, Ryan…for a while now. Feelings other than friendship. And I completely understand if you don't feel the same way about me, but I…I needed you to know that before you moved in with me. Because I know the last time I hinted at my feelings for you, it pushed you away to Emma."

Ryan shook his head. "Morgan—"

I held up my hand. "Wait, let me get this out, please, while I have the nerve to do it. It's really okay, and I don't want this to ruin our friendship if you don't feel anything for me. But I thought you deserved to know. I can always have Hunter come and stay with me if that changes things."

Ryan closed his eyes for only a moment, though it felt like an eternity. When he opened them again, I sucked in a breath at the emotion I saw in his gaze. He took a step closer and cupped my face in his hands.

"Morgan, I never meant to hurt you that morning. I was fighting my own feelings for you at the time, because I thought it was the right thing to do. You were in college, I wasn't sure how Blayze would feel about it, and a million other stupid reasons were going through my head. I never, for the rest of my life, want to see that look of hurt on your face again."

"It's okay. I acted like a child, and I only want to be open with you about how I feel now to let you know that I'll be okay if you don't—"

My words were cut off when Ryan's mouth pressed against mine.

The kiss started off slow, but when his tongue swept over my lower lip, I opened to him. The feeling of his tongue against mine caused me to moan into his mouth and grab his forearms. Every bone in my body felt as if it had turned to molten liquid. Ryan deepened the kiss and turned me so that I was pushed into Tay's side, who remained steadfast.

When he finally eased back, we both gasped for air. Ryan leaned his forehead on mine and closed his eyes. He drew in one deep breath after another—and so did I. That was the most amazing kiss of my entire life.

Then he started to speak, and my heart nearly beat out of my chest at his words.

"You take my breath away, Morgan. Your smile, your laughter. Your take no prisoners attitude. The way you love so deeply. And when you look at me...*fuck*, when you look at me, I want to tell you how it makes me feel." He placed his hands on either side of me, pinning me against Tay. "When you look at me, it's all I can do not to pull you into my arms and kiss you senseless. Yesterday morning, waking up with you in my arms? It felt so goddamn right, and I wanted to tell you that. Then last night, in that dress—I was sure you could see all over my face how much I wanted you."

I blinked back tears as I looked up at him. "You really want me?"

He let out a humorless laugh. "If I thought I could take you right now, I would."

I licked my lips and smiled provocatively. "What's stopping you?"

Groaning, he dropped his forehead back to mine. "My first time making love to you is not going to be out in a field."

My stomach clenched with a desire so strong it stole my breath. Lifting a hand, I slid my fingers through Ryan's hair and closed my eyes. In the midst of all the crap that had happened since I'd moved into my apartment, something beautiful was rising up out of it.

◆ ◆ ◆

Tina and Bobby insisted that we stay for lunch. It was nice to visit with them, and even though Ryan and I tried not to let how we felt about each other show, it was obvious his parents were picking up on it.

After Ryan had packed up a few things and put them in his truck, Tina hugged me goodbye. "You take care of him."

"I think it's going to be the other way around," I said with a soft smile.

Tina grinned. "I've never seen my son look at anyone the way he looks at you, Morgan. I'm glad he finally woke up and realized it."

I frowned. "Finally?"

Tina waved her hand at me. "Please, that boy has had a thing for you for as long as I can remember. Just ask your mother. We both saw it years ago."

He'd mentioned having feelings for me two years ago, but... Blinking rapidly, I opened my mouth to say something but nothing came out. I was too stunned.

Tina chuckled. "Don't look so shocked. Now, you be careful—and keep your eyes and ears open."

"I will." I hugged her again and then kissed her on the cheek. "Thank you for lunch."

"Anytime," Tina said, making her way over to Bobby.

"Don't worry about us, everything will be fine out here," Bobby was saying to Ryan. "We've got three horses leaving this week and no new ones coming in, so take it easy, son. You deserve some time off."

"I need to come back and check on my brew," Ryan said.

Bobby laughed. "Don't trust me to do it?"

"You'll drink it all," Ryan said in a totally serious voice.

I looked at Bobby then at Tina for confirmation. She simply winked.

"You'll call me if you need anything?" Ryan asked his parents.

"Ryan, you're only fifteen minutes away. How do you think we managed when you lived in town?" Tina asked.

Ryan hugged his mother then kissed her on the cheek. "I love you, Mom."

"Love you back, sweetheart."

He moved to his father, and they exchanged a quick hug. Once we were in the truck, I studied Ryan. "Are you sure about this?"

He reached for my hand, lifted it to his mouth, and kissed my wrist. Goosebumps instantly swept over my body. "Stop worrying."

"I don't want you to think I'm pressuring you into anything."

Ryan looked at me with a stunned expression. "Morgan, have you forgotten the reason I'm staying with you? Some lunatic is *stalking* you. And I offered to stay. You're not pressuring me into anything, okay?"

I sighed. "I *had* forgotten. At least for a little bit."

He squeezed my hand. "I'm glad you were able to forget. How about I see if we can get reservations at Le Vacher for tonight?"

"Shut up! Are you serious?"

"Let me call Bradford," Ryan said with a chuckle. "If he can get us in, I'll owe him one."

"That would be amazing. Do you think Georgiana and Blayze could join us since they'll be in town for the interior design meeting?"

"I'll see what I can do."

I squealed and bounced in my seat while Ryan let out a laugh that was music to my ears.

Chapter Ten

*R*YAN

While Morgan and Georgiana had their meeting, I stepped outside to call Bradford. I knew I was going to be calling in a pretty big favor, but the way I saw it, he owed me for introducing him to Savannah Henderson, one of the local newscasters here in Hamilton. I'd gone to high school with her, and we worked out at the same gym. The moment Bradford first saw her, he'd been smitten. One introduction later and the two of them had been dating ever since.

"Make it quick, Marshall," he said when he picked up. "I've got twenty-five quiches in the oven."

I chuckled. "I don't suppose you could arrange a table for four this evening, could you?"

"If I said no, Savannah would have my ass for it, so my only choice is to say yes. Give me the details." I could hear him moving around the restaurant kitchen as he issued a command to someone.

"It's a double date: Blayze and Georgiana, and me and Morgan."

"Wait—Morgan? Not Blayze's little sister Morgan?"

"The one and only."

It suddenly got quiet, and I heard a door shut. "Dude!" he said. "Blayze is okay with that?"

I smiled. "Yeah, he is."

"Wow! That's great, Ryan. I'm happy for you. I know you've had feelings for her."

"I'm never going to live down the night I got drunk and spilled my guts to you, am I?"

Bradford chuckled. "Let's just say if I ever need to bribe you, I've got some good shit on your ass."

I laughed. "Morgan's had a rough day or two, and she mentioned she's dying to try out Le Vacher. So this is me calling in a favor."

"It's not a problem at all. We always keep a couple of tables free every night for things like this that pop up. I'll give your name to the hostess. If possible, can we make the reservation for a bit later? Like maybe eight?"

"Eight is great. I really appreciate you doing this, Bradford. It means a lot to me."

"It's not a big deal. So…are you guys official?"

I couldn't help the grin that spread across my face. "As of today, yes. Actually, I'm moving in with her temporarily, until we get some things worked out."

"Holy shit! I haven't even made that jump with Savannah yet. Although, I do spend more time at her place than my own. I should probably talk to her about it, but things are going so good with us, I don't want to rock the boat."

"Trust me, moving in with Morgan wouldn't have been my first move in a new relationship. I'll explain it all later. I don't want your quiche to burn."

"Fuck! The quiche! I gotta run. I'll see the four of you tonight!"

"Thanks, Bradford. See ya later."

He hung up without saying goodbye, but not before I heard him yelling, "The quiche!"

I chuckled and hit End.

When I stepped back inside the store, I saw Morgan and Georgiana walking around with the interior designer, Joyce.

"Perfect. Now that we have everything ready to go, I don't see any problems on my end," Joyce said. "It looks like the dressing rooms and your office still need to be painted, but everything else is pretty much finished, right?"

"They're working on the punch list the rest of this week, but we can start moving in inventory. Will the benches we ordered for the dressing rooms be in on time?" Georgiana asked.

"Yes, I've double-checked, and they'll be here. The only thing that might not arrive on time is the light fixture that'll hang above the register."

"That's not a big deal," Morgan said as she moved around the large, nearly empty space. "I love that we kept the original walls and ceilings. It's one of the things I love about my apartment as well."

Joyce grinned. "Well, if you guys are all good with everything, I'm going to head out. I'll do the final walk through with you when the time comes. It's always good to have a second pair of eyes on things."

Georgiana reached her hand out for the other woman's. "Thank you so much. It's truly been a pleasure working with you."

Joyce smiled at them both. "The pleasure's been all mine."

I held the door open for her and said goodbye as she breezed through.

"Well?" Morgan asked, a hopeful look on her beautiful face.

"Reservations for eight tonight. That was the best he could do."

Georgiana and Morgan both let out a squeal as they danced in place.

"Perfect! That gives me time to get home, change, and do my hair," Georgiana said.

"You know what dress you want to wear?" Morgan asked as she and Georgiana fell into a conversation about dresses, shoes, and what to do with their hair. I took advantage of the moment and checked my email.

I hadn't mentioned it to anyone yet, but Bradford and I had submitted rental paperwork on a building a few doors down from Morgan and Georgiana's place, though we had yet to hear back from the owner. With everything that had been happening lately, however, I wasn't sure the brewery was a path I wanted to go down right now. Everything had changed now that Morgan was in my life.

Too focused on my email, I didn't hear Blayze walk in. He hit me on the back, nearly causing me to drop my phone. Shit! I needed to pay better attention, especially when Morgan had a damn stalker out there.

"Jesus, you scared me!" I said as I pushed my phone into my pocket.

Blayze ignored my outburst. "Did you get your stuff moved in?"

"Yeah. I didn't bring much—a couple bags of clothes and some bathroom stuff. Speaking of moving, Morgan would like to move Titan to my folks' place so she can ride him more often. Maybe we can work out a day and time to get that done?"

"Sure thing. I can have Hunter do it. He's already going stir crazy, and he hasn't been home a full week yet. It didn't take him long to decide to stay in the guesthouse. My mother was coddling him too much, or so Hunter says."

I laughed. "He'll be okay doing it with a broken ankle?"

Blayze huffed. "Please. He was out on a horse this morning, helping me round up some cows. My mother was livid. You'll never believe what he told me, though."

"What?"

Blayze glanced around and nodded for me to follow him outside. From the look on his face, whatever news he was about to share was going to be interesting.

"What's going on?" I asked after he closed the door to the shop.

"Hunter said this producer from LA called him. They're planning on doing some kind of social dating experiment on a new streaming network. They want to do it here in Hamilton—and have *Hunter* be the bachelor that a group of women vie for."

I blinked a few times as I let all of that soak in. "Wait. They want Hunter to be on a reality TV show?"

Blayze laughed. "Yes! Apparently it's some new streaming network. And they want this show to launch it."

"What did Hunter say?"

"No, at first."

I raised a brow. "At first?"

Blayze smiled. "They offered to make a hefty donation to Dad's foundation."

"Holy shit." I shook my head in disbelief. "Does Brock know?"

"Not yet. To be honest, I'm not really sure how my parents will feel about it. I mean, the money would be amazing, but I told Hunter he shouldn't do anything he's not comfortable with. Especially when he described it as him and his dick getting treated like a lab rat in a dating experiment."

I couldn't help but laugh. "He doesn't have to ask anyone to marry him at the end, right?"

"Nope," Blayze said with a shake of his head. "But if he ends up dating one of the girls for at least a month after the show ends, they both get some kind of bonus."

"Interesting. I'll be curious to see if he does it."

"You and me both."

The door to the shop opened and Georgiana stuck her head out. "Hey, I didn't know you were here."

Blayze walked over and kissed her. "You ready to leave?"

"I am! Ryan got us reservations for eight tonight, so I need to go home and get ready."

Swinging his gaze to me, he asked, "Bradford was able to make it happen?"

"Yeah, he said they normally hold a table or two for special guests, but he couldn't get us in until eight."

"Works for me. We'll meet you and Morgan there?" Blayze asked.

"Why don't you guys come to Morgan's first, then we'll all head over together. That way, we only have to park one car."

Morgan stepped out of the shop. "Alarm is on. I'm locking up." When she faced the three of us, she had such a glow on her face. I was so glad she wasn't thinking about the cat on her doorstep—or the unknown nutcase who'd left it there.

"Everything's all planned. Blayze and I will meet you guys at your place, and we'll go to the restaurant together," Georgiana told her.

"Perfect! You better get going. Dinner is in a few hours."

After everyone exchanged goodbyes, I took Morgan's hand and we walked down the alley to the back of the building to head up to her place. All evidence of the cat was gone, and the only difference was the new doormat that Lincoln had bought and set up earlier while we were out at the ranch.

Once inside Morgan's apartment, we both moved toward the kitchen, neither of us saying a word. She reached into the fridge and pulled out a water. "Want one?"

"No, thanks." I stepped toward her. "Why do you suddenly seem nervous?"

She let out a light chuckle. "Because I am. Usually people date first, then move in together."

Smiling, I brushed a piece of hair behind her ear. "We can go as fast or as slowly as you want, Morgan."

Nodding, she whispered, "I know. It's just…I feel like this is a dream. I've wanted you to look at me like this for so long, and now…" Her voice faded.

"And now what?"

Those blue eyes lifted and met my questioning gaze. "I don't want to mess this up. I don't want you to regret anything, or to have regrets myself…even though I'd love to have you take me into my room to do all kinds of wicked things to me."

I groaned and shut my eyes.

She placed her hand on my shirt and fisted it. "I also like the idea of knowing you're here, in my place, always nearby. Does that make sense?"

Opening my eyes, I lifted her hand and turned it, kissing her wrist. "Yes, sweetheart. It makes sense. How about we relax and get ready for our date tonight? I'll stay in the guest room, you stay in your room, and I'll meet you back out here whenever you're ready."

A wide grin erupted across her beautiful face. "It's going to be really hard, knowing you're in the shower on the other side of my apartment. Naked and wet."

I rubbed the back of my neck. "You have to stop saying things like that, Morgan, or I'm going to say *fuck it* and make you mine right here in the kitchen."

Her eyes widened and her nostrils flared slightly. In her baby blues, I could see that she wanted me just as much as I wanted her, and something about that knowledge flooded me with a happiness I'd never known. It felt like an empty space in my chest was slowly filling up.

After one more heated look, she sighed. "Okay. You go get ready and I'll meet you back out here in a little while."

I leaned down and kissed her nose. "Sounds good."

◆　◆　◆

It didn't take me long to get ready. I had planned on taking Morgan to Le Vacher at some point anyway, so I'd packed a pair of dress pants and a shirt, along with a tie and dress shoes. My phone buzzed while I was grabbing a water, and I glanced over at it on the kitchen counter.

Bradford: I'd love to pair some wine with tonight's dinner, unless you have something else in mind?

I smiled as I typed back my reply.

Me: I will definitely leave the wine pairing to you, my friend.

He sent me a thumbs-up emoji in response.

"What has you smiling?"

When I glanced over to Morgan, who was standing in the door to her bedroom, I nearly dropped to my knees. She looked gorgeous.

"Wow. Morgan, you look beautiful."

I saw a hint of pink infuse her cheeks. "Thank you. I designed this dress. It's part of our exclusive line."

I took in the black dress she was wearing. It hugged her curves in the most delicious way. The front fell to her knees while the back of the dress hung a bit lower. It was off the shoulder...and shit if it didn't showcase her cleavage to perfection.

I cleared my throat. "Do you have a wrap or something to wear?"

She frowned. "A wrap?"

Nodding, I made my way over to her, slowly taking in every single inch of her skin. Stopping in front of her, I ran my finger gently along her exposed cleavage. Hearing her suck in a breath had my dick growing hard in my pants.

"If a single guy looks at you the wrong way tonight, I might have to kill him."

She chuckled. "This is the very first dress I ever designed. When Georgiana saw it, she suggested having the fabric crisscross like this on the bodice. It gives the illusion that it hugs my waist more."

"It's stunning, Morgan. I'll be honest, though, you'd look beautiful in a potato sack."

She smiled. "Thank you, Ryan."

I brought my hands to her waist and pulled her to me. "The moment we get back here, I'm going to slowly unwrap this dress from you."

She bit down on her lower lip. "Then it's a good thing I have a little present underneath for you."

I raised my brows. "A present?"

Morgan nodded as the doorbell rang. That would be Blayze and Georgiana. Damn them for being on time.

Tossing a grin over her shoulder as she walked toward the door, she said, "You don't see any panty lines for a reason."

It took me half a second to realize what she meant, then I had to reach for the counter to hold myself up.

Morgan looked through the peephole before opening the door. "Georgiana, you look stunning! You're wearing one of my dresses!" she exclaimed.

Georgiana spun around in a light blue dress that reminded me of an old-fashioned design. Maybe from the 1940s or 1950s. It looked amazing on her.

"What's the matter with you?" Blayze asked, walking up to me. "You hot or something? Your face is all flushed."

Morgan looked like she was trying not to laugh as she turned her attention back to Georgiana. "Is it comfortable?"

Georgiana nodded.

Clearing my throat, I forced a casual smile for Blayze. If he knew some of the thoughts I currently had running through my head about his sister, he'd murder me. "It's a bit hot in here. You guys ready to head over to the restaurant?"

Blayze gave me an assessing look before he finally turned to his sister. "You look beautiful, Morgan. Your design as well?"

She beamed with happiness, and I had to put a hand over my heart to rub at the sudden ache I felt. I was so damn proud of her, and I knew she and Georgiana were going to do great things with the store, as well as with Morgan's designs.

"Yep! It's the very first dress I ever designed, in fact, with some alterations suggested by your future wife."

Blayze grinned. "My two talented girls. I couldn't be more proud."

"Let me grab my handbag. Be right back!" Morgan said and dashed into her room.

"Don't hurt yourself too bad staring at my sister like that, Marshall."

"*Blayze*," Georgiana warned as she wrapped her arm around his.

I brought my hands up. "I wasn't thinking anything."

Georgiana let out a bubble of laughter while Blayze scoffed, "Please. It's written all over your face."

"Stop it," Georgiana demanded as she pulled Blayze toward the door. "Your sister is stunning, and you can't blame Ryan for thinking so, either."

Blayze huffed. "If that's what you think *he's* thinking, you're naïve, Georgie."

Laughing again, she kissed Blayze on the cheek. "It's Ryan, remember?"

When Morgan came out of her room, she was holding a sweater and her purse. "Did you bring a sweater, Georgiana? It's going to get chilly tonight."

"I did," Georgiana replied. "It's in the truck."

I waited for everyone to step outside before I set the alarm. I took one quick look around the apartment and then shut the door, locking it behind me. I took another quick look around the courtyard below…and attempted to push away the sudden strange feeling I had, pricking at the back of my neck.

Chapter Eleven

MORGAN

The moment we walked into Le Vacher, Georgiana and I gasped. It was everything I expected it to be, with a very industrial, French vibe. Exposed white bricks and planked walls gave it a warm feeling, and I was immediately drawn to the entire wall of windows that looked out on what was sure to be a beautiful view of the sunset over the mountains in an hour or so. White marble tables were sprinkled throughout the restaurant, with a long bar in the middle. The kitchen was on the right side of the bar and open so we could see into part of it. At the back of the restaurant was a wide staircase that led to a space for private events.

I glanced toward the kitchen and saw a handful of people moving about. Two men—one who looked to be in his early forties, and the other in his mid- to late-twenties—moved together with synchronized ease. Both men had brown hair while the older gentleman sported a sprinkle of gray.

"I take it the younger one is Bradford," I said as the hostess led us to a table in the corner. It was a cozy, very romantic spot for lovers on a date.

"That's him," Blayze answered.

Ryan held my hand as we walked, and I couldn't ignore the way my stomach flipped at the gesture. I wasn't sure which I liked better, when he put his hand on my lower back, or when he held my hand. I loved them both, if I was being honest.

"Can I start you off with water or anything from the bar?" the hostess asked.

"I'll have an old fashioned, please," Georgiana requested.

The hostess looked at me. From what I'd read on the restaurant's website, I knew they had locally brewed beer, and I also knew it was Ryan's. His father had encouraged him to build a small structure on the ranch that housed everything he needed to make his beer, and Le Vacher was the only restaurant in town that carried it—so far. "I'll have the local IPA, please."

Ryan's head shot up and he looked at me. I winked, and a wide smile erupted across his handsome face.

"I'll have the same," Blayze stated.

Looking up at the hostess, Ryan nodded. "Make that three."

She asked for ID from all of us, then quickly headed toward the bar.

Our waiter, Carl, appeared minutes later with our drinks and asked if we wanted to hear the specials. Once he was finished describing an array of amazing-sounding cuisine, we ordered. Blayze requested the Moroccan-style lamb shank, Ryan went with steak frites, and Georgiana and I both opted for pan-seared salmon.

"I'll have your salads out in a few minutes," Carl said as he gathered the menus.

"This place is beautiful. It's hard to believe it's here in Hamilton," I said as I glanced around the restaurant.

My gaze caught on a stunningly beautiful woman sitting at the bar. Her blonde hair was pulled up in a French twist. She was dressed in a black pencil skirt and an amazing white blouse that fit as if it had been sewn onto her body. Everything about her screamed "famous" or "model."

"I wonder if we can get her to model some of our new designs," I said as I took a sip of my beer and casually motioned for Georgiana to check out the woman.

"Savannah?"

I gaped at Georgiana. "You know her?"

She nodded. "She's Bradford's girlfriend. You'll know exactly who she is once you get a good look at her."

Right at that moment, Savannah turned and looked directly at our table. A wide grin spread across her face, and she slid off her tall chair and made her way toward us.

"The newscaster on channel twenty-four!" I exclaimed.

"That's her," Ryan confirmed with a chuckle.

"Hey, you guys," Savannah said when she stopped at our table. "Bradford mentioned you'd be coming in tonight."

Ryan and Blayze both stood to greet her, and Savannah laughed and motioned for them to sit. My goodness, chivalry wasn't dead after all, at least not with those two.

"Savannah, I'd like for you to meet Morgan Shaw," Ryan said as I pushed my chair back.

Reaching her hand out for mine, she said, "Please don't stand. It's a pleasure to finally meet you, Morgan."

"Finally?" I asked.

"Ryan and Blayze speak about you so much, I feel like I know you already. And of course, Georgiana," Savannah added with a sweet smile on her face.

"Is this person bothering you?" A male voice behind me made me to jump. "Sorry about that!" He stepped toward Savannah and kissed her—rather passionately—in front of everyone. Granted, we were tucked away in a corner, but it was nice to see a man who wasn't afraid to show his feelings.

"I hope you're Bradford?" I said, laughing slightly.

"I better be, or Savannah's in trouble," Bradford quipped while he slid his arm around her waist. He glanced around the table. "Everything okay so far?"

"Everything's great," Ryan answered. "I appreciate you getting us in tonight. I owe you."

Waving off Ryan's words, Bradford replied, "It's the least I can do for friends. Now, you have to introduce me to the lovely lady. Don't tell me you're Ryan's date?"

My cheeks heated. "I am. Morgan Shaw."

Bradford's grin widened as he looked at Ryan then back to me. "Morgan, I've heard so much about you from your brother. It's so nice to meet you." He reached for my hand and kissed the back of it lightly. "Ryan mentioned you've been wanting to try out our little restaurant. I hope you enjoy the food. If not, I had nothing to do with the cooking."

We all laughed, and Savannah beamed up at Bradford. You could tell she was in love, and from the way he returned her look, he was as well. They made a cute couple.

"I've taken the liberty of ordering the table a bottle of wine to go with the meals you picked out. If you don't care for it, please let me know, and I can have Savannah give it a shot. She really should be a sommelier with how well she knows her wine."

Savannah lightly hit his chest. "Stop it." When she looked back at the table, she explained, "My grandparents own a vine-yard in Sonoma, so I grew up around wine."

I smiled at her. "You know, Georgiana and I were talking about doing a wine and cheese night at the boutique once it opens. It would be wonderful to get your input."

Savannah's eyes lit up. "I would love that! Thank you, Morgan."

Bradford kissed Savannah on the cheek. "I need to get back to the kitchen. You let me know if you need anything, okay?" he said, glancing around the table.

"Will do. Thanks, man," Blayze said.

Before he left, Bradford looked back at me. "It really was great meeting you, Morgan. And whatever it is you're doing to make this guy smile like that—" Bradford nodded to Ryan—"keep it up!"

I felt my cheeks heat again, and Ryan took my hand in his.

Kicking off my heels, I let out a groan as I headed toward my room. I needed to get out of this form-fitting dress and into something with an elastic waist. "I'm so full, I feel like I'm going to pop!"

Ryan nodded. "I could have gone without dessert, but when Bradford showed us that crème brûlée, I knew I was a goner."

"I thought for sure Blayze was going to throw up when we finally left."

Ryan laughed and took off his jacket.

"Bradford and Savannah are really nice," I said.

"They are." He pulled his tie loose. "Maybe we can try and get together sometime. They're both always so busy, but I do know Savannah loves to hike and camp. Bradford, though...his idea of camping is at a five-star hotel with endless amounts of bread and cheese."

It was my turn to laugh. "I had an amazing night. It was exactly what I needed."

Ryan smiled, and I felt my heart jump in my chest. Then he slowly moved toward me, and my breathing picked up. I wasn't entirely sure why I was so nervous. No, that was a lie. The very idea of being with Ryan caused me to go breathless as my heart hammered in my chest.

"Are we moving too fast?" he asked softly, coming to a stop only inches away.

All I could do was shake my head.

Lifting his hand, Ryan wrapped a lock of my hair around his finger. "God, your hair is so soft." He let out a sigh. "I can't tell you how many times I've wanted to touch it to see if it's as soft as it looks."

Okay, why was that so freaking hot?

I swallowed and placed my hand on his chest. The feel of his heart pounding made me realize he was as nervous as I was. My eyes moved up and met his. "I want this more than anything, Ryan."

His eyes grew darker, and I could instantly tell he wanted it just as much.

Cupping my face with his hands, Ryan leaned in and kissed me. The kiss caused an explosion of feelings even before he deepened it. When he did, I had to grab onto his arms to keep my body from swaying.

Tearing his mouth from mine, he placed soft kisses along my jaw, then down my neck.

"Ryan," I gasped as his hands lowered, one cupping my breast through the dress. "Yes. Oh God, yes!"

He yanked my body flush against his, and I felt his desire press into my stomach. I had never wanted anyone as much as I wanted this man.

"Bedroom," I whispered, and Ryan reached down and lifted me into his arms. He practically sprinted into the bedroom, but once there, he gently placed me back down.

He ran his finger along my neck as he stared at a spot below my ear. "Your heart is beating as fast as a hummingbird's wings."

All I could do was be honest with him. "I've never felt this way before…about anyone."

His eyes snapped up to meet mine. I could see so much emotion in those caramel eyes of his. Want. Passion. And something I was afraid to label because I so badly wanted it to be true.

"Neither have I, sweetheart."

My heart couldn't possibly beat any harder. I saw Ryan's chest rise and fall, and there was something wonderful about knowing that I made him feel as crazy as he made me.

"Turn around, Morgan. I want to see what presents are under this dress."

I smiled and did as he said. Tingles raced across my body when I felt his fingers start to undo the back of my dress. And, good Lord, when he softly kissed my shoulder, I jumped and let out a giggle.

"Are you ticklish?"

With a shake of my head, I whispered, "No. But when you touch me like that, it feels…" My voice trailed off.

He placed another kiss on my skin, then another, letting the bodice of my dress fall to my waist. "It feels like what?"

"I don't know how to explain it. It feels like a jolt of delicious electricity. Like a million emotions rolled up into one amazing feeling."

He moved his fingers softly over my skin as he unclasped my strapless bra, allowing it to fall to the floor. I leaned against his back, and when his hands came around and cupped my breasts, I moaned.

"Jesus, Morgan," he whispered as he played with my nipples and nestled his face into my neck.

"That feels so good," I panted. "I need more, Ryan. Please...I need more."

Suddenly, my dress was pooled at my feet, and Ryan was letting out another long moan that seemed to go straight to the core of my stomach as it tightened with desire.

I drew in a deep breath and turned to face him. I was completely naked—and about to give my heart and soul, as well as my body, to my lifelong crush.

He locked his gaze on mine for the longest time before he finally looked slowly down my body. His breathing picked up and he rubbed at his chest. I loved that he was so open to showing his emotions to me. It filled me with even more desire, if that was at all possible.

"You're beyond beautiful, sweetheart."

My cheeks heated, and I reached for his shirt to unbutton it. I chuckled when my shaking hands struggled to open the first button.

Ryan moved my hands away, then ripped the shirt open with one quick jerk, causing buttons to fly everywhere. I would have laughed if I hadn't been captivated by his insanely gorgeous body.

"You're...so...fit."

Laughing, Ryan cupped my face in his hands, and I looked up at him. "Fit?"

Feeling my face heat, I said, "It was the first word that came to my mind, but the more I stare at you, the more I want to run my tongue over every inch of your perfectly chiseled body."

His brows rose. "That's a much more erotic image than *fit*."

I winked.

With shaking hands, I fumbled with his belt and pants until Ryan clearly couldn't take it any longer. He pushed my hands away yet again and started to take off his pants. When his dick sprang free, I couldn't stop the whimper that slipped from between my lips. My eyes locked on his hard length, and I fought the urge to run my tongue over it. For now, I swept my thumb over the drop of precum at the top and put it in my mouth, closing my eyes as I groaned at the taste of him.

"Fucking hell, are you trying to make me come before I'm even inside you?"

My eyes sprang open, and I shook my head.

"Sit down on the bed, Morgan. I want my second round of dessert."

A chill raced through my body and caused me to shiver as I took a few steps back until I was sitting on the edge of my bed. Ryan fell to his knees, and I gripped the comforter in my fists. I held my breath, watching him slowly spread my legs apart.

Staring at me, he licked his lips, and I felt a rush of wetness between my legs.

He ran his hands up my thighs and whispered, "You're so perfect. So beautiful."

"Ryan," I pleaded, silently begging him to touch me. I didn't care if he used his fingers or his mouth, I just needed to feel him.

He opened me completely, and a part of me was amazed I wasn't the least bit embarrassed by his actions. I'd never had a guy give me oral sex, nor had I ever given it. Hell, the most I'd ever done was let a guy touch me and make me come with his fingers.

Sex, especially oral, was something that seemed far too personal and intimate, and I'd never felt that connection with any of the guys I'd dated in the past. I always wanted to be a hundred percent sure when it came to giving myself to a man. And not any man could have that part of me.

A thought suddenly occurred to me. Had I purposely saved myself for Ryan?

"Hey, where are you?"

Startled back to the present, I moved my gaze to his. "Right here. With you."

Ryan smiled, and butterflies swarmed in my stomach. "You were somewhere else. Talk to me, Morgan."

"Ryan...I've never..." I swallowed hard. "I've never done this with anyone."

"Oral sex?" he asked.

I shook my head, then nodded, then shook it again.

He laughed. "Is that a yes or a no, sweetheart?"

Pulling in a deep breath, I exhaled and explained, "I've never given myself to anyone. I'm still a virgin. Call me old fashioned, but...I've been waiting."

Ryan's eyes grew wide as he sat back on his heels. "Waiting?" he asked, sounding somewhat awed.

"I've dated, and I've let guys touch me, but I wanted to be sure that I gave myself to the right man."

Ryan blinked a few times before he slowly shook his head. "Morgan...are you sure?"

It was my turn to cup his face in my hands. "I've never been so sure of anything in my entire life, Ryan. I want you. I've wanted you for as long as I can remember, and I think…I think that's why I've been saving myself. Maybe that's stupid and naïve, but I want you to be the man I give my body to."

His eyes turned dark with desire as he smiled softly. "You have no idea how many times I've dreamed of you, Morgan. Of this very moment."

"What are you waiting for then?" I asked, giving him a soft smile. Dropping my hands, I spread my legs for him and waited, ignoring the way my heart was pounding in my ears.

Ryan moved forward, his hands once again on my thighs. "You'll tell me if it becomes too much or if you change your mind?" He ran a finger through my folds, and I sucked in a breath.

"It won't. I mean, I *will* tell you…but I won't change my mind."

He looked up at me and whispered, "So damn wet for me."

I closed my eyes and dropped my head back when I felt him slip a finger inside of me. When his thumb rubbed over my clit, I once again grabbed onto the comforter as if it would keep me grounded.

"Watch me, Morgan. I want to see your face when you come apart on my tongue."

Oh. My. God.

Never in a million years did I imagine those words could nearly make me explode. I tilted my head back down and locked my gaze with his. Ryan smiled, then leaned in and gave me a deep, long lick between my lips before he closed his mouth over my clit, and I nearly jumped off the bed.

"Ryan!" I gasped and pushed my hand into his hair as I closed my eyes.

I snapped them open again when I realized he'd taken his mouth off me. When I looked at him, he flashed me a hotter-than-hell grin. "Don't stop watching me, Morgan. I meant what I said. I want to see you come."

"I'm already so close, Ryan. I feel like I'm about to explode."

A wicked gleam appeared in his eyes as he covered me once again with his mouth. The feeling of his fingers sliding inside of me was heaven. Both of my hands were now in his hair as I stared down at him between my legs, licking and sucking and moaning like he couldn't get enough of me. It was the most erotic thing I'd ever seen or experienced. My body was winding up so tightly, I knew I was about to experience the best orgasm of my life.

I was going to kill my friends for not telling me how good this could be.

"Ryan! Oh God, Ryan. Yes… Yes!" I shouted, not even sure if I knew any other words at the moment. All I knew was that I wanted more. I needed more. I needed to come, but I also needed Ryan inside of me.

Then he did something with his fingers as he licked my clit. I felt the build-up and wanted to close my eyes and throw my head back, but at that moment, he looked up. His eyes were filled with a heat and passion so full of fire that I felt it through my entire body. Not looking away, I fought to get closer, shame-lessly shoving my hips into him.

Then it happened. The most intense, glorious orgasm hit me.

"Ryan! I'm coming. Oh God!"

His eyes turned dark, and he held me tightly to him as I tumbled over the ledge. His name fell from my mouth over and over as he continued to bring me the greatest pleasure I'd ever felt before. Somehow watching him bring me to orgasm made everything more intense.

When it was too much, I fell back and scrambled to get away. I needed him to stop, but at the same time, I needed him to keep going.

It was only then I realized that I had moved up the bed and that Ryan had followed, spreading my legs open once again. I was lying back on my pillows, attempting to remember how to breathe. I let out a cry and looked down to see his mouth back on me. His tongue flicked my sensitive clit, and I gasped.

"Ryan…I can't! Not again…oh God, *yes!*"

His fingers were back inside of me as he sucked on my clit. The different position allowed me to move my hips more freely. The feel of my clit sliding against his soft tongue, and the memory of watching him make me come had me ready to explode yet again.

"Jesus!" I screamed out as another orgasm rolled through my body. I squeezed my eyes shut and moaned out his name.

I felt Ryan ease over me, between my legs. My eyes snapped open at the feeling of him at my entrance.

He smiled softly down at me. "It's going to hurt, but I promise the pain will go away quickly."

I nodded and wrapped my legs around him, pulling him closer. "Ryan…I need you."

He kissed me, and I tasted myself on his tongue. Moaning into my mouth, he pushed gently inside of me, and I gasped at the intrusion. It hurt, but somehow it still felt good.

Lifting his mouth off of mine, he asked, "Are you okay?"

"Don't stop. Please, don't stop!"

The feel of Ryan filling me was both pleasure and pain. The pleasure was winning out quickly, though. He stilled, and I felt the fullness of him stretching me. I never wanted the feeling to go away.

"Ryan! It feels so good…"

He buried his face in my neck and laughed softly. "It's about to feel even better. I need a second, though."

I moved my fingers softly over his back. "What's wrong?"

He drew in a breath and lifted his head to look into my eyes. "You're so tight, Morgan. So goddamn tight…" He groaned softly. "I'm afraid if I move, this will be over way too soon."

I felt myself smile. "Don't hold anything back. I want all of you."

He dropped his forehead to mine. "Morgan." My name sounded like a plea.

"I'm yours, Ryan. I'm yours forever."

His mouth covered mine with a moan, and he slowly slid out, then pushed back in. I gasped and tightened my legs around him.

"More," I gasped against his lips.

"Fuck!" he growled out as he thrust faster. "It feels amazing! I don't want to hurt you."

I pushed my fingers into his hair, my other hand clutching his shoulders as he moved faster still.

"Feels so good," I panted and moved my hips in the same rhythm. "Ryan…more…I need more!"

"Morgan," he gasped and grabbed my leg and pulled it up, opening me to him even farther.

"Yes! Oh God, that feels so good!" I cried out.

His eyes met mine. "Tell me what you want, sweetheart."

I thrashed my head back and forth as the feeling of another orgasm started to build. "You! Ryan, I want more of you. Please! Go faster and harder. I need *more*!"

He did as I asked, and the sound of our bodies slapping together was such a turn-on. I was almost there. I could feel my body tightening up.

"Morgan…baby…I need you to come."

All I could do was shout his name while the feeling built more and more until I exploded, crying out in pleasure.

"Oh God, Morgan! You're gripping me so… *Fuck*, I'm going to come." With a guttural groan, Ryan cried out, "I'm coming!"

"Ryan! Yes!"

His hips bucked as he pounded into my body. "Feels… so…good!"

I wanted to agree, but I was so overwhelmed, I couldn't find the words to speak. We had come together, and I swore the heavens crashed down into my room because all I saw was stars.

Ryan slowed his movements until he came to a stop. I wrapped my legs around him, not wanting him to leave me yet.

"Don't move," I whispered. "I want to stay like this forever."

His face was buried in my neck, and I was warmed by the feel of his hot breath hitting my skin.

After a few moments, he lifted his head and our gazes met. He stared at me, and there was something in those eyes of his that I'd never seen before. It filled my entire body with warmth.

"It's never felt that good before, Morgan. That…beautiful. It's never been that intense."

Tears pricked at the back of my eyes, and I fought to keep them at bay.

He rested his body on his elbows and brushed a piece of my hair away from my face. "Thank you for giving me such a beautiful gift, sweetheart."

I lost the fight to hold my tears back and felt them spill over. Ryan brushed them away with the pads of his thumbs before he pressed his mouth to mine. The kiss was soft and tender but filled with so much emotion, I felt like I was being swept away with it all.

I opened my eyes when he slowly drew his mouth away from mine.

Every ounce of my body wanted to tell him I loved him. That I had always loved him...

But he suddenly went rigid—and a look of worry washed over his face. I knew what the problem was, what he was thinking. In the heat of the moment, we hadn't used a condom.

Placing my hand on the side of his face, I smiled. "I'm on the pill."

"Morgan, I'm so sorry, I...I wasn't even thinking. I've never in my life had unprotected sex. Shit, I was so swept up in it."

I pressed my finger to his lips. "It's okay. I wanted to feel you, Ryan. To feel all of you, and I don't regret it for a second. It felt so good to be with you raw like that."

He rubbed his nose against mine. "It *did* feel good. So goddamn good, Morgan." He sighed. "Let's go take a shower?"

Biting my lower lip, I asked, "Together?"

He nodded, and I felt almost bereft when he pulled out of me. I wanted to protest the loss, but instead, I smiled as I watched him stand. Damn, if the man didn't have the most amazing body. Was it possible to want him again so soon?

Ryan reached for my hand, and I slowly moved off the bed. I felt a small bit of pain between my legs.

"Are you okay?"

"I'm more than okay," I stated as I lifted onto my toes and kissed him. "I've never felt so amazing."

Ryan brushed some hair from my face and was about to say something—

When we heard glass breaking and then a car alarm going off.

"What the fuck?" Ryan said as he rushed out of my room. Grabbing his pants on the way, he called out, "Get dressed, Morgan!"

I stood there for a few seconds, too stunned to move. What was happening? One moment I was in a blissful heaven, and the next there was chaos.

The sound of the car alarm finally penetrated my shock, and I rushed over and opened my dresser drawer. I hadn't even finished unpacking all of my clothes yet. I grabbed a pair of sweatpants and a long-sleeve shirt and threw them on.

I ran out into the living room. "Ryan? Ryan?"

The back door wasn't closed all the way, and my heart started to pound. I looked around. Where was my phone?

"Fuck!" I cried out as I frantically looked for the clutch I'd taken to dinner.

The door flew open, and I nearly screamed until I saw it was Ryan. He looked pissed.

It was then I noticed the alarm had stopped.

"What happened?" I asked, watching his gaze bounce around the apartment until he finally found what he was looking for. "*Ryan!* What happened?"

He grabbed his phone and finally glanced at me. His expression instantly softened and he stalked over, pulling me into his arms. He moved his hand softly, comfortingly over my back. "Shh, I'm sorry, sweetheart. Everything's okay."

"Was that your truck or my car?"

He kissed the top of my head, then leaned back so he could look at me while he talked. "It was my truck. Someone threw a rock through the driver's side window."

I sucked in a breath. "What?"

"And we need to call the police."

Fear instantly spread through my body. "Why?"

Ryan looked as if he didn't want to answer my question, but he did. "There's a note tied to the rock, and I don't want to touch it."

I covered my mouth with my hand. "Oh my God."

"Let me call the police, then I'll call Blayze."

I grabbed his arm. "No! I don't want him or my parents rushing over here this late. Let's call the police and wait to tell my family for now."

Narrowing his eyes, Ryan said, "Your father will kill me if we keep this from him."

"Just for tonight! Please?"

He nodded, then called nine-one-one as I stumbled over to the sofa and sat down. Wrapping my arms around my body, I sat there, completely stunned that something had happened again. *Already*.

"Why is this happening?" I whispered as I closed my eyes and tried to go back to the place I'd been only minutes ago... safe in Ryan's arms.

Chapter Twelve

THE RINGMASTER

How could she let him touch her?

I'd seen the way her eyes lit up when I observed them from afar in the restaurant. She hadn't even realized I was watching. Of course, she hadn't noticed *any* of the times I'd watched her.

I noticed everything, though. Like the moment his hand had touched her knee under the table...and she'd smiled! Why was she encouraging him?

And now he was there with her. *Living with her.* That whore! How could she do this to me?!

Staring up at her back door, I shook my head. "I won't let him have you, Morgan. Not when you're mine."

Chapter Thirteen

RYAN

I wasn't sure how I could go from being the happiest I'd ever been to being so pissed off I wanted to kill someone. When I found the person doing this to Morgan, I was going to rip them to pieces with my bare hands.

I was sitting across from Morgan, who was on the sofa talking to the detective who'd shown up not long after the police had arrived. One of the cops had read the disturbing note tied to the rock. He hadn't wanted to read it in front of Morgan, but she'd insisted. My stomach still lurched when I thought about what the anonymous person had written.

She's mine, and you fucking touched her tonight at the restaurant. I saw you slip your hand under the table and touch WHAT IS MINE! Leave Morgan alone, or I'll make you pay, you fucking bastard!

The detective's voice pulled me from my thoughts.

"You haven't noticed anyone following you at all?"

Morgan shook her head. "No. I'm usually pretty aware of my surroundings."

"Did you notice anything off at the restaurant this evening?" Detective Billings asked me.

I shook my head. "I texted my friend, Bradford, and asked if he might have noticed anything."

"What did he say?" she asked as I saw her write down Bradford's name.

"He said he hadn't, but he was in the kitchen most of the night. He did step out a few times to talk to us and his girlfriend. He's going to ask Savannah if she noticed something, and he'll check their security cameras as well."

"Savannah is the girlfriend?" Billings asked.

I nodded.

"And have you noticed anyone following *you*?" she asked me.

"No, but to be honest, I haven't been paying attention. I will be now."

Morgan wiped away a tear. "He threatened you," she said softly.

Detective Billings turned back to Morgan. "I don't want you to worry, Morgan. I know the note is scary, but most of the time it's all talk. He's trying to scare Ryan away from you."

"And if that doesn't work?" Morgan asked.

"Keep your eyes open, and pay attention to your surroundings. If you see anyone who looks off, or makes you feel uncomfortable, or if you suspect someone is following you, you let me know right away. And if you feel like you might be in danger, you call nine-one-one."

Morgan nodded. "I will."

"I'm going to see if we can get footage from any of the businesses around the area. With everyone having security cameras these days, it's harder for people to sneak around and not be noticed."

I stood when Billings did. "Thank you, Detective Billings, for all your help."

She gave me a polite smile. "Of course. If you or Morgan think of anything else, call my cell." She handed each of us her card.

Nodding, I replied, "We will. Thank you."

I followed her to the front door, where she paused and turned back to me. "You mentioned that Morgan was having someone come out to install cameras?"

I nodded. "Yes."

She glanced over at Morgan before she focused back on me. "I'd make that happen sooner rather than later, if it was me."

My stomach twisted into knots as I gave her a nod.

When she stepped outside the door, I followed. Lowering my voice, I asked, "Do you think she's in any real danger?"

Detective Billings gave me a sober look. "I think you both are."

◆ ◆ ◆

I sat in the chair and watched Morgan sleeping peacefully on the sofa. After the police and Detective Billings left, Morgan's will to be strong disappeared the moment our eyes met. My heart broke in fucking two, and all I wanted to do was take all of her fear away. The best I could do was hold her when she asked me to. The sound of her sobs nearly did me in as I tried to comfort her and told her there was no way this guy was going to harm her or me. And I fucking meant it. I'd do whatever I needed to do to protect her. She was *mine*, and after tonight, there was no doubt in my mind…I loved her.

After Morgan finally cried herself to sleep on the sofa, I let her rest and called Blayze, filling him in on what was going on. To say he was pissed was an understatement. We both agreed to not tell Brock about what happened tonight. If he found out, he'd force Morgan to move back home and that would only make her angry with her parents. Blayze and I both knew she wasn't going to budge from this apartment, so we agreed to give it a week. If nothing else happened, we'd tell Brock and Lincoln about the vandalism to my truck then.

Morgan stirred and let out a soft sigh as she nuzzled deeper into the pillow. I rubbed at the back of my neck and tried like hell to think if I had missed anything at the restaurant.

I'd called Bradford, as well, and told him what had happened. He'd asked if we needed anything and even offered to let me use his BMW while I got my truck fixed. I told him it wasn't necessary. He was with Savannah when I'd called, relaxing after a long night at the restaurant. When he'd asked if she'd noticed anything out of the ordinary, she'd said she hadn't, but mentioned one of the waitresses had said something about a man standing for a while outside the restaurant. She'd assumed he was waiting for someone to get off shift. Bradford had assured me he'd check their security cameras tomorrow.

Pulling out my phone, I looked through my contacts until I found the person I was searching for. I stood and quietly headed for the back deck so I could make the call and not wake Morgan. This was a conversation I didn't want her to hear.

A deep male voice answered. "Ryan."

Rubbing at the tension in my neck, I said, "I need your help, and I need it kept on the down low."

He paused for only a heartbeat. "What do you need done?"

A few minutes later I ended the call and drew in a deep breath. The cool mountain air felt good in my lungs. I glanced down at the parking lot below and scanned the area. That motherfucker had been somewhere down there. Probably watching us when we got home. My truck was gone, long since towed away and taken to Carl's body shop in town. I knew Carl would take care of it quicker than the dealership. I shut my eyes and gripped the railing of the deck hard. When I opened them again, I let out the breath I'd been holding.

I turned to open the door of the apartment—before I suddenly paused, taking one more look around the parking lot.

I could have sworn someone was watching me, but after scanning the area, I didn't see anyone.

Chapter Fourteen

Morgan

I rolled over and stretched. The slight pain between my legs caused me to smile as the memory of last night flooded my mind. All too quickly, it was chased away by the memory of the stalker and what he did to Ryan's truck.

Sitting up, I looked to my left, and for a moment, nothing else mattered. Ryan was lying there, sound asleep. I remembered him carrying me to bed in the early hours of the morning, then crawling in next to me and pulling me against him. That feeling of safety had caused me to drift back to sleep almost instantly.

Now I was waking with him by my side, and I wanted it to always be like this.

I rolled over carefully and propped my head on my hand as I watched his chest rise and fall. I chewed on my lip and focused on his mouth. The same mouth that had been all over my body last night, making me feel things I'd never felt before.

Squeezing my legs together tightly, I slowly exhaled. I wanted to pinch myself to see if I was dreaming. Was Ryan really here? Had last night actually happened? I lifted the sheet a bit. One quick peek revealed he was naked.

Holy mother of all get out. Ryan was sleeping *naked* next to me.

Drawing in a deep breath, I eased my hand under the bedding and gently grasped his length. He was somewhat hard already.

Ryan let out a soft moan as his hips jerked slightly. I couldn't help but smile, knowing I was the one making him moan with pleasure. Was I brave enough to give him oral sex? I could…but would I do it right?

I squeezed a bit tighter, slowly working my hand over his hardening dick. Ryan mumbled something in his sleep, and I leaned in closer.

"Morgan," he whispered softly, and my chest nearly burst. "Morgan… I love you."

My hand stilled, and it took everything I had not to squeal in excitement. I blinked several times as I stared at his mouth, willing him to repeat the words.

He suddenly stretched, and I pulled my hand away and dropped back on the bed. I closed my eyes and pretended I was asleep. I felt the bed move, and then a soft fingertip moved down my cheek and along my jawline.

"My sweet Morgan."

His words caused my heart to flutter, and all I wanted to do was scream for him to repeat those three words he'd just said! I needed to know that I'd actually heard it and hadn't been mistaken.

A soft kiss on my forehead had me blinking my eyes open. Ryan's caramel eyes seemed to catch the sunrays that were filtering in through the window, and when he smiled, my God, the whole room lit up.

"Good morning, sweetheart."

"I love it when you call me that."

He raised a brow. "Really?"

I nodded. "And I love when you put your hand on my lower back to guide me somewhere. And when you softly kiss the tip of my nose."

Ryan chuckled. "Are you always this open and honest in the morning? Because if so, I'll start making a list of questions to ask you as soon as you open your eyes."

"Does this mean you'll be sleeping in my bed with me every night?"

He brushed a strand of hair back from my face. "I'd love to fall asleep and wake up next to you every day…if that's what you want too."

"It is," I quickly stated. "I barely remember you bringing me in here last night."

He gave me a soft smile, but it didn't fully reach his eyes.

I placed my hand on his bare chest—and nearly jerked it away when I felt that electricity between us. Passion quickly filled Ryan's eyes and a sense of boldness swept over me. I pushed him back, pulled the sheet down and got up on my knees. I pulled my shirt up and over my head. Ryan must have taken off my sweats because I was only wearing a pair of panties. I quickly removed them and crawled over his body.

"Morgan," he said in a raspy voice.

"I want you, Ryan."

He closed his eyes and groaned when I sat on him, his hard cock nestled between my legs. I could feel his heat, and it instantly flamed my own desire.

I lifted up and reached for him, working myself onto his cock. I was so wet, I knew it would be easy to take him. "Tell me if I do something wrong."

He nearly laughed. "Trust me, you won't."

I lifted myself back up, then down. I'd seen a porn movie or two in my life and had an idea of what to do.

"Do what makes you feel good, Morgan. You're in control."

Those words did something to me. A sense of power overtook my nerves. I placed my hands on his chest, bent low, and rubbed my clit against him. It was glorious, and if I kept that up, I'd be coming in no time.

Ryan grabbed my hips and started to move. I sat up and grabbed my breasts and Ryan growled.

"Morgan," he gasped, watching me play with my nipples.

"Don't stop!" I said, loving the way he filled me so completely as he thrust into me from below for several amazing minutes. "Ryan—I'm going to come," I cried out. I felt him grow bigger inside of me, shocked that my orgasm was racing up on me so fast. I dropped my hands back to his chest while he rocked his hips faster and harder.

"I'm coming!" I shouted as he gripped my hips, crying out my name.

I dropped my head to his chest while we both dragged in deep breaths of air. "I didn't think it could be better than last night," I said.

He drew in a deep breath. "Neither did I." Rolling us over, he held his body weight off me and pressed his forehead to mine. "Morgan…"

The way he said my name was filled with so much emotion, it caused a warmth to heat my chest. I opened my eyes and stared into his.

He opened his mouth, then shut it. I knew it was too soon. Hell, he hadn't even been in my apartment for twenty-four hours. We'd gone on our first official date only last night and made love for the first time.

Yet, I could see it in his eyes.

I lifted a hand and ran my fingers down his cheek. "Will you move in with me? And I don't mean temporarily. I mean for always."

A wide smile grew across his handsome face. "Yes." I giggled when he kissed my nose. "Let me brush my teeth, so I can kiss you properly."

I brought my hand up to my mouth. "Oh my gosh! Does my breath stink?"

He laughed and kissed me quickly on the lips before moving off me and reaching for my hand. "Teeth, then shower."

As we headed into the bathroom, Ryan's phone rang. He glanced over at it. "I need to get that."

I saw the name "Nox" on the screen and wondered who it was. I hadn't ever heard Ryan mention that particular name before.

With a serious expression, he grabbed his phone. "I'll be right back."

I nodded. "Okay."

As I shut the bathroom door, I heard Ryan say, "Nox, thanks for getting back to me so quickly."

Turning on the shower to let it warm up, I quickly brushed my teeth. Ryan was off his call within ten minutes or so, but I'd already hopped in the shower and gotten out by then. Since I didn't need to wash my hair, I was faster than normal.

When he stepped into the bathroom, his expression was sober.

"Is everything okay?" I asked, wrapping a towel around my body.

Ryan nodded and turned the shower back on. "Yeah. Just some business I needed to take care of."

"You look tense. Is there anything I can do?"

He smiled, and the tension in his expression instantly faded away. "Seeing your beautiful face makes me happier." He stepped close to me, cupping my cheek with his hand. "I want to kill the person who's doing this to you."

The reminder made me frown. "I know. Why would anyone be stalking me?"

Ryan shook his head as he stepped into the walk-in shower and started to soap up. So much for our happy shower time. "Someone sick in the head. I hate that I don't know if this person is someone you know or not. I want answers."

"So do I," I said on a sigh. "Can we do something fun today? I mean, unless you need to head to the ranch for work."

Ryan's face lit up. "I'd love to do something fun. What did you have in mind?"

"I don't know. Something silly and crazy. Once the boutique opens, I'm afraid I won't have very much spare time. I should be designing some new pieces today, but I need to do something mindless."

"About the only fun and crazy thing to do in Hamilton is go to Ravalli's."

I nodded. "Well, that *could* be fun. Maybe we should see who can come with us since it's a Saturday. Do a little bowling or have a cornhole competition."

Ryan held up his hands. "Oh no. No competing."

I crossed my arms over my chest and huffed. Ryan turned his back toward me, but I was positive he heard my displeasure. "Why not?" I asked.

He turned off the shower and stepped out. My eyes took in his wet body with greed. Lord, the man was fit and so damn handsome. He was crazy muscular from all his time at the gym and from working at the ranch. It honestly looked like his *abs* had abs. Could he truly be mine? *Was* he mine? I was certainly his.

"Keep looking at me like that, and I'm going to throw you over my shoulder and take you back to bed."

My face heated, and I dragged my gaze away from him as he began to towel off. "Tell me why we can't compete."

Ryan gave me a look. "Morgan, you get crazy when you compete in anything. Remember when you sent Hunter to the ER because you broke his nose after he bought the last railroad in Monopoly?"

"He knew I had the other three and wanted that last one. And besides, he cheated! He deserved to be punched."

Ryan stopped drying off and gave me another look—one that said I was making his point very clear.

"Okay, I'll admit I'm a little competitive. But I promise I won't be today. Let's see who can join us! Please?"

Wrapping the towel around his waist, Ryan looked like he was on the verge of saying no. My eyes traveled down his body, and my earlier idea from the bedroom hit me. I walked over to him and undid the towel, letting it drop to the floor.

He raised a brow. "What are you doing, Morgan?"

I grinned naughtily as I stroked my hand along his hardening length. I had no idea what I was doing, but I was pretty sure once my mouth was on his dick, I'd have Ryan agreeing in no time.

"Please?" I said, kneeling in front of him.

"Morgan," he warned.

I licked up the underside of his dick, and Ryan let out a heated hiss. "Christ. If you think doing this will…"

His words faded as I took him into my mouth, and then he let out a moan. I could taste the saltiness of his precum, and it did something to me. Made me feel brave and sexual in a way I'd never experienced before.

Ryan moaned out my name as I worked him with both my mouth and hand. "Morgan. God, your mouth feels so fucking good!"

His words drove me on, and I took him in deeper, sucking a little more. He buried his fingers into my hair and gasped, guiding my head to the rhythm he enjoyed most.

The way he moaned and the ripple of his stomach muscles had me clenching my thighs together. I could come simply from watching him.

I glanced up to see that Ryan's eyes were closed, a look of pure pleasure on his face. I was doing that. I was making him feel good. It was *my* name tumbling out of his mouth…and that made me feel the sexiest I'd ever felt in my entire life.

Ryan tugged at my hair. "Morgan, I'm going to come… you…you might…"

I took him in deeper and sucked even harder, causing Ryan to let out a growl of pleasure that went straight to my core. The moment he came, I quickly swallowed his cum until there was nothing left to take from him. I gave him one last long suck before I released him.

Ryan stumbled back to the counter and held onto it. "Jesus Christ, Morgan."

I stood and smiled. "I've never done that before."

Ryan drew in a few deep breaths. "I should marry you right now."

Laughing, I inched closer. He'd kissed me after oral sex, would he let me kiss him now? Reaching for him, I paused.

Ryan's eyes flared, and he covered my mouth with his, moaning as he deepened the kiss.

Good gracious, why was that so hot? My clit was throbbing so hard, I desperately wanted to come. Ryan picked me up and set me on the counter as if reading my mind. He slipped his hand between my legs and pushed his fingers inside me, causing us both to sigh in pleasure.

He drew his mouth away from mine. "Do you need to come, sweetheart?"

I nodded, and being the wanton woman I'd somehow become in two days, I spread my legs and met his gaze. "I want your mouth on me."

Ryan closed his eyes and groaned before he bent low, placing his head between my legs and giving me the most intense orgasm yet. I had to put my hand over my mouth to keep from screaming.

When I finally came back to my senses, his mouth was already back on mine, his hand in my hair, pulling my head back so that I was open to his exploring tongue. I'd just had an amazing orgasm, but my body was still on fire. I still felt wound up, as if I could come again, and again, and again.

"You're so fucking sexy, do you know that?" he whispered against my mouth.

"Ryan, I want you."

And without a word, he lifted me off the counter and carried me into the bedroom, where he made slow, sweet love to me.

Chapter Fifteen

RYAN

"You cheated!" Morgan cried out as she pointed at Hunter. All her younger brother did was laugh.

"How do you cheat at cornhole, Morgan?" He looked over at Blayze and winked.

"I saw that! I saw the wink! You two are cheating. Georgiana, did you see the wink?"

Looking up from where she'd been staring at her nails, Georgiana sighed. "I didn't see a wink. Maybe we should try bowling again?"

Savannah leaned close to me and whispered, "Has she always been like this?"

Nodding, I replied, "I'm afraid so."

She sat back in her seat and then smiled when she saw Bradford returning.

Leaning down, he gave her a quick kiss. "Sorry, that was the restaurant calling. The footage from outside does show a guy standing there, but it looks like he was just smoking. After looking at the indoor footage, I'm afraid it isn't much help either since there are a few areas of the dining room where the cameras can't see. At least four tables. Though, the guy would have had to know that ahead of time in order to not be seen."

"That's a scary thought," Savannah said and Bradford nodded in agreement, sitting down next to her.

"I'm sorry I couldn't be of any more help, Ryan," he said.

"Dude, you've done more than I could have asked for. I appreciate you having someone check the cameras."

"For sure, no problem at all."

"Ryan, if there's anything you need us to do, please don't hesitate to ask," Savannah offered. "I know I just met Morgan, but I like her. I don't think I've ever seen you this happy."

I smiled as I watched Morgan argue with Blayze over his last throw. "I think I've known for a long while that Morgan's the one."

"The one?" Savannah and Bradford asked together. They both smiled at me, and I laughed.

With a half shrug, I replied, "It's hard to explain. I feel this connection with her that I've never felt with anyone else."

"I get that." Savannah linked her fingers with Bradford's.

He leaned in and kissed her again. "I love you."

Savannah's face lit up. "I love you too."

"Gag me," I whispered, right before Savannah smacked the back of my head.

Blayze came over and sat down, grabbing his beer and nearly downing it. "Are you sure you want to date my sister? Why in the world would you agree to this when you know how she is? Having Hunter here to top it off is like pouring gasoline on a fire."

I couldn't very well tell him I'd agreed to cornhole because his little sister had given me the best blowjob of my life. So, I went in a different direction. "She needed the distraction. She tossed and turned all night and hardly slept."

When Blayze slowly turned to look at me, I realized my fuck up.

"And how do you know this? Did you sleep in the living room chair and watch her all night?"

I cleared my throat and sat up straighter. If I needed to take off running, I was pretty sure I could beat him. "No, I carried her to bed around two in the morning."

"And he slept in the same bed as me," Morgan said, walking up and sitting down in my lap. She gave me a bright grin before she kissed me. "And then, in the morning, we—"

"Oooookay! How about we all head back inside for a friendly game of pool!" Georgiana interrupted as she fought to get the beer bottle out of Blayze's hand.

Savannah and Bradford both laughed and then stood and headed back into the building. Hunter stared after them, an expression on his face I couldn't interpret. I wasn't sure if he was looking at Bradford or Savannah, but…God, I hoped he wasn't developing a thing for my friend's girl.

I was distracted from that thought when Blayze elbowed me in the side.

"The only reason I'm not killing you right now is because I want this to work between the two of you. I love you both, and there isn't anyone I trust more than you, Ryan. But…" Blayze turned to Morgan. "If you ever even *attempt* to talk about your sex life with my best friend, I will beat him to a pulp."

"Hey!" I croaked out.

Hunter walked over with a slight grin, but then pointed to me and put on a serious expression. "That goes for me too."

Morgan stood and looked between her brothers. I saw her evil grin—and I knew something explosive was about to come out of that mouth of hers.

She patted Hunter on the chest, then glanced at Blayze. "Just be glad it was Ryan I lost my virginity to and not some rando in college."

Hunter closed his eyes. Blayze snapped his head around to look at me while Georgiana casually stepped between us.

Swallowing hard, I held my breath. Blayze looked around his fiancée, pointed at me and said, "You fucking better have made it special for her."

I blinked a few times.

Morgan sat back down on my lap and kissed me. Looking directly into my eyes, she softly said, "He did...multiple times."

"For fuck's sake, Morgan!" Blayze bitched, pretending to gag.

My heart squeezed in my chest as I cupped Morgan's face and kissed her tenderly.

"Ugh, I don't want to hear *or* see this." Hunter turned and walked into the building. I saw Georgiana wiping a tear away while Blayze simply smirked and then gave me a quick single nod before he and Georgiana followed Hunter.

Smiling at Morgan, I shook my head. "Are you trying to get me killed?"

She chuckled. "I can't help it. I love to tease them, especially Hunter. That man doesn't think he'll ever fall in love."

I pulled my head back in surprise. "What do you mean?"

We both stood, and Morgan wrapped her arm around my waist as we started for the building. "Exactly that. He doesn't think he's meant to find love. I don't know why. I think he *believes* in love. At least, I hope so. He sees it with our parents and aunt and uncles. Our grandparents. Blayze and Georgiana. But for some reason he doesn't think he'll ever find it himself."

"Did he tell you that?"

"Not in so many words, but it's amazing what a man who's had too much whiskey will confess to his litter sister."

I stopped us right before we got to the door. "Did Blayze tell you about the TV thing they want Hunter to be part of?"

Morgan's eyes went wide with curiosity. "Like…a reality show?"

I nodded. "Yeah."

"What kind? Are they going to follow him around on the circuit?"

Not wanting to let Blayze or Hunter miss out on seeing the look on their sister's face when they told her about the show, I shrugged. "You need to ask Blayze or Hunter. I'm not sure on all the details."

She narrowed her eyes and nodded. "I will. Now I'm intrigued."

Kissing her on the forehead, I replied, "I knew you would be."

◆ ◆ ◆

Nearly two weeks had passed, and it was finally the opening day of A La Chic Boutique. No more notes had shown up, no more vandalism had taken place. Blayze attributed it to the new security cameras, and the fact that I was living with Morgan.

At Morgan's insistence, I had started back at my folk's ranch yesterday. Only half a day at a time for now. There were so many people at the store getting ready for the opening, I felt it was safe to leave for a few hours. Every night, I looked forward to spending time with Morgan. We spent almost every single evening at home, cooking side by side and talking for hours. Then we made love before she fell asleep in my arms. It was fucking blissful. There were times I thought maybe it was all a dream.

Now I got to watch all of Morgan's hard work finally pay off. I'd taken a few days off to help around the store, and so did Blayze. So far today, the store had enjoyed a constant stream of people coming in and out. Even Savannah had stopped by with her news crew earlier, recording a story for the evening news.

Standing toward the back, I watched Morgan and Georgiana talk fashion with their customers up front. They were both clearly in their element.

"It's nice to see them both so happy," Blayze said as he stood next to me.

"It is," I agreed. "I meant to ask, how's the book writing going for Georgiana?"

Blayze grinned. Georgiana had been a freelance reporter before she'd settled down in Hamilton with Blayze. She'd worked for fashion magazines, including *Vogue*, but had also written for a few sports magazines, mainly focusing on professional bull riding. Her true passion was fashion, though according to Morgan, Georgiana also loved reading, and she was currently writing a romance novel.

"She's almost done."

I looked at Blayze. "No kidding? What happens next?"

"She has a few friends in the publishing industry, but she's decided to self-publish. She's trying to get it finished before the wedding. Not sure when exactly she'll publish it, though."

Blayze and Georgiana were due to get married at the end of summer. They'd both wanted things to settle down with the store before Georgiana jetted off for a week on her honeymoon.

Avery rushed by with a dress in her hand, making both of us smile. "I'd say you might have another fashion diva in the family," I said.

"Definitely. I mean, even though Avery isn't blood related, she's still like a little sister to me and my siblings. And Morgan is crazy protective over her. It's nice to see her involving Avery in the store."

I nodded. Avery's older brother, Bradly, had always been on the shy side. But Avery was larger than life, exactly like her father, Dirk. "Bradly still riding for his school?"

Blayze nodded. "Yep, but boy does he want to drop out and go on the circuit. Dirk won't let him, though."

Before I could reply, my phone buzzed in my pocket. Blayze's phone went off at the same time. My heart dropped as I looked at the screen. Blayze glanced at his, cursed—and looked at Morgan.

"She doesn't have her phone on her. I have it," I said, pulling it out of my other back pocket, already knowing what he was about to ask me. We made our way out the back door and to the private staircase that led to the two upper floors.

Before we even reached the steps, Morgan's phone rang in my hand. It was the alarm company, and I answered the call. "No, no one's home, but we're almost there. Yes, pull up all the cameras."

I raced up the steps, Blayze right on my heels. I unlocked the door off the deck and opened it. As soon as I stepped into the living room, my heart thundered when I saw the other door to our place had been kicked open.

"Fucking hell!" I said as I started toward the door.

Blayze was behind me—until he suddenly shot toward the door we'd just entered. "There he goes!"

I could hear sirens from the cops who must have already been on their way. I only prayed they came around back and not to the front of the store. I didn't want to ruin Morgan and Georgiana's opening day.

I scanned the rest of the apartment, not knowing if the person Blayze saw had entered alone. I checked the master bedroom last—and froze. I placed my hand to my mouth to keep the bile down.

At that moment, Avery texted me and Blayze.

Avery: What's going on? I see a police car out back.

Thank God they hadn't stopped in the front.

Me: don't let Morgan or Georgiana know keep them distracted...someone broke into Morgan's place

Avery: Okay. I'll be sure they don't come to the back room.

Me: thx

With that taken care of, I backed out of the bedroom, not wanting to touch anything. Turning, I raced to the back deck. I nearly fell down the steps when I saw Blayze on top of someone, struggling to hold him while the police attempted to cuff the guy. He started shouting something I couldn't hear.

"You got him!" I yelled, racing down the steps.

"He paid me five-hundred bucks to break in and leave it! I swear I don't know who he was!"

Skidding to a stop, I looked at Blayze as he stood and pushed his hands through his hair.

He drew in a few deep breaths. "This guy said he was paid to break in and leave something on Morgan's bed. Did you see anything?"

I looked down at the young guy—a kid, really—whom the cops were lifting to his feet. "I swear, it's the first time I've ever broken into someone's house!" he said.

"What was his name?" I growled as I walked up to the kid.

He looked scared to death. "I don't know!"

"What did he look like?"

Shaking his head, he replied, "I didn't see his face. It was covered with a ski mask. He gave me the cash—it's in my pocket. Then he gave me the stuff to put on the bed."

"Did you write the note?" I asked.

"Note?" Blayze and one of the cops asked at the same time.

The kid shook his head. "No! He only gave me the stuff to leave behind, I swear! He told me to put everything on the bed."

"What the fuck?" Blayze spun to look at me. "What's up there?"

I swallowed back the bile that rose in my throat, my voice shaking as I said, "He scattered rose petals on the bed, and right in the center there's a note…and a goddamn animal heart."

"Did you touch any of it?" a cop asked sharply.

Looking at the man like he was an idiot, I bit back, "Of course not."

"I'm gonna call Detective Billings," Blayze said, sounding furious. "Go back to the store. Make sure the girls don't find out."

"What about the fucking shit on her bed?" I asked.

Blayze exhaled. "The cops will take it. I'll stay with them. Just keep the girls away. I'll call my mom and have her stop by before closing and offer to take the girls out to celebrate. I'll call my Dad as well to let him know what happened."

Nodding, I looked at the kid who was being put in the back of the police car. "Blayze, as soon as you find out what the note says…"

He put his hand on my shoulder and gave it a squeeze. "I'll tell you. Go, before they come looking for us."

"Don't forget to call a locksmith to repair the door."

Blayze nodded.

As I turned to head back toward the store, I fought to keep the worry and fear off my face. The last thing I wanted to do was upset Morgan on today of all days.

Chapter Sixteen

MORGAN

To say I was flying on cloud nine would be an understatement. The opening of A La Chic Boutique had been a huge success. I'd even gotten a custom order for a dress from the mayor's wife. A custom order! I kept pinching myself to make sure I wasn't dreaming.

I shut the door behind the last customer and locked it before turning around and falling against the surface. Georgiana stood there, a smile so big and bright on her face, I couldn't help my childlike reaction.

"Oh my God!" I yelled as I jumped up and down and clapped my hands. Georgiana did the same, and we rushed to each other and hugged. Then we both proceeded to talk at the same time while my mother stared at us with a bemused expression.

"You got a custom order! From the mayor's wife!"

"I know! I don't even know what to think right now!"

Clasping our hands, we started to jump together now, all while turning in a circle and squealing.

"Oh my gosh, can someone do something? They're going to blow my eardrums out!" Avery shouted.

My mother laughed and walked over. "I'm so very proud of you girls. Let's get everything cleaned and locked up. Your father wants to take everyone out to eat."

"Praise be to the Lord above," Avery said. "I'm *so* hungry."

I pulled my little cousin into a hug. "Thank you so much, Avery. I don't think we could have managed today without your help."

She beamed at me. "It was nice having a job where I don't have to muck out a stall."

Georgiana chuckled as I hugged Avery once again. She was about to turn sixteen, and I could already tell she'd been bitten by the fashion bug.

I glanced over to where Ryan, Blayze, and my father stood near the back of the shop. The three of them had their heads together...and they all looked very serious.

"Is everything okay?" I asked as I made my way over. All three instantly plastered on smiles. They weren't fake, but something was for sure going on.

"Everything's great, pumpkin," my father said, pulling me in for a big hug. "I'm so damn proud of you both."

I drew back and looked into his blue eyes. "Thank you, Dad. We couldn't have done this without you and Jeff."

Georgiana's father, Jeff, had gone in with my father on purchasing the building that housed our boutique. It would take a while to pay them back, but if we had days like today at least a few times a month, we'd be paying that debt off quickly. Not that they wanted us to pay them back, but Georgiana and I had decided we intended on paying at least half of it back, if not all of it.

"Let's head to dinner. I have a surprise for you both," Dad said as he looked at my mother and winked. "Is the surprise ready, Lincoln?"

Mom laughed. "Indeed, it is."

"Then let's head on out!" Blayze said before he dipped Georgiana and kissed her. "I'm so proud of you."

She blushed and whispered something I couldn't hear. From the look on my brother's face, no one was *meant* to hear it.

Warm arms wrapped around me from behind, and Ryan kissed the side of my neck, sending a zing of warmth down my spine. "I packed an overnight bag for you," he whispered.

Turning in his arms, I raised a brow. "Really? And why would I need an overnight bag?"

Ryan glanced to make sure no one was in ear shot of our conversation. "I plan on celebrating long into the night, and I wanted to take you somewhere romantic."

Smiling, I tilted my head. "Anywhere with you is romantic. You don't think our own bed is good enough?"

I could see his eyes light up. "I love when you say *our* bed. *Our* apartment."

"It *is* all ours."

He searched my face and grew serious. "Someday I'm going to give you your dream home, Morgan."

I reached up and ran my finger along his jaw. "My dream home is anywhere you are, Ryan."

He leaned his forehead against mine. "I wanted to say this at the right moment, in the right place, but I can't hold it in any longer. Morgan…I love you. It might be way too soon to say that, and I don't want you to think I'm casually tossing it out there, because I've never told another soul that. Well, except my parents."

Tears slipped free and rolled down my cheeks. Ryan wiped them away before he kissed me.

"Come on, you two lovebirds! I'm starving!" Avery shouted.

We both laughed, but I grabbed onto Ryan's shirt before he could step away, meeting his gaze. "I love you, too, Ryan."

He kissed me once more before something hit me in the back of my head.

"Hey!" I shouted as I turned to glare at Avery.

"Come on! I'm riding with you two, and everyone else has already left."

Ryan set the alarm while I made sure Georgiana had taken the money from the register. Then we were out the door and on our way to celebrate.

Our celebratory dinner was at Le Vacher, and my entire family was there. Aunt Timberlynn and Uncle Tanner. Uncle Ty and Aunt Kaylee. Uncle Dirk and Aunt Merit, Grams and Grandpa, as well as Lily, Bradly, Joshua, and Rose. Savannah joined us while Bradford went back and forth between greeting everyone and running to the kitchen to make sure everything was okay. My father had booked the entire restaurant for our small private party—last minute, from what Savannah told us.

Georgiana let out a delighted scream when her parents, Jeff and Callie, came walking into the restaurant shortly after we got there.

"Mom! Dad!"

"Now the party can begin," my father said fondly, kissing me on my cheek.

And party we did. The meal was delicious, the wine perfect, the laughs many. But despite my happiness, I couldn't help noticing that something seemed off with Ryan. He was putting on a good show, yet I could tell something was bothering him. I went over after chatting with Rose and sat down beside him.

"You know, I can't find my phone. I must have left it in the office at the shop."

He smiled and pushed a loose piece of hair back behind my ear. "I have your phone. I put it in your bag. I'm so proud of you, Morgan."

I took his hand in mine, studying him. "Thank you, but… what aren't you telling me, Ryan?"

His eyes darted over to where my two brothers were talking with my father. When I glanced at them and then back at Ryan—I could see it.

"Something happened."

With a shake of his head, he replied, "Don't ask me anything right now, Morgan. Let's enjoy dinner, and when we get to the cabin, we can talk."

My heart started to pound. "Is everyone okay?"

"Yes," he quickly assured me. "Yes, sweetheart, everyone and everything is okay. I want you to enjoy this evening."

"Why do I suddenly want to be alone with you, safe in your arms?"

Placing his hand on the side of my face, he leaned in to kiss me, but we were interrupted by Bradford calling for everyone's attention.

"A little bird told me our two guests of honor both love crème brûlée. So, to honor their successful first day, I give you…dessert!"

A few waitstaff appeared, carrying trays full of my favorite dessert. Ryan tapped my nose with his finger. "I love you."

And just like that, all my worries seemed to float away. "I love you too."

◆ ◆ ◆

Ryan drove up a long driveaway to a stunningly adorable cabin that was lit with some amazing outdoor lighting. He parked, and I looked at him. "We're staying here?"

"We are. Rose told me about it…and made all the arrangements."

"What kind of arrangements?" I asked.

He winked. "You'll see."

Jumping out of the truck, Ryan jogged around and opened my door, then got two bags out of his backseat. Taking my hand in his, he led me to the front door. It was a small cabin, and I loved the idea that we would be all alone here, with nothing and no one to bother us.

Ryan typed in a code on the electronic lock and opened the door. One step inside and my hand flew to my mouth and I gasped at the sight before me. White lights were strung up all the way around the one-room cabin, with small LED tealights and candles placed throughout the room. Next to the bed were huge bouquets of flowers that filled the space with the most beautiful scents. It reminded me of my mother's flower garden back on the ranch.

Tears pricked the back of my eyes as I scanned the room. A small table sat near the kitchen area, and on it were two champagne flutes and a bucket of ice holding a bottle of champagne. Soft music played in the background, and I stepped farther inside to take it all in.

That's when I spotted a box on the bed with a large red bow. I turned to face Ryan. "I get a present?"

"All the way from London."

My eyes widened. "London?"

"From Lady Mary Douglas. She sent something to both you and Georgiana. It was delivered to your parents' house, and Rose brought it with her when she decorated in here earlier."

"When did you plan this?"

He chuckled. "A week or so ago. I told Rose I wanted to take you somewhere special to celebrate, and she happens to know the guy who designed and owns this cabin. He rents it out."

I rushed over to the box and gently untied the bow. If this was something from Mary, it was either going to be stunningly beautiful or very naughty. Maybe both. I slipped the lid off the box—and drew in a sharp intake of air.

It was a black lace bodysuit with a plunging neckline. Swarovski crystals were placed in small heart-shaped patterns across the bodice, and they seemed to catch every bit of light possible. The lingerie actually shimmered in the candlelight.

"What is it?" Ryan asked as I quickly shut the lid.

Facing him, I felt my cheeks heat, though I wasn't sure why. Over the last two weeks, the things Ryan and I had done would make a nun beg for forgiveness. Let's just say he was a good teacher, and I was an eager student. "It's lingerie."

His brows rose. "Do I get to see it?"

I smiled. "Yes, when I put it on."

Those light brown eyes of his turned dark with desire. "I think you should go put it on then while I start a fire. It's a bit chilly outside and getting colder in here."

"A fire would be amazing. Do you have my bag?"

Ryan nodded and picked up the overnight bag he'd packed for me. I took it and headed toward the bathroom, carrying the gift box from Mary. When I walked into the surprisingly massive, spa-like bathroom, I nearly groaned.

"Bathroom of my dreams!"

I swore it was larger than the rest of the cabin. A large oval soaking tub sat in the middle of the space. Directly behind it was the largest walk-in shower I'd ever seen, and the far wall was all windows. I couldn't even imagine the view during the day.

"Okay, this is super cool."

Putting my bag on the counter, I opened it to see what Ryan had packed. My heart squeezed as I saw all of my everyday necessities. He actually paid attention to all the products I used, and that meant more to me than any romantic cabin filled with flowers and candles.

After quickly washing off my makeup, I pulled my hair down from the bun I'd fashioned early this morning and let it fall around my shoulders. I pulled off my heels and nearly sighed with relief when my feet hit the cold tile floor. Next came the dress.

I started to slip it off…and paused, my gaze moving to the windows. Despite the soft white shades in place, and the fact we were in the middle of nowhere, my entire body shivered as an eerie feeling swept over me. I kept my dress on as I walked over to the light switches. There was a remote control sitting in a holder attached to the wall. I pressed the down button, and waterproof shades lowered over the large wall of windows, blocking any view into the bathroom.

Once the shades came to a stop, I let out the breath I hadn't even realized I was holding.

Carefully slipping out of the dress, I placed it on the counter. I took the lingerie out of the box and nearly moaned at the feel of it. Silk and lace. Two of my favorite things.

I glanced over at the shower, thinking of my favorite person right outside the door, and smiled.

Putting the nightie back into the box, I grabbed a towel and wrapped it around my body before heading to the bathroom door and opening it silently. Ryan was bending down, getting the fire ready. He had already changed into a pair of sweats and a T-shirt. I watched the muscles in his back and arms flex as he placed the logs into the fireplace to start the fire.

I reached up and pinched myself. Today had been an absolute dream. The boutique opening, Ryan telling me he loved me. And now this romantic little getaway.

Not taking my eyes off of him, I studied every move he made. Once he got the fire going, he stood and stared into the flames, rubbing at the back of his neck. Something was still bothering him.

"Do you want to take a shower with me? It's big enough to fit a small party in there."

Ryan turned slowly and let his eyes roam over my body. Then he moved so quickly, I hardly had time to realize what he was doing before he'd pulled the towel off and picked me up. I wrapped my legs around his body, and he walked us back into the bathroom, kissing me with so much passion and urgency, my body felt like it was going to catch on fire.

He placed me on the counter that didn't have all of my stuff sprawled on it and ran his hands all over me. He caressed my body so tenderly, I couldn't help but moan out his name.

"Touch me," I whispered as he placed soft kisses down my neck. "Ryan, please."

He spread my legs apart and pushed two fingers inside me, then he placed his mouth over my nipple and teased it with his tongue and teeth. Dropping my head back, I relished the moment. There was nothing I loved more than Ryan's mouth on me, doing things I dreamed about.

"I want to fuck you right here."

I sucked in a breath at his dirty words. Ryan was always so gentle and caring, but there was something about this version of him that I absolutely loved.

"Yes. Now!"

He pushed his sweats down to reveal his hard cock. I licked my lips at the sight of it, thick and ready.

Pulling me closer to the edge of the counter, Ryan took himself in his hand, pumped a few times, then positioned himself at my entrance. He slid inside in one go, and I let out a small scream.

When he paused, I grabbed his hair and pulled his head back. "Don't stop!"

Doing my bidding, he thrust fast and hard, forcing me to hold onto the counter. Knowing we were out in the middle of nowhere, I moaned and cried out his name with abandon. There was something incredibly hot about being so raw with one another.

"Fuck, Morgan. I crave you constantly. I can't...get... enough of you," he said in time with his thrusts.

"Yes. Harder, Ryan. Please! Harder!" I cried out.

The loud sound of our bodies slapping together only caused my build-up to happen faster. It wasn't going to be long before I exploded. I dropped my head back as I shouted his name.

"I need you to come, sweetheart."

"I'm so close!" I cried out.

Then I felt his thumb press against my clit, and everything in me exploded.

"I'm coming! Oh my God, I'm coming!"

I felt myself pulsing around Ryan's cock as he grew bigger inside me and then gasped my name, both of us coming together in our most intense sex yet. I cried out my pleasure while stars seemed to explode in the bathroom, my orgasm feeling like it lasted for an eternity.

When Ryan stopped moving, I dropped my forehead to his and gasped in breaths of air. Once I could finally breathe, I lifted my head and looked into his eyes.

"Wow," I managed to say, running my fingers through his hair. "I liked that, a lot."

He laughed. "Me too, but I didn't hurt you, did I?"

"No! It felt amazing. There's something so hot about you losing control like that. And I must admit, the dirty talk nearly had me coming on the spot."

He winked. "Duly noted."

The sparkle in his eyes from our lovemaking—no, our fucking—seemed to quickly fade away, and that worry from earlier was back.

"Let's take a shower," I said. "Then I want to talk about why you seem so bothered tonight."

Ryan glanced toward the middle of the bathroom. "I have a better idea. Let's take a bath."

Chapter Seventeen

THE RINGMASTER

I balled my fists at my sides as I watched the two of them walk into the cabin. I quickly made my way around the back, finding a bathroom with a large wall of windows. The moment Morgan stepped inside, my heart soared. She stood in front of the windows, and I could just make out the lines of my sweet girl's silhouette.

I watched her move about the space, and my cock grew harder when she started to undress. She paused, looked out the windows, and froze.

Standing perfectly still, I barely breathed. My hand trembled slightly, making my binoculars shake. Morgan moved back toward the door, then the shades slowly took her from my view.

"Motherfucker!" I growled. I leaned back against a tree and ran my hand through my hair. How could she be with him after I showed her what she was doing to my heart? *How?!*

I lifted my gaze back to the cabin and glowered. "I'll right this terrible wrong, my sweet girl. I'll save you from him... soon. Then you'll be mine forever."

Several minutes later, frustrated as fuck that I couldn't see her, I thought about leaving—until Morgan's screams of pleasure made me stop.

Quickly lowering to the ground, I leaned against the same tree as I frantically ripped off one glove and tore at the button of my pants. Releasing my stiff cock, I gripped it tight, closing my eyes and envisioning Morgan while I pleasured myself.

When she cried out that she was coming, I groaned and spilled into my gloved hand, moaning her name.

Dropping my head back against the tree, I sighed deeply and whispered, "Tick-tock goes the clock."

Chapter Eighteen

Morgan

I leaned back against Ryan's chest and closed my eyes, enjoying the feel of his body and the warm water as he moved his fingers lightly up and down my arms.

"Are you ready to tell me what's going on?" I asked.

He sighed. "First, I want you to know that Blayze and I didn't want to ruin opening day, and that was the *only* reason we kept this from you."

I tensed. "Kept what from me?"

"The alarm for your apartment went off today."

I sat up and turned to look at him. "What? Was it a false alarm?"

From his somber expression, I already knew the answer.

"It was about an hour or so after your opening," he said. "Blayze and I rushed up the back steps to the apartment. When we got in, the front door had been kicked open. Blayze saw someone run out and went after him, and I made sure the rest of the apartment was clear."

I felt the blood draining from my face. "Was it?"

He nodded. "But they left something on the bed."

Suddenly cold as ice, I wrapped my arms around my body and shivered.

He rubbed my arm. "Let's get out of this water and get warm. I'll finish telling you everything."

My entire body was numb. Ryan got out and wrapped a towel around his waist before he gently lifted me out of the tub. I was unable to move. The idea that someone had broken into our home and was in our bedroom…it was too much. *Too damn much!*

I was barely aware of Ryan drying me off and slipping one of his T-shirts over my head. Barely registered him asking me to lift my legs so he could help me don a pair of panties. When he lifted me again and carried me in his arms, only then did I notice he'd tugged his sweats back on.

Setting me gently on the sofa, he kissed my forehead. "Let me make you some hot tea."

I nodded, then dropped back against the sofa and watched Ryan move about in the little kitchen. Before I knew it, he was handing me a cup of tea.

"What was in the bedroom?" I asked, my voice wooden.

Ryan looked away and drew in a long breath before he exhaled and focused his attention back on me. "It was a heart."

I gasped. "As in…a *real* one?"

He nodded. "Detective Billings said it was taken from a deer or some other animal, according to the kid who broke in and left it."

I covered my mouth with my hand to hold back the bile that was building.

"There were also some rose petals thrown onto the bed and a note."

I closed my eyes and focused on breathing slowly so I wouldn't throw up. When I opened them, I softly whispered, "What did it say?"

He swallowed hard and pulled out his phone. "Billings sent it to me. It said, um…" Clearing his throat, he went on. "When I see you with him, you rip my heart out. I love you, and I know he has blinded you. So I'll wait a little longer for you to see the light."

Ryan closed his eyes briefly, then opened them and finished, "Tick-tock goes the clock…until you're mine, Morgan."

Tears streamed down my face. Ryan tossed his phone to the coffee table, sat down beside me, and pulled me onto his lap, holding me tightly.

"He was in our apartment!" I sobbed.

"No. It wasn't him. Blayze tackled the guy right as the police showed up. It was a young kid who said a guy offered him five-hundred dollars to break in and put all that shit on the bed. He didn't see his face, said he had it covered with a ski mask. At the station…he also told the detective that the guy had given him a hand-drawn layout of the apartment, so he'd know which room to put everything in."

I looked at Ryan in horror. "How does he know the layout of the apartment if he hasn't been in it?"

He slowly shook his head. "I don't know. Detective Billings is going to start questioning all the construction guys who worked on the apartment."

Closing my eyes, I rubbed my temples to ease the headache that was building. "I can't believe this. It's been so quiet…I thought maybe he'd forgotten about me and moved on."

Suddenly remembering my feeling in the bathroom, I jerked my gaze up to look at Ryan. "He's here," I blurted out.

With a confused expression, Ryan shook his head. "No, Rose was here earlier, but that's it."

I frantically shook my head. "No, Ryan, he's *here*! I felt someone watching me through the windows in the bathroom. He's here—or he was. Watching. I know he was. I felt it in my core."

Ryan reached for his phone and hit a number.

"Did you see anyone following us?" he asked into his cell. "Morgan thinks he was watching her. Fuck! Well, he might be here anyway… Yeah. I'll meet you outside."

He hung up, kissed me on the mouth quickly, then lifted me and deposited me on the sofa. "Stay inside, Morgan—and put some pants on."

"Wait! Who was that? Who are you meeting outside?"

"I'll explain in a bit. Don't come outside—do you hear me? No matter what, do not come outside. And lock the door when I leave."

Swallowing hard, I watched Ryan reach for his bag, and then gasped when I saw what he pulled out. "Why do you have a gun?" I asked, panic filling my voice.

He returned to the couch and kissed me again. "I'll explain everything once I come back in. Please don't come outside. Promise me."

"Ryan, you're scaring me."

His expression softened as he cupped my cheek in his hand, his thumb moving softly over my skin. "I'm being cautious. That's all."

And just like that, he turned and rushed out the door.

I jumped up and locked it, then stood there for a moment, listening. The sound of a car door shutting had me racing to the window. There was a car parked beyond the range of the outdoor lights, so I couldn't see who got out, but it was definitely a man. He was a bit taller than Ryan. They spoke for a couple of seconds, then both of them went off in different directions.

Spinning around, I raced to the bathroom so I could search for pants and my phone. Slipping on a pair of lounge pants, I grabbed my cell and tapped Blayze's number.

"Hey, is everything okay?" he answered.

"No! I mean, I don't know! Why does Ryan have a gun?"

"What?" Blayze asked, clearly confused.

"Ryan met some man outside the cabin because I told him I felt like I was being watched in the bathroom. He called someone, said he'd meet him outside, then he got a *gun* out of his bag, Blayze, and went outside to meet this man!"

"Morgan, calm down and take a few deep breaths, okay? First of all, you have a stalker doing all kinds of crazy shit to you, of course Ryan has a gun. It's not the first time you've ever seen him with a gun."

I closed my eyes. "I guess so, but he was hunting then. But yes, I see what you mean. It was just a shock to see it."

Blayze exhaled. "The guy is most likely Nox. A friend of ours."

Nox? Why did that name sound so familiar? Then I remembered. It was the name on Ryan's phone a couple weeks back. "Who's Nox?"

Blayze cursed. I heard him moving, then the sound of a door shutting. "Nox is someone we met in college our freshman year. He's probably the smartest guy I've ever known. Anyway, he ended up leaving school and went to work for the government. Doing what, I have no idea. I'm not sure Ryan does, either…but maybe. He and Ryan had a closer relationship. Ryan actually spent a whole summer with Nox, but don't ask me why.

I never asked. All I know is, if Ryan called Nox for help, it was either to assist in finding the guy doing this to you, or to…" His voice trailed off.

"Or to what?"

He sighed. "Watch you."

"Watch me? As in, follow me around?"

"Morgan, don't get upset with Ryan. He only wants to keep you safe."

"But if he has someone watching me, why didn't they see the kid break into the apartment today?"

"Because he probably had his eyes on you in the boutique."

"Ryan isn't involved with the government, is he?"

Blayze laughed. "No, I promise you he's not. He is, however, very proficient with a gun, and I think that has everything to do with Nox. From the little Ryan has told me about the summer he spent with the guy, I'm pretty damn sure he was attempting to recruit Ryan for something. He said no—and I'm even *more* sure that was because of you."

"Me?" I asked.

"Morgan…Ryan has had a thing for you ever since you were a teenager. He may not have admitted it to me, maybe not even to himself, but it was always obvious that most of the decisions he's made in his life have had everything to do with you."

I closed my eyes and fought the tears that threatened to escape. "He's out there right now, Blayze. What if that lunatic is still here? I would die if anything happened to Ryan!"

"Trust me when I say that Ryan can take care of himself."

I heard the lock disengage, then the door to the cabin opened and I let out a huge sigh of relief. "He's back." My eyes jerked over to a large man dressed entirely in camo. "And…he has GI Joe with him."

Blayze actually laughed at that. "Everything okay?"

"Blayze wants to know if everything's okay?" I called out.

Ryan smiled and nodded, though the smile didn't quite reach his eyes.

At the same time, Nox shook his head. I instantly liked the guy.

"Yeah, it's okay," I said, not wanting to worry Blayze. "I'm sorry I interrupted your evening. I'll talk to you later."

"I love you, Morgan."

"Love you too."

Hitting End, I stood and approached Nox. Jesus, the man was huge, and not the type of guy I would want to be on the wrong side of. He was all muscle and at least six two, with brown hair that was cut in a military style. His eyes were a beautiful light blue, but there was something in them that said he'd seen his fair share of terrible things. Holding out a hand, I said, "I'm Morgan Shaw."

"Nox Miller. It's a pleasure to finally meet you in person, Morgan, although I wish it was under different circumstances."

I forced a weak smile. "Me too. Since Ryan is clearly lying... Was he out there?"

Nox shot a bemused look in Ryan's direction. "I see what you mean."

Raising a brow, I gave Ryan a questioning look. He ignored it and said, "Someone was here; we found fresh tracks behind the cabin...and whoever they are, they got sloppy when they took off and left these behind."

Ryan raised a pair of binoculars up by the strap. I instantly wrapped my arms around my waist. He *had* been here—and he'd been watching us. Had he seen me in the bathroom? The thought made me sick to my stomach. "Do you think you can get prints off of them?" I asked.

Nox shook his head. "Already checked it with a UV light and got nothing. My guess is he wore gloves. The only reason he probably dropped them was because Ryan and I likely surprised him. I could hear him running, but he already had a good lead on us."

"I didn't want to leave you alone here, in case he's working with someone," Ryan added.

My eyes widened. "Working with someone?"

Ryan walked over to me and rubbed his hands up and down my arms. "I don't think he is. I was just playing it safe."

I let out a shaky breath. "This is insane! Does this guy not have a damn life? How in the hell did he know we were here?"

"He didn't follow you, I can tell you that," Nox stated. "That leads me to believe he already knew you'd be here."

"How?" Ryan and I asked at the same time.

"Who all knew you were planning this evening?" Nox asked Ryan.

"Morgan's cousin Rose, and her friend who owns this place. I told Blayze…and that's it. I didn't tell anyone else."

Nox nodded. "Could Rose have told someone?"

Ryan shrugged. "I mean, it's possible, but she's been up at school taking summer classes. She only came down this afternoon to decorate for us."

"Oh God! He could've been here while Rose was out here by herself!" I said, filled with sheer panic at the thought. I couldn't let anyone else get hurt by this psycho!

"Hey," Ryan said, pulling me to him and hugging me. "Don't think like that, okay? We don't know for sure that he didn't follow us here."

I saw the look Nox gave Ryan. He knew we hadn't been followed, so that meant this crazy asshole had to have known where we'd be. He somehow found out about the cabin and came here earlier. Maybe even while my cousin was here alone.

"I've got two of my best guys on their way already, Morgan," Nox said. "Only I have been shadowing you so far, but with your permission, I want to have one of my guys with you at all times."

"All times?" I asked as Ryan eased back and slid his arm around my waist. "Like, as in…a bodyguard? Do you think that's necessary?" I looked up at Ryan.

"Yes. I definitely think so, sweetheart. This guy knows the layout of the apartment, and he somehow discovered we were going to be here tonight. That means he's closer to us than we realized. For your safety and my sanity, I agree with Nox. You should have someone with you when I'm not around."

I shook my head. "I don't want this nutcase to know he's scaring me or intimidating me to the point that I need a bodyguard."

"Morgan, having a bodyguard isn't a sign of weakness," Nox argued. "This guy isn't messing around, and it seems like he's starting to get more daring, maybe even a little desperate. Now that Ryan's in the picture, the closer you two become seems to only make the guy angrier."

"How long do you think he's been stalking me?"

Ryan and Nox both looked at each other, then at me. Nox shook his head. "I'm not sure. Maybe he saw you on break from school, maybe he saw you a few weeks ago when you returned…it's impossible to say."

I blew out a frustrated breath. "It pisses me off that this guy is dictating part of my life."

"I know, but if he made a mistake tonight, maybe he'll make an even bigger one next time."

"That's the part that scares me," I said softly. "The next time."

Ryan laced his fingers with mine. "Do you think you can find anything out from the binoculars?" he asked Nox.

He gave us a one-shoulder shrug. "I'll see if I can, but they're a pretty everyday, run-of-the-mill set. Anyone could have bought them from a number of stores." Nox gave me a sympathetic look. "I hate to do this, but I think the two of you should probably head back to your place where there's plenty of security. Nothing says the guy won't try to come back here tonight."

"Even if he sees you and knows we have someone watching?" I asked.

Ryan squeezed my hand. "If he had the balls to hire someone to break into the apartment while the store was having its grand opening, God knows what else he might do."

Nox nodded. "Ryan's right, Morgan. You're safer at your place. Plus, we can have a uniform drive by every so often. Send a message to our guy that your place is being watched as well."

Looking into Ryan's eyes, I frowned. "I'm sorry this ruined the night you had planned."

He leaned down and kissed me on the forehead. "It doesn't matter where we are, as long as we're together."

Chapter Nineteen

RYAN

When we arrived back at the apartment, Morgan walked straight to our room. I wasn't sure what she was expecting, but it was clear Blayze—or maybe Brock—had taken care of everything. The entire old bed was gone, replaced with a new one, along with brand-new sheets and a comforter. The whole room smelled of lavender.

I walked in and stopped behind her, wrapping my arms around her body and resting my chin on her head. "You okay?"

"Who did all of this?"

"I think it was Blayze or your father. Maybe both."

Her body melted into mine. "I want to be brave, Ryan. I don't want this lunatic to make me afraid to be in my own home."

"I know," I whispered. "I'm so sorry we haven't found out who he is yet."

"What if it's someone I know?"

Turning her, I narrowed my eyes. "What makes you say that?"

She chewed on her lip. "When you mentioned he had to know the layout of the apartment, it got me thinking. I went to school with one of the construction guys. He used to have a crush on me, and during our senior year, he asked me out."

"Did you go out with him?"

Shaking her head, she replied, "No. I only liked him as a friend." "What's his name? I'll make sure Detective Billings checks him out."

She gave me a look. "It's David Keller."

"The guy you introduced me to? Doesn't his father own the construction company that worked on the entire building?"

"He does."

Frowning, I said, "Didn't he also mention having a girl-friend?"

Morgan began chewing on her thumbnail. "Yes, but that doesn't mean anything."

"That's true. I'll call Billings in the morning and give her the information. Doesn't hurt to find out where he was earlier today and this evening."

She nodded, then sighed. "I'm exhausted."

Taking her hand in mine, I led her over to the bathroom. "Get ready for bed, and I'll double check the alarm and check in with Nox."

Morgan yawned. "I'm too tired to do anything but crawl into bed."

I walked over and pulled the covers down. Morgan climbed into the bed and lay on her side, her hand tucked under her face. I knew she was going to fall asleep fast. It was nearly two in the morning, and the store would be opening at ten tomorrow.

"I'll only be a few minutes," I said.

She mumbled something as she snuggled deeper into the pillow. I kissed her on the forehead, whispered that I loved her, and then headed back into the main living area. After one quick check that all the doors were locked and the alarm was set, I texted Rodney, who was sitting in a vehicle in the back parking lot next to my truck. He'd arrived shortly before we got back to the apartment.

Me: I'm heading to bed. Everything's locked up and secure.

Rodney: I've got a guy up front, and I'll be back here. Try to get some sleep.

Me: Thanks, Rodney.

I pulled up the security alarm app and looked at each camera. Once I was sure everything was up and running, I headed to the bathroom and quickly changed for bed. After climbing under the covers, I wrapped my arm around Morgan and drew her against my body. She sighed in contentment as I kissed the back of her head and whispered again that I loved her.

I was both mentally and physically exhausted...and it only took a few moments before my eyes drifted shut.

A week and a half later, I slowly walked up to the gelding I'd been working with on my parents' ranch. "Okay, buddy. Let's hang out a bit, shall we?"

Ranger was standing next to a log, his lead draped over his neck so that if he wanted to walk away at any time, he was free to do so. I leaned over his back and gave him a bit of my weight before removing it. He didn't make a move. Trying again, I put more weight on him.

He lifted his front leg and kicked at the dirt once before looking back at me. I couldn't help but smile.

"Was that permission, or a 'stay the fuck off my back'?"

He whinnied, and I nodded. "Permission it is."

Walking to the other side, I repeated the process until I eventually draped my entire body over him. Ranger bopped his head a few times but remained where he was. Each horse was different when it came to saddle training. Some were curious about what the end game was going to be. Others, well…they simply didn't want anyone or anything on their backs.

I picked up the blanket I'd left on the ground and showed it to Ranger. "See, it's a blanket. Go on, smell it."

Ranger bounced his head with excitement.

"Yeah? I think you're going to love going for rides."

I ran my hand down his neck and along his body, then back and forth over his back. Gently placing the blanket on him, I moved back to his front. I gave him a good scratch behind his ears and laughed when his upper lip quivered.

"You're not bothered by that blanket at all, are you, boy?"

Ranger lifted his head and started to nibble on my baseball cap.

"Oh no, this is one of my favorites. I take it you're not a Seattle Mariners fan?"

"I like him already."

Turning, I caught sight of my mother. "Why, Tina Marshall, are you saying *you're* not a Mariners fan?"

My mother stroked Ranger's neck lovingly. "Indeed, I am. How's it going?"

"Good. He's one hell of a smart horse. Doesn't seem to mind the idea of something on his back. I think I'll have him saddle trained in no time."

Smiling, she looked the horse over. "Good. He's a pretty boy, and his momma is missing him."

My phone vibrated in my back pocket. Pulling it out, I said, "I need to take this, it's Bradford."

"Of course, I'll keep Ranger company and tell him all about the Boston Red Sox."

Rolling my eyes, I swiped the screen. "Hey, what's up?"

"I've got good news and bad."

Rubbing the back of my neck, I decided to get the bad news out of the way. "Give me the bad."

"The building we were hoping to rent? They sold it. I guess that's why they never got back to us—they already had buyers on the line. The new owners are planning to open a toy store."

I should have been upset by Bradford's news, but something inside me felt a sense of relief. Ever since Morgan and I got together, my future felt like it was shifting. I was starting to suspect my love of brewing beer had mostly been a substitute to keep me busy while I waited for something I could never put my finger on. I still enjoyed brewing...but now I knew what that *something* was. Morgan.

"A toy store?" I asked.

"Yeah," Bradford laughed. "But Lance wants to keep selling your brew at the restaurant."

Smiling, I said, "That's great. I really appreciate you going the extra mile for me, Bradford."

"Nonsense. You make a damn good beer, and Lance knows it."

"Thanks, dude."

"And the good news," he said. "Have you heard of Rockies?"

"The new bar that recently opened?"

"That's the one. The owner was in here last night with his wife. He ordered your beer and loved it. Wanted your information before he left."

"No shit," I said. "That's crazy."

Bradford mumbled something to someone. "Sorry, had to answer a question. Listen, I hope you don't mind, but I gave him your number. I hate to say it, Ryan, but our dream of opening our own place might be slipping through our hands. Things are going so good for me here at Le Vacher, Lance has been talking about bringing me on as partner. I'm not sure I should turn him down on the chance we may or may not be able to open our own place anytime soon."

I cleared my throat. I needed to be equally honest with Bradford and tell him where my own head was at lately. "Dude, don't pass up the chance to be a partner. The idea of owning our own restaurant was great when we first came up with it, but to be honest, right now, I'm so focused on Morgan and our relationship—and this bullshit stalker she's dealing with—that I can't even think of starting a new venture."

"Fuck, I forgot about that. How's she doing? I should probably have Savannah reach out to her. Do you think maybe she could help? Before she made anchor, she was an investigative journalist."

Glancing back to make sure everything was okay with my mother and Ranger, I replied, "Morgan's okay…for now. The guy seems to go quiet for a week or so, then does something to scare the living shit out of her. I wish we could figure out who the hell it is."

"Dude, I can't even imagine. If someone was doing that to Savannah, I'd want to rip his fucking head off and shove it up his ass."

"Exactly. I hope the police catch him before Blayze or I can get to him. Or Brock. Hell, Morgan's father would probably gladly go to prison for killing the guy."

"I'd feel the same way if it was my daughter. At any rate, if you or Morgan ever need anything, you let us know."

Smiling because I really did have some awesome fucking friends, I said, "I will. Hey, what are you and Savannah doing Sunday? Blayze and I were thinking of taking the girls four-wheeling. The boutique is closed. I wasn't sure if you're working or not?"

"I actually have Sunday off, and that sounds like a hell of a lot of fun. Being able to spend more time with Savannah would be great." A heavy pause followed before he continued, "I bought a ring."

"No shit!" I said with a laugh. "Dude, you're going to ask her to marry you?"

"I am. Just trying to figure out when and where to do it. I want it to be special for her."

"How soon are you planning on doing it? The place we're thinking of four-wheeling has a beautiful overlook of the Bitterroot Mountains. I'll even film it on my phone if you want."

Bradford let out a roar of laughter. The last time we went fishing, I'd pulled out my phone to record him reeling in a giant catch and the entire time, all you could see was either the water, part of Bradford's head, or my coat.

"If I actually want to remember the moment, I might get Georgiana or Morgan to do the filming. You really wouldn't mind if I asked her during your outing? She wouldn't see that coming at all."

"Dude, do it!"

I could hear the excitement in his voice when he said, "I'm going to." Another pause, then, "Shit! I'm going to ask her to marry me! I gotta go!"

"What's wrong?"

"I think I'm gonna throw up!"

The line went dead, and I pulled my cell back to see that he'd hung up. Laughing, I turned and headed back toward Ranger and my mom. I stopped abruptly when I saw my mother on Ranger's back, letting him walk around the enclosure at his own pace.

I let out a soft laugh and shook my head as I resumed walking. Ranger met me halfway, giving me a vocal greeting. I smiled at the horse. "You're lucky your good taste in women overrides your bad taste in baseball."

Chapter Twenty

MORGAN

Folding my arms over my chest, I refused to budge while my brother and Ryan both glared at me.

"Morgan—"

I held up my hand to stop Ryan. "I'm already going to be with you, my brothers, Georgiana, Bradford, Savannah, and Hunter's little...*friend*."

We all glanced over to see the blonde hanging all over my brother, several yards away. I shook my head and muttered, "Buckle bunny if I ever saw one."

"Buckle what?" Savannah asked with a confused expression.

Bradford grinned. "That was my reaction the first time I heard it. That's what they call women who follow the cowboys around at rodeos."

"Why buckle bunnies?" Savannah asked.

Georgiana answered that one. "They tend to go for the guys who win."

"Ohhh," said Savannah, nodding her head and looking back over at Hunter and his...friend.

"Is it weird that her name is Bonnie? Do you think they call her Buckle Bunny Bonnie?" Georgiana asked with a giggle.

Ryan sighed in frustration. "Morgan, I still don't think it would hurt to have Rodney come with us."

"He's right, Morgan. You won't even know he's there." This came from Blayze.

I huffed in disagreement. None of my friends or siblings could relate to my frustration. They didn't have to deal with a shadow every minute of the day.

"Not to join the ranks of overpowering men, but I agree with them. It doesn't hurt to have him tag along," Bradford said with a soft smile.

Rolling my eyes, I threw my hands up. "I just don't think it's necessary. And I feel bad. He's the only one without a date!"

Rodney laughed but quickly covered the sound with a cough. "It's really okay, Ms. Shaw."

After it was settled that Rodney would, in fact, be coming along, we all piled into our vehicles and headed toward the Bitterroot National Forest, where they had OHV trails for four-wheelers.

Once there, Hunter had to explain to Bonnie nearly a dozen times how to drive an ATV. She finally asked if she could ride on his.

"Why don't you guys use ours, and we'll take the single ones," Georgiana finally suggested. "It's against the law to ride double on a single four-wheeler."

Bonnie jumped and clapped her hand. "Thank you so much, Ginger!"

She frowned. "It's Georgiana."

Bonnie flashed a fake smile. "I was close."

Georgiana shot her a dirty look, then turned to Blayze, who gave her a look that said, "Let it go."

After finally getting Buckle Bunny Bonnie on a four-wheeler, we were off on the trails, with Rodney driving not too close but not too far behind, either.

Not even thirty minutes into the ride, Hunter pulled over. I stopped as well, since I was behind him. "What's wrong?"

He sighed. "Bonnie needs to use the restroom...*now*."

I looked at her and snarled my lip as she crossed her legs and bounced. "I have to pee so bad!" she said. "But I am *not* walking into those woods by myself."

Hunter made what sounded like a growl and pointed into the trees. "I can see you. Just go right there."

Bonnie looked insulted. "Right off the trail, so everyone and their mother can see me? I don't think so."

Ryan came driving up beside me. "Hey, what's going on?"

"Bonnie has to pee, and she's afraid to go alone," I said with a roll of my eyes.

Ryan glanced from me to Rodney.

Rodney nodded. "I'm pretty sure he isn't here, or we'd know if he was following us."

"Who?" Bonnie asked.

I took off my helmet and shot my younger brother a look that said he was going to owe me big time.

"Come on, Buckle—um, Bonnie, let's go."

Walking into the woods far enough for her to pee, I pointed to a spot. "Watch out for poison ivy."

"What?" she screeched.

I could *not* understand what Hunter saw in this girl besides her fake-ass boobs. She had to be good in bed. That was the only possible reason I could figure why she was here.

Motioning for her to go, I said, "You're fine. Squat and pee."

Bonnie mumbled under her breath, and I swore she said something like, "His dick better be big." I covered my mouth to keep from gagging.

"No one can see, right?" she called out.

I closed my eyes and silently asked for patience. "No one can see. Just pee!"

Bonnie was giving me a blow by blow of her peeing experience in the woods when the sound of a stick breaking caused me to turn and look to my left.

My heart dropped to my stomach when I saw a man standing behind a tree. The only thing I could see was that he was wearing…on my God. Was that a ski mask?

I did the only thing I could think of—I screamed my lungs out.

"Jesus Christ, what is it!?" Bonnie yelled as she tumbled back onto her ass. Then *she* started screaming. I turned back and the guy was gone.

Five seconds later, Rodney was running past me and after the guy.

Hunter and Ryan both raced toward me. Ryan grabbed me by the arms as Hunter skidded to a stop next to me. They both asked at the same time, "Are you okay?"

"Is *she* okay?" Bonnie yelled. "Are you seriously asking that? I fell on my ass. My naked ass!"

Hunter and Ryan ignored her.

"I'm fine," I said, taking a shaky breath. "It's okay. Go help her, Hunter."

Hunter made his way over to Bonnie. "Shit! You fell in poison ivy."

My mouth fell open as I stared at Bonnie, sitting on the ground with tears streaming down her face. I shook my head. "And I thought *I* was having a bad day."

◆ ◆ ◆

Ryan paced furiously in the parking lot as we waited for Blayze to get off the phone. Rodney had chased after the guy through the woods, but he'd lost sight of him, having to double back only to tell us the guy got away.

"Ryan, please stop pacing," I said, wringing my hands together in my lap. "We're not even sure it was him. I could have seen a hunter."

He gave me a look. "It's not hunting season. And last I checked, hikers don't wear ski masks in the middle of the summer."

I couldn't argue with that.

Blayze walked over, shaking his head when Ryan looked at him. "They don't have cameras at the entrance of the park."

"Fuck!" Ryan said before slicing his hand through his hair.

"How did he know we were here?" Hunter asked.

Ryan looked around our small group. His eyes landed on Bradford and Savannah.

"I didn't tell anyone, I swear," Bradford said.

Savannah shook her head. "I wasn't even aware we were coming here until this morning when Bradford said he had a surprise day planned for us."

Guilt hit me hard, knowing I had ruined Bradford's plans to ask Savannah to marry him. Ryan, so excited for his friend, had told me all about it yesterday.

Spinning around to face Rodney, Ryan said, "He had to have followed us."

"There's no fucking way we were followed. I would know, Ryan. And *you* know I would."

Scrubbing his hand down his face, he shouted, "How the fuck did he find out then?"

Their exchange reminded me that I never did ask Ryan how he knew Nox and Rodney so well. I still only knew the little Blayze had told me.

Everyone looked around at one another, though none of us had an answer.

"Is your apartment bugged?"

All eyes swung toward Bonnie, who was trying desperately not to itch her ass.

"What did you say?" Blayze asked.

She shrugged. "If the guy keeps showing up everywhere, maybe he has a bug in your house. Or in your car. My father works for the FBI, and you wouldn't *believe* the places they find hidden bugs and cameras."

Ryan turned to Rodney. "We know he has the layout of the apartment. It would make sense that he bugged it."

"I'm on it," Rodney said, already dialing his phone. "Nox, we need to sweep Morgan's apartment for listening devices."

When Ryan looked at me, I put a hand to my mouth. The idea that this man could've been listening to everything in the apartment, for *weeks*, made my stomach roil.

Every conversation, every phone call, every time Ryan and I made love…

I jumped off the tailgate of Ryan's truck, raced over to the grass, and threw up.

Ryan, my brothers, and Georgiana were instantly at my side. When I couldn't possibly throw up anymore, I straightened and looked out into the woods. With every ounce of strength I had left, I screamed at the top of my lungs.

"Fuck you, you sick motherfucker!"

◆ ◆ ◆

Sitting at the dining table in my apartment, I held my mother's hand while my father tried to convince me to stay out on the ranch. He even said that Ryan and I could stay in the guest house together, if we wanted.

After Rodney had asked Nox to sweep our place for listening devices, he was informed that Nox had already done so… and that he'd found nothing.

We still had no idea how this guy was showing up everywhere we went.

"Dad, as safe as you think the ranch is, this guy could get onto it from anywhere. It doesn't make sense to have Morgan stay out there," Hunter said. He'd joined us minutes ago, having detoured to take poor Bonnie to Urgent Care before dropping her off at her hotel where she'd promptly passed out from the drugs they'd given her.

Ryan was pacing back and forth again, like he had been in the trail parking lot. I could see his mind working overtime.

"I've got to agree with Hunter, Dad," Blayze said. "I think Morgan is better off here, where there's security and cameras and she's closer to the police."

"And no listening devices were found?" my mother asked in disbelief.

Nox walked in through the front door in time to hear the question. He shook his head. "Nothing. We didn't find any bugs anywhere in the store or on the second level of the building, either."

Tears burned at the back of my eyes. As much as I didn't want them to find any, it would have explained how the guy knew nearly every move we'd made so far.

Nox had left the front door open, and Detective Billings walked in. She made her way past everyone, coming straight to me. With a smile that said she was so sorry this shit was happening, she sat down in the seat my father vacated for her.

"David Keller checks out as clear. Every time there was an incident, he had a reliable alibi."

"Was it his girlfriend?" Nox and Ryan asked at the same exact time.

Billings smiled slightly and shook her head. "He's been out of town working in Boise on a project his father's company has there. His girlfriend went with him since she telecommutes and can work from anywhere. There are multiple people who can vouch that they were there during each incident. I checked again just now, and they're still in Boise."

"Fuck," Blayze mumbled.

"You thought it might be David Keller?" my father asked.

"At the time, he seemed like a reasonable suspect," Ryan said. "He liked Morgan in high school, she turned him down when he asked her out, and he would have access to the whole building."

My father rubbed his chin, seemingly lost in his thoughts.

"Dad?" I asked. "What are you thinking?"

"It's something Rose said to me when I saw her out riding yesterday."

"Rose?" Hunter asked.

Dad nodded. "I mentioned something about a few missing calves, and she casually said they were probably in the one place we'd least suspect them to be…"

Frowning, I asked, "How do missing calves have anything to do with any of this?"

He looked at me, then around the room. "Maybe the person we're looking for is so obvious, we're simply *overlooking* them."

"Them?" Ryan asked. "You think it's more than one person?"

Dad glanced at Ryan. "I think if this guy already paid someone to do his dirty work *once*, how do we know he's not paying multiple people to keep tabs on Morgan, you, Georgiana...? Hell, all of us."

The idea caused me to shiver.

A light knock on the still-open door had us all turning to see a young girl standing there with a bouquet of flowers. "Sorry, the door was open. I have a delivery for Ryan Marshall?"

"That's me," Ryan said as he walked toward the delivery girl. She handed him the huge bunch of lilies.

Detective Billings followed Ryan. She put her hand on his arm when he reached for the card and shook her head. Putting on a glove, she pulled the card off the bouquet and opened it.

She turned the card for Ryan to see—and I watched his expression turn furious.

"What does it say?" I asked as I got up and walked to his side. Billings showed me the card. I read the neat print and nearly dropped to the floor when my knees buckled.

Did you know, Ryan, that lilies are the traditional funeral flower? Tick-tock goes the clock...soon she'll be mine, and I'll right this wrong once you're gone.

Chapter Twenty-One

RYAN

I sighed as I looked over at Lucas, the bodyguard Nox had insisted I let tag along with me everywhere. Everyone's biggest fear was now that the psychopath would try to do something to *me* to get to Morgan.

It was the beginning of August. Weeks had gone by with nothing from the douchebag. I wasn't about to let my guard down, though.

A La Chic Boutique was still going strong, with a steady stream of business. The line that Morgan had designed exclusively for the shop was their bestseller, with many of their customers wanting one of every design. They had customers as far away as England—after Lady Mary was photographed in a dress she'd purchased from A La Chic Boutique.

"How's it going?" my father asked, approaching the enclosure and leaning against the fence.

Taking my cowboy hat off, I wiped the sweat from my brow and then replaced it. "She's stubborn and wants to go where she wants to go."

Dad laughed. "I believe that's why the owner brought her to us."

I tried to smile but couldn't seem to muster enough energy. "How did the breeding go with the new mare?"

He nodded. "Good. She was a bit pissed at first, but they managed to take care of business on their own."

"I'm telling you, that front pasture needs to be renamed the love pasture. You need to breed, then shove them out there."

Dad let out a good belly laugh, then opened the gate and walked into the corral. "Want me to give it a try?"

"I'm sorry, Dad. My mind isn't really here right now, and she knows it."

He nodded and glanced over at Lucas. "Is it the scary-looking soldier near the barn who's causing you to lose your focus?"

I chuckled. "Lucas is a nice guy, and I know he's only doing his job. Everyone seems to think with all the added security and everything that maybe the nutcase gave up…but I know he hasn't. I feel it in my gut, Dad."

"What do the police think?"

I sighed. "Detective Billings doesn't think so either. I feel guilty that I'm not with Morgan, but at the same time, I can't follow her around everywhere she goes. The last thing I want to do is smother her."

"How's Morgan holding up?"

That time, when I smiled, I meant it. "She's the toughest woman I've ever met, Dad. She's stubborn, so she wants to keep living life as normal. She was up at six this morning to head to the gym. She asked me to stay home. I think she needed some time alone, and I don't blame her. I can tell she's worried about me since the last note he sent was directed at me. But I can take care of myself, and I've told her that."

"That's what you love about her, Ryan. Her strength and that stubbornness."

I slowly shook my head and looked down at the horse. Sliding off, I gave the mare a good scratch behind her ears and then let her wander around the pen while I walked over to the fence.

"In all the years that I've wondered what life would be like with Morgan if we ever started dating, I never dreamed I'd move in with her before we even went on a first date. Or that we'd have someone following us around, watching our every move. I love her so much, Dad…and I think I have for some time. A part of me wants to whisk her away and be free of all of this."

He put his hand on my shoulder and gave it a squeeze. "Then do it. Take her somewhere."

"I can't. She's got the boutique, and I don't want to take her away so soon after they opened."

"Four days, Ryan. Go somewhere for a long weekend."

"A long weekend…" I mused, the idea instantly taking root.

"How about you let me and your mother plan something? You won't even know where you're going until you get to the airport."

I rubbed the back of my neck. "It's tempting. I'd have to ask Georgiana if I could maybe steal Morgan for a couple of days. They're closed on Sundays."

Dad smiled. "This weekend then."

I let out a humorless laugh. "Dad, that's in two days."

He frowned. "Because no one has ever planned a last-minute trip? I've got this. And you clearly need this as much as Morgan does."

I inhaled deeply…and for the first time in a couple of months, I finally felt like I could breathe without a vise squeezing around my chest.

"I'll leave a little early and talk to Georgiana about it. Thanks, Dad."

My father grinned. "You know we've always adored Morgan, but seeing how happy you both are together, even with all this mess, it makes me and your mother just as happy. You deserve nothing more than unconditional love, Ryan, and I know Morgan gives that to you."

I chuckled. "It feels like this should be a conversation for after we've dated for a year. Our relationship has been on supersonic speed since day one."

He threw his head back and laughed. "It feels like you've been dating forever, if you ask any of us."

My phone rang in my back pocket. I pulled it out and glanced at the screen. "It's Georgiana," I said as I swiped my finger across the surface to answer the call.

"Hey, Georgiana," I said as my father motioned to me, letting me know he'd take care of the mare.

"Ryan!" Her voice was filled with panic.

My heart dropped at the sound—and I instantly took off running toward my truck. It was then I noticed Lucas also racing toward the driveway, his own phone to his ear and a look of utter panic on his face. He beat me to the truck, opened the passenger-side door, and jumped in.

"What's wrong?" I said into the phone.

"She's gone! *She's gone!*" Georgiana shouted. "He's knocked out! He's bleeding and…and…she's gone!"

My head was spinning as I jumped into the driver's seat, started the truck, and took off down the drive.

"Georgiana, I can't understand you—what's going on?"

It sounded like she dropped the phone, then I heard Nox's voice.

"Ryan."

"Nox! What the fuck is going on?"

"Take Lucas's phone. I'm on that line. Someone calm her down—and call Blayze!"

It sounded like total chaos in the background. I tossed my cell onto the dash and took the phone Lucas was holding out for me.

"Nox, what the fuck is happening? Where's Morgan?"

"Rodney was drugged. He was in the back of the store in the office, drinking some coffee that Avery brought back for everyone. Apparently, it's a daily thing she does. The police are already at the coffee shop now, investigating and talking to whoever made the drinks. When Rodney passed out, he hit his head on something. The women all heard the noise, and it was Avery who went back and found him. She started to yell for help, but someone grabbed her from behind and put a cloth over her mouth, knocking her out as well. We're assuming chloroform."

He paused. "Ryan...Morgan happened to be the one who walked to the back to investigate. Georgiana said they both heard Avery yelp, and they thought she might have hurt herself. Georgiana was helping customers, so Morgan went to the back...and that's when someone grabbed her."

My heart dropped to my stomach. "The cameras?"

"The camera in the office shows everything I just told you. The guy was waiting outside the frame to subdue Avery, so we only have a shot of his back. Same thing when he abducted Morgan. The outside camera captured a delivery van pulling up. The guy gets out, but we can't see his face. He has his head down, a hat on, plus he's holding a number of boxes. It was a UPS van, so no one thought twice about it. It usually shows up around this time to make deliveries. Whoever this guy is, he's been watching closely. He had this whole thing planned out to almost the minute...the coffee run, the package delivery..."

"What about Morgan?" I shouted.

"A few minutes later, the same guy is on camera leaving the building, carrying a passed-out Morgan in his arms, and putting her in the van. He knew where the cameras are because he never once looked in their direction. He drove off and the police have an APB out on the van. But my guess? He's already ditched it."

Anger and fear fought for control as I handed the phone back to Lucas and pressed down harder on the gas.

"We should be there soon," I heard Lucas say. He sounded far away, like he was talking through a tunnel.

"Morgan," I whispered, fighting to hold back the tears that were pricking the back of my eyes. "I'll find you, Morgan. I swear to God, I'll fucking find you."

◆ ◆ ◆

I slumped on the sofa in our apartment and buried my face in my hands. Almost eight hours had passed since Morgan was kidnapped.

Eight fucking hours.

I'd driven the streets aimlessly most of that time, looking for any trace of the van. Nearly everyone in her family had packed into the apartment after the abduction while we'd regrouped, working to come up with a plan. Lincoln and Brock were clearly trying to be strong for everyone else, but I had seen it written all over their faces—they were scared. I was scared. Every single person in the family was scared. Some crazy-ass guy had Morgan. *My* Morgan.

If he put a single finger on her, I would kill him with my bare hands.

We'd all gone out to look for Morgan, but it had been fruitless. Now, the apartment was quiet, and I was drowning in my thoughts. Thoughts I shouldn't be lost in at a time like this. Hunter, Blayze, Brock, Ty, and Tanner—and all their women—were still out searching. Dirk had been at the police station for the last four hours, trying to stay updated so he could pass along information. FBI agents from the office in Missoula had been called in, and they'd left after interviewing me, only moments ago.

A light knock on the door had me looking up to see Bradford and Savannah standing there. She rushed over and sat on the sofa, wrapping her arms around me. "I did a piece on her kidnapping on the six o'clock news."

"Thanks, Savannah."

Bradford was holding a couple of baking dishes. He walked into the kitchen and put them in the refrigerator, then made his way back over to me. "Put it in the oven on three-fifty to warm it when you're hungry."

All I could do was nod.

"Is there anything we can do, Ryan?" Bradford asked as he sat down on the seat opposite the sofa.

"No," I said, my voice sounding raspy. "Everyone's out looking, but no one knows what the fuck to look for. I drove around for hours, but it was fucking pointless."

Savannah squeezed my hand. "We're going to find her, Ryan."

I dropped my head back…and for the first time in my adult life, let my tears fall freely. "I tried so hard to keep her safe!"

"No! Oh, Ryan, *no*," Savannah said as she pulled me closer, holding me tightly. I didn't give two fucks that Bradford was there; I cried like a goddamn baby. "This is *not* your fault. And she's going to be okay. She'll be okay," Savannah repeated over and over, rocking me gently.

After a good five minutes, I pulled myself together and wiped my face, letting out a frustrated groan. When I glanced at Bradford, he was looking down at his phone. His expression was so odd, it caused me to pause.

Had he heard something? Was it about Morgan? My heart started to damn near beat out of my chest.

"What's wrong?" I asked.

Jerking his attention away from the phone, he shook his head. "I'm sorry, Ryan. It's the restaurant—an emergency in the kitchen. God, I'm so damn sorry, but I might have to help get this handled before the dinner rush."

I let out a relieved breath. "Dude, please don't stay here on my account. Go take care of the restaurant."

Bradford shook his head and was about to argue when Savannah said, "Sweetheart, go. I'll stay here and make sure everyone gets some food. It's okay."

He looked so torn as his gaze bounced from me to Savannah. He finally nodded and stood. "I'll call before I come back to see if I should bring any more food."

I tried to smile but couldn't quite manage it. "It looks like you brought enough to feed an army."

Bradford smiled, though I saw the concern in his eyes. "Have you *seen* how many people are in the Shaw family?"

That time, I chuckled slightly. "Yeah, I have."

Savannah stood and walked Bradford to the door. They spoke softly for a minute before he leaned down, kissed her, and slipped out the door.

Day turned into night and I stayed on the sofa, completely numb, wanting to go out and look for Morgan but also not wanting to leave again in case someone had an update.

Savannah had done as promised and fed everyone who came and went. She was also really good at keeping Lincoln busy.

Needing a few moments of peace, I stood to go sit in the bedroom. But before I could get there, Blayze walked up to me. "Detective Billings is here. She wants to talk to you."

Turning, I saw the detective standing just inside the apartment, speaking to Brock. They were talking in hushed voices, and the next thing I knew, Brock was motioning to Hunter and Ty. They walked outside in a rush.

"What's going on?" I asked, making my way over to the detective.

"I need to talk to you, but it would be best if we do it outside."

"Morgan?" I asked, my voice cracking as I silently begged God for her to be okay.

"We haven't found her…yet. Let's take this outside, away from everyone else."

I frowned, about to deny her. The family had a right to know what was going on.

Detective Billings gave me a silent pleading look before she whispered, "Not in here."

Turning, she headed out the front door. I followed her down the steps and over to her unmarked car. She motioned for me to get in, so I did.

"What's going on?" I asked.

"There are cameras in the building."

Confused, I asked, "What building?"

She pointed to our building. "The FBI found two in the store and four on the second floor. They're in the attic space now, above the apartment. There are two in the living room, and one in each bedroom and bathroom. They don't want to disconnect them yet in case the kidnapper finds out we know about them."

A sick feeling swarmed my body. How in the fuck had Nox missed the cameras? "He's been watching us?"

She nodded. "That's how the bastard knew everywhere you were going, what your plans were. Ryan, he's been watching the two of you..." She cleared her throat and went on. "He's been watching you together."

I threw open the door to the car, leaned out, and threw up.

Chapter Twenty-Two

THE RINGMASTER

I'd had the cabin prepped for months. Painstakingly made sure it was perfect for her. There was a design table for her to keep making her pretty dresses. A king-size bed where we would finally be joined as one. A big kitchen, because I knew my Morgan wanted to learn to cook. Then there was the huge bathroom. I'd recently added the large soaking tub after seeing how she loved to take baths.

Shutting the door, I walked over to the bedroom. Morgan had woken up four hours ago. I'd watched her screaming over and over for help, but I knew no one would hear her so far out of town. There were no windows in the room and no way for her to get out. She eventually started to sob, finally crying herself back to sleep.

My hand shook as I slid the key into the lock and opened the door. I was finally going to have her all to myself. After almost three years of wanting and waiting, I'd be able to feel those lips on mine once more.

The sound of the door opening caused Morgan to jump up and run to the farthest corner of the room. It was dark inside.

"Let me go!" Morgan cried. "Please! Just let me go!"

Reaching over, I turned on the light switch and watched and waited as my beautiful girl's eyes adjusted to the bright light of the room.

When she finally stopped blinking, her eyes went wide and her mouth dropped open in shock.

"I've been waiting a long time for this moment, Morgan."

She slowly stood, a confused expression crossing her perfect face as she said one word...but that word was music to my ears.

"Bradford?"

Chapter Twenty-Three

Morgan

I stood there in shock as I stared at the man I had come to know the last couple months. Ryan and Blayze's friend. *My friend.*

My entire body started to shake when he shut the door and locked it. "I'm a little hurt you don't remember me, Morgan."

With a shake of my head, I said, "I *do* remember you. You're Bradford. Ryan and Blayze's friend. Savannah's *fiancé.*"

He lifted a brow. "I'm not *your* friend?"

"Yes," I quickly said. "What are you doing here? What's happening? Where am I?"

Slowly moving through the room, he stopped on the other side of the bed and sat down.

"You don't remember me? Our kiss meant something to you—don't deny it."

I blinked in confusion. "Our kiss?"

He tsked as he slowly shook his head. "I uprooted my entire life to move to Hamilton. Then I had to befriend your brother, and it didn't take me long to figure out old Ryan boy had a thing for you. Every time you came home from school, I saw the way he looked at you. And *you*—you looked at him the same way. But I can forgive you. I'd forgive you for anything… even giving your virginity to him."

I pressed my hand to my mouth as my chest constricted in fear. After a long pause, I dropped my hand and asked softly, "How do you know that?"

He smirked. "Because I know *everything*. I know you let him take that gift that should have been for me."

"Wh-what? How?" Did *Ryan* tell him that he took my virginity? No…no, he'd never do that…

"Oh, Morgan. I've been watching you ever since the night you kissed me."

"What are you talking about, Bradford? I've never kissed you! I only met you two months ago!"

Anger contorted his features and he stood. "Why don't you remember?!" he shouted.

I jumped and pressed my fist to my mouth to keep from crying again. Bradford started to pace across the room, his face blood red.

"The minute you walked into that party, I realized instantly you were supposed to be mine."

What in the world was he talking about?

"Then the way you smiled at me, so sweetly, I knew you weren't like any of the other whores in that place. Your innocence poured off you in waves…delicious, exciting waves…"

I stared at him, utterly confused.

"*You* flirted with *me*, Morgan. Made me hard as a damn rock for you." Bradford gave me a smarmy grin, and my eyes went to his mouth.

I'd seen that smile before! But where? Where had I seen it?

I slowly shook my head. I couldn't remember, damn it!

"Maybe we should kiss so you can be reminded. I see the way you're thinking so hard, trying to remember where we met."

Pressing myself against the wall, I shook my head. "I don't want to kiss you."

His smile faded. "Why? Because of *him*? Do you know what it did to me to watch you fucking him night after night!?"

My entire body went rigid. "What do you mean?"

He laughed, low and dark. "You like to be on top. And you like it when he licks that pretty pussy of yours."

My stomach lurched, and I instantly covered my mouth. I was going to get sick. Throw up right there. "Oh God...no. Please, no!"

"Every time I saw that bastard, I wanted to strangle him with my bare hands. He took what was *mine*. I hated him for that," he seethed. "I tried to crush his little dream of owning his own bar. I wanted that power over him. But when I told him—he couldn't have cared less! That was because of *you*, Morgan. All because you couldn't keep your legs closed and wait for me."

The room started to spin, and I felt like I was going to pass out. He'd been watching us. Watching us in our own home.

"Are you okay there, princess?"

My gaze jerked up when he took a step toward me. I held out my hands. "Stay away from me! Don't you dare touch me!"

Another step. Then another. The closer he got, the more my heart raced in my chest. Bradford grinned.

Then—it hit me where I'd seen that smile before.

"*Rich?*"

Bradford stopped. His smug grin slowly spread into a wide smile. "You remember."

"I don't...I don't understand."

He stood right before me now, lifting his hand to touch my face. I jerked back. Grabbing a lock of my hair, he rubbed it between his fingers. "Do you call this honey brown? Golden brown? I never could figure out if your hair was light brown or dark blonde. But it's just as soft as I thought it would be."

Once more, I felt the urge to throw up.

"The night you walked away from me, I vowed to win your love. I followed you around campus as much as I could... and you were clueless. Even followed you to Hamilton that first Christmas break. Stayed in this very cabin. That's when I saw you looking at Ryan with lust in your eyes." He closed his own eyes, his brow furrowed as if in pain. "I wanted you to look at *me* like that. I saw a glimpse of it the night he brought you to Le Vacher. You let your eyes move over my body, and I saw it—you wanted me."

My eyes widened in horror. "No! I'm in love with Ryan."

"Shut up!" he yelled. "Don't you *ever* say that again! Never!" He started to pace the room again. "I had the chance to go to France. Develop my culinary skills, but I had to pass it up to move to fucking Hamilton. I had to stay close to you so when you graduated and moved home, we could be together. Then that fucker ruined *everything*!"

"What about Savannah? I thought you loved her?"

An evil laugh slipped from his mouth. "Savannah was a cover. Yeah, she's a good fuck. But she's a little whore. Anything I want to try, she'll do it for me. It's really pathetic, actually. She means less than nothing to me. She was only a warm place for me to stick my cock. I used to close my eyes and pretend it was *you* riding me. It was you I was sinking into." He gave me another smirk. "Savannah fell so fast, I knew she'd be the perfect thing to take any suspicion away from me. Sure, she'll be hurt when I never show up again, but she'll get over me. They always do."

My voice cracked as I asked, "What do you mean, when you never show up again?"

He paced back toward me. "After I make you mine, we're leaving Hamilton."

Tears slipped free and rolled down my face and I shook my head.

"Oh, princess," he said, putting his clammy hand on the side of my face. I had to fight the urge to jerk away. If I did, I knew it would only make him more angry. "We can't stay here. We need to start a new life together far, far away. The longer we stay, the sooner that fucking family of yours, or Ryan, will find us. They've been out all day looking for you."

He frowned. "Poor little Ryan was all torn apart when Savannah and I stopped by to bring him some food I'd made. I am, after all, the caring and concerned friend. I was watching you on my cameras trying to figure out how to get out of this room while that dumb fuck was sitting right there." He let out a sick-sounding laugh. "While he was crying in Savannah's arms, I was sitting directly across from him, watching you on my phone. Imagine how pissed at himself he'd be if he knew that!"

My chest squeezed so tightly I had a hard time breathing. Oh, Ryan. I closed my eyes and tried not to picture how worried everyone was.

"Avery…is she okay?"

"She's fine. And so is that stupid-ass bodyguard of yours. I have to admit, the addition of Nox and his merry band of military men threw me off, and I had to lay low for a bit. I thought I was finally going to be able to grab you when we went four-wheeling."

I sucked in a breath. "That was you?"

He smiled. "When that stupid idiot Bonnie had to go to the bathroom and you offered to go with her, I knew it was my chance. The fucking bodyguard was so busy staring at Bonnie's ass, he never noticed me slipping through the woods."

"How did no one know you were gone?"

He shrugged. "I ran back to my four-wheeler and met back up with Savannah. Told her I took a wrong turn. She didn't even notice I was gone for a few minutes."

As much as I didn't want to think about it, I asked, "That's how you knew all of our plans? The camera in my apartment? How?"

"*Cameras*. Plural. And that was the easiest part. All I had to do was show up the same time as the team from the security company. Told them I was hired by your dad to install additional cameras as backup. No one even questioned when I added a few more."

I gently massaged my temples. My head had already been pounding; now it was throbbing. And I was still a little woozy from whatever he'd used to knock me out. It wasn't as bad as when I first woke up, though.

"Do you have a headache?" His voice almost sounded tender.

"Yes."

"I'll get you some Tylenol. I also have a gift for you."

He took a few steps backward before turning to leave.

"I thought your name was Rich?"

Pausing, he glanced over his shoulder. "It is. Rich Bradford. Now…I'm going to need you to get undressed, so you can put on your gift."

Panic instantly filled my entire body. Before I could think of anything to say, he shut and locked the door behind him.

Sliding down the wall, I buried my face in my hands and cried. "Please find me, Ryan. *Please*!"

The door opened seconds later, and Bradford or Rich or whoever the hell he was stepped inside with his hands full. There was a small table and two chairs on the other side of the room near the door. He put a glass of water and bottle of Tylenol on the table, followed by a gift box and a plate of food.

"I need to call Savannah. I have to let her know my mother's fallen ill and I had to leave town—and that I won't be back for at least a week."

I wiped away the tear that rolled down my cheek. The last thing I wanted was for him to see me as weak.

"Come over here, Morgan."

Knowing how unhinged this guy was, I decided to do as he said. I slowly made my way over to the table. I opened the unopened bottle of Tylenol and took two. The smell of the quiche on the plate made me both hungry and sick to my stomach.

"Open your gift."

Swallowing hard, I reached for the white box. It took everything I had to keep my hands from shaking. When I took the lid off, I pulled tissue paper to the side and stared at the light blue lingerie. I jerked my head up to look at him.

"I picked it out for you. Stupid Savannah found it hidden in my closet and thought it was for her. She almost put it on, but I couldn't have her tainting it. I lied and told her I was saving it for a special occasion. Then I had to distract her with sex."

He looked up in thought and laughed. "I guess it wasn't really a lie. I *am* saving it for something special. For the first time we make love."

"No," I said. "I am not doing that with you."

His eyes filled with anger. "Yes, you are. I've waited *three fucking years* to have you. I would have had you that very first night if your goddamn friend hadn't shown up. I could see it all over your face then—you wanted me."

I shook my head. "Bradford, I—"

"Don't call me that!" he shouted. "You call me *Rich*. That's the name I want to hear from those pretty lips." When he tried to touch my mouth, I stepped away.

Scowling, he tried to grab me and I cried out, "I'm pregnant!"

Bradford froze. "What?"

I pressed my hand to my stomach, and I prayed with all my heart that I could lie well enough for him to believe me. "I'm pregnant with Ryan's baby."

He pushed his hand through his hair, clutching at the strands, his face a mask of fury. "It's because you were careless! You let him fuck you without a damn condom! What the hell were you thinking?!"

I stood perfectly still, afraid of what he might do.

"Fuck!" he shouted. "This ruins *everything*! Now I have to raise *his* goddamn child?!"

A small piece of me relaxed, knowing that he believed the lie. Now I had to hope he wouldn't want to be with me if I was carrying another man's child.

"Brad—*Rich*, if you let me go, I won't tell anyone it was you who took me. You can slip away and no one will ever know."

He gave me an incredulous look. "You think this changes things? I'm still gonna make you mine. Whether you're pregnant or not."

My eyes went wide, and nausea filled my chest yet again.

"But it changes my plans for the immediate future. I'll need to rethink a few things."

"I thought…" My voice trailed off. What could I say? This man was completely insane. A monster.

He narrowed his eyes. "Are you lying because you thought that would keep me from making love to you?"

"Do you really want to force me to have sex?" I countered. "You'd be raping me, Rich. Is that what you want?"

Staring at me, he looked confused and almost tormented. "I don't ever want to hurt you, Morgan. If you're not ready yet, that's okay. I've waited this long; I can wait a little longer. But a part of me doesn't believe you're pregnant." A slow smile pulled at the corners of his mouth. "Maybe I'll go to town and get a pregnancy test."

Fuck. Fuck. Fuck.

He walked over to me, causing me to back away until I hit the wall. He cupped my cheek, and I had to close my eyes to keep from gagging at his touch.

"I would never hurt you, Morgan. I love you. You'll see that soon. You'll see how destiny has brought us together."

He slid his hand to the back of my neck and into my hair. Grabbing a fistful, he pulled hard enough to jerk my head back, and I let out a small scream. His mouth covered mine, and before I even knew what was happening, his tongue was everywhere.

I pressed my hands into his chest and shoved with all of my might, but it was useless. He pushed closer to me, covering my body with his. I could feel his erection, and felt powerless to do anything. There was no space between our bodies to thrust my knee into his groin, so I pushed harder with my hands.

As quickly as it began, it stopped. Rich turned and walked to the door as I frantically wiped at my mouth. "I'll be back, darling." He pointed to the quiche. "Eat up—you'll need your strength."

The door shut, and I looked at the table. Lunging forward, I picked up the plate and threw it as hard as I could against the door. "Fuck you, you goddamn lunatic!" I screamed.

Chapter Twenty-Four

RYAN

I sat with my head in my hands, devastation choking me, and vowed yet again to kill the fucker who'd taken my Morgan.

The FBI had tapped into the apartment cameras and put the feed on a loop with most of the lights out, making it appear that everyone had gone back out to continue searching. After that, they let us back into the apartment. Currently, Brock, Hunter, Blayze, Georgiana, Rose, and Lincoln were all talking quietly among themselves in the living room. Savannah was also still there, but she'd gone into the stairwell to take a call.

Minutes later, she walked back into the apartment with a confused look on her face.

"What's wrong, dear?" Lincoln asked.

Savannah glanced over at her. "Bradford left."

"What do you mean he left?" Blayze asked.

She shook her head. "He just called me and said his mother was sick and he had to leave town. I told him I'd go with him, but he said no. That he's already halfway to Missoula to catch a flight home."

"What's wrong with her?" I asked.

"I don't know. He was very short and kind of…cold toward me. Said he'd be gone at least a week."

Lincoln handed Brock a cup of coffee. "I'm sure he was just worried about his mother, Savannah. He's probably afraid. It sounds serious, if he had to drop everything and leave so quickly."

Savannah nodded slowly and sat down.

Turning to Lincoln, I couldn't help but notice how tired she looked. "Lincoln, if you want to go lie down, the guest room is quiet."

She offered me a gentle smile. "Thank you, Ryan, but I can't sleep right now."

"Should I heat up some more of the food Bradford made?" Savannah asked.

"Ryan, you should eat," Brock said.

I shook my head. "I don't think I can keep anything down."

He looked at me with a world of understanding.

Blayze stood. "I might have some food. I'm starting to get a headache."

Hunter walked over a few minutes later and handed me a beer. I took it with a grateful nod. He sat down next to me… and didn't say anything for the longest time. Then he cleared his throat, and when he spoke, his voice was low. "Ryan, I've been thinking. How well do you know Bradford?"

I was so surprised by his question, I didn't answer right away. "I mean, we were going to go into business together, so I'd like to think I know him pretty well. Why?"

Hunter's brows pulled down. "It's just…I always got a weird vibe from him. And more than once I caught him looking at Morgan and…" He looked over to Savannah who was standing in the kitchen, then back to me. His voice was so low now I had to lean in to hear him. "It gave me the creeps how he looked at her. If he didn't think anyone was watching, he was practically eye-fucking her. I noticed it at Ravalli's, and the night we went to Le Vacher to celebrate the opening of the boutique. He…watched her. And I remember thinking it was so odd, especially when he was with Savannah."

I rubbed at the back of my neck. "Hunter, you can't possibly think it was Bradford. I mean, he was with us when Morgan spotted that guy in the woods when we went four-wheeling."

"Yeah. But I *also* remember Savannah saying something about how he disappeared for a bit. Something about turning down the wrong trail. Ryan—there's only one trail up there."

I frowned. "I didn't know he disappeared that day."

"Savannah said it was only for like five minutes. And at one point, I remember passing him because he'd fallen back behind everyone else."

Letting out a disbelieving laugh, I shook my head. "It can't be him, Hunter. I think we're all so desperate to find Morgan, we're grasping at straws."

Hunter sliced his fingers through his hair. "Maybe. I just find it odd that Morgan is gone and he suddenly had to leave town. Did you even *know* anything about his mom? Was she sick?"

"He doesn't talk about his parents much. I've never met them. All I know is that he apparently comes from a lot of money."

The door opened, and Stella and Avery entered. Poor Avery had been a mess since all of this began. After being released from the hospital—Merit and Dirk had insisted she be looked at—she'd stuck to Blayze's side like glue. At least until Stella came over and finally talked her into leaving the apartment. They'd gone to Albertsons to pick up some drinks and more food.

Avery's gaze caught mine as she walked by. I stood to help both ladies with the groceries, and so did Hunter.

"Let me get that, Grams," Hunter said as he took the bags from his grandmother. I took the three out of Avery's hands.

"Are you okay?" I asked her.

Tears filled her eyes, but she blinked them away. "I'm okay."

"Oh, Savannah!" Stella said, greeting her in the kitchen. She glanced around the living room. "I figured Bradford would have beat us here. Are you waiting for him?"

With a sad smile, she replied, "No, he had to leave town earlier. He's on his way to Missoula to catch a flight home. His mother's sick."

Stella and Avery both paused and shared a confused look. Suddenly, my blood turned to ice in my veins.

Hunter placed the bags on the counter and looked at his grandmother. "Why did you think he'd beat you here?"

Stella frowned. "We saw him at Albertsons not ten minutes ago. He was looking at pregnancy tests. He said it was for Savannah and that he was in a rush to get back to her."

"Me?" Savannah said in shock. "I…I can't have kids. And Bradford knows that."

My heart felt like it dropped to the floor. Everything clicked into place. "Motherfucker. It's him!"

"I knew it! I fucking *knew* it!" Hunter seethed.

"Wait—what's going on?" Blayze asked, glancing between me and Hunter.

"Hunter just told me he had a strange vibe about Bradford," I said. "Saw him looking at Morgan a few times, and it gave him a weird feeling."

Savannah let out a disbelieving laugh. "You can't possibly think Bradford took Morgan?"

I turned to her. "Why was he at Albertsons when he *just called* and told you he was already on his way to Missoula? He said he was halfway there, Savannah. And who the hell would he be buying a pregnancy test for, if not you?"

I felt sorry for Savannah as soon as I saw the look of absolute devastation on her face, but right now my only focus was on finding Morgan.

I pulled out my phone as Blayze said, "Hold on. So you think Bradford was stalking Morgan this whole time?"

"I didn't until this very moment," I replied.

"What do we do?" Avery asked, her voice shaking.

I hit Detective Billings's name in my contacts and put the phone on speaker. While it was ringing, I sent Nox a text with three words:

It's Rich Bradford.

Several minutes later, while Billings spoke to Savannah, I packed a bag with the things Nox told me to bring. Reaching under the bed, I pulled out my gun safe, entered the code, and took out my revolver.

"What do you think you're going to do?" Hunter asked from where he stood in the doorway.

"I'm not waiting around for the police to fucking interview people when I *know* it's him. It all makes sense. He was at the restaurant the first night we got a note. He went missing during the four-wheeling trip." I looked at Hunter. "He was the one who approached me and Blayze when we first met. And thinking back on it, whenever Morgan's name came up, he asked a ton of fucking questions—but he was so good, he also asked a lot of questions about *you*. And not that long ago, he claimed we lost out on the building we were trying to rent for our brewery and restaurant. I think the whole brewery thing was a ploy to get closer to Morgan."

Hunter scrubbed his hand over his face. "This is so fucked up. Does that mean he knew Morgan before he met you and Blayze?"

"I don't know." I shook my head. "That's the part I can't figure out. But I fucking know that Rich Bradford didn't just happen to stumble into our lives."

"Rich?" The question came from Rose, who now stood next to Hunter.

I threw the bag over my shoulder. "That's his name. Rich Bradford. He likes to be called by his last name."

She looked away and stared at nothing as if in thought, then her gaze snapped back to me. "Morgan told me about some weird guy she met at a frat party, Halloween of my freshman year. She said he was dressed in a really cool costume, but his face was painted so she couldn't see what he looked like. He asked her to dance, then asked her for a kiss. She thought it would be a harmless peck, but he was…um…he pulled her close…and she said he was aroused. She shoved him away, then luckily her best friend showed up and they left. I think she only told me the story because it creeped her out so much. But she warned me to be wary around guys I didn't know. She happened to mention his name was Rich."

Hunter and I looked at each other. "There's your connection," he said. "He knew her from college."

The room felt like it tilted. "There's no way it could be the same guy. All these years later?"

Hunter gave me a look. "Just like there was no way it could be Bradford less than fifteen minutes ago?"

My phone buzzed with a notification. Nox was here. "I need to go. Hunter, make sure no one tries to follow me."

"Why can't I go with you?" he asked.

I shook my head. "Because it's too dangerous."

"Do you even know where to look?" Rose asked.

I knew if I told them Nox had already found records for a certain purchase Bradford made a year ago, everyone would go swarming after me with guns blazing, including the police. There was no way I was going to risk Morgan's life like that.

"No. But I'm going to find her and bring her home before the fucking sun comes up."

Pushing past them both, I made my way through the apartment.

"Ryan? Ryan!" Detective Billings called out.

Ignoring her, I gave Blayze a nod and started out the front door and down the steps. Before I climbed into Nox's truck, Detective Billings called out my name once more.

Stopping, I turned to look at her. "I can't wait around anymore. I need to find her."

Her eyes went to Nox. "Listen, I don't even want to know who this guy is, but it's pretty damn clear he has some kind of military background. What I *do* need to know is that you're not going to do anything illegal."

With an impatient shake of my head, I said, "We won't do anything illegal."

"Then if you know where she is, why won't you tell me?"

I prayed that the next words out of my mouth would sound convincing. "We *don't* know. Listen, if I find anything out, I'll call you. I won't do anything illegal, but I can't promise I won't kill him the moment I see him."

She closed her eyes and sighed. "Uh, *murder* is illegal. Why would you tell me that?"

"Tell you what?" I climbed into the truck, but she grabbed the door before I could shut it.

"You *will* let me know if you find anything, right?"

"Of course I will."

She looked over at Nox. "If you need someone to have your back, just call."

Nox nodded.

Billings looked back at me and exhaled. "If I discover where she is, I'm heading out. Even though I have a feeling you're already heading there now."

Nox leaned over me to talk to the detective. "Sirens come racing in, and you know damn well what'll happen."

All she did was give him a single nod.

Before I shut the door, I promised, "I'll text you."

Billings shook her head, turned, and walked back to her car. Nox put his truck in drive, and we pulled out.

"What did you find out?" I asked.

"Like I told you, he bought a cabin right on the outskirts of town a little over a year ago. It used to be a rental. Looks like he stayed there several times before he purchased it from the couple who owned it. Talked to the woman briefly. She said whenever he was in town the year prior, he'd stayed there. When he made them an offer they couldn't refuse, they sold it to him."

"Fucking bastard. He must have had this planned for at least a year."

"Where the fuck is he getting his money?" Nox asked. "Chefs get paid shit wages."

"His dad. Or maybe his paternal grandparents. He mentioned his dad's parents both came from money. The grandfather's family hit it big in the railroad industry, and the grandmother's in oil. His grandparents live here, and his folks are in Billings."

Nox shook his head. "None of them live here. They're all in New York City."

"Jesus. The bastard lied about everything. And I fucking fell for it!" I felt sick to my stomach for maybe the tenth time since this all started. "He met my parents, Blayze's parents... and I never thought twice about why we didn't meet any of his family. What about Savannah?"

"Rodney's still looking into her, but from what we can tell, she's clueless about all of this. My guess is he used her as a cover."

"Stella said she saw him at Albertsons. How's he getting around without being seen by any traffic cameras?"

"My guess?" Nox said as he headed south out of town. "He ditched his vehicle and is driving something else."

"The police are going through camera footage of Albertsons' parking lot. Maybe they'll see what car he got into."

"Doesn't matter. I'd bet my left nut he's at that cabin with her."

Nox drove like a bat out of hell down the highway as I stared out the window. If Bradford had harmed a single hair on Morgan's body, I was going to kill him.

Nox glanced over at me. "Ryan, I need to know your head is in the game. Emotions can be overwhelming. You go in there running on your feelings and you risk Morgan getting hurt—or worse, killed."

Turning to look at him, I drew in a slow, deep breath. "Back in the day, I decided not to work with you because of her."

He nodded. "I know. That's why I'm worried."

"I appreciate all the training you gave me that summer, and for taking a chance on me, Nox. I'm sorry if I let you down."

A humorless chuckle slipped from his mouth. "Ryan, you never let me down. The kind of work I do isn't for everyone." He paused. "Can I ask you something?"

"Of course you can."

"Blayze has no idea how we actually met, right? He still thinks it was in college?"

"Yeah, he thinks we met in college. I never told anyone the truth."

He gripped the steering wheel tighter. "You never told anyone that the CIA tried to recruit you?"

I hadn't been surprised when Nox had approached me about the CIA. I'd gotten top scores on both college entrance tests. I was on our high school shooting team and had won countless tournaments. Plus, I spoke Russian since my grandmother had started teaching me when I was a toddler, and I'd taken four years of Spanish in high school. I was a walking fucking advertisement for the CIA.

Lifting my brow, I asked, "Did *you*?"

"Touché." He let out a long breath. "Will you tell Morgan?"

"Only if she asks."

"You know she's going to after this, don't you?"

I smiled. "She might have a few questions."

"Well…let's hope we get there before Billings and the Feds figure out what we already know."

My phone buzzed seconds later. I pulled it out to see a text from Blayze. "They found the car he was in. Traffic cams have him headed south, out of town."

"Better floor it. If they found the car he was driving, it won't be long before they figure out everything else."

Chapter Twenty-Five

Morgan

I heard the sound of a door shutting and I sat up in bed, my heart instantly hammering in my chest. I'd been racking my brain trying to think of a way out of here. I knew I needed to convince Bradford to let me out of this room if I stood any chance of escaping. I highly doubted anyone suspected he was the person who took me. He'd fooled us all.

I stood and reached for the wall to steady myself. I was still feeling a bit off and my head was pounding even though I'd taken the Tylenol he'd brought for me.

I had no idea what time it was since I had no clue how long I'd been knocked out, and there weren't any windows in the room to indicate the time of day. It had been around nine in the morning, or maybe closer to nine-thirty, when he'd taken me from the shop. I'd been out cold for the drive to the cabin, but Bradford had said we'd have to leave so we wouldn't be found, and that gave me hope that we really *were* still in Hamilton. And he hadn't been gone very long on his trip to town. Maybe…a half hour or so?

The bedroom door opened, and Bradford stood there. He looked *pissed.*

"I ran into your fucking grandmother at the store."

My heart felt like it stopped. If he harmed her in any way, I'd dig his eyes out with my fingers and shove them down his throat.

"If you hurt her, I swear to God, I'll make you pay."

He jerked his head back in surprise. "I didn't fucking hurt her! Now…come on."

I blinked at him a few times. "What?"

"Come on. You're gonna pee on the stick."

"I'm sorry…?"

He held up a box. "Did you think I was joking about the pregnancy test? We're gonna find out if you were lying to me or not. Then we have to leave. If your grandmother tells Savannah she saw me in town, everyone will know it was me."

He held the door open, and I took in as much of the living room as I could without moving.

"Don't even think about it, Morgan. We're in the middle of nowhere."

"We can't be that far from town. You weren't gone long."

He shot me a dirty look. "Get out here—now!"

I swallowed the lump in my throat as I made my way over to the door. "You do realize those tests aren't always accurate."

When I walked by him, he put a hand on my lower back and I quickly stepped away. He then grabbed my arm and guided me to a large bathroom.

"I added the tub just for you, when I saw how much you loved to take baths."

My skin crawled at the idea of him watching me in my bathroom. "How often did you watch?"

He winked. "Not often enough, thanks to Savannah." A wicked smile grew on his face. "She used to sit across from me on the sofa, working, while I'd have the cameras pulled up, watching you bathe...watching you fuck that asshole. God, it made me so damn hard, I'd have to give in and take her right there on the sofa. She thought I was being spontaneous and romantic." He laughed. "It was *you* I thought about, every time. Not her."

I shook my head, my voice sounding small when I asked, "How could you invade my privacy like that?"

He shrugged. "It was like watching porn. As much as I hated seeing him touch you, it still got me off. And hearing you scream out your orgasm at that cabin? I got off on that too."

I stumbled over my feet so badly, he had to catch me. "I knew you were there that night!"

All he did was laugh. I wanted to tell him he was a sick, twisted fuck, but the last thing I could afford to do was piss him off.

He tossed me the box, and I caught it. "Sit and pee."

My mouth dropped open. "With you in here?"

He leaned against the doorjamb. "I've seen you naked plenty of times, Morgan."

I couldn't help it, I snarled my lip at him.

"What's the matter?" he said with a smirk. "You don't like knowing I was watching you?"

Folding my arms over my chest, I retorted, "Would *any* woman like to know a man was watching their every move? Their most intimate moments?"

"Some might."

"Well, I'm not one of them. What you did was *wrong*—and illegal."

"I hardly think I need to worry about a few cameras now. Not after kidnapping you."

Standing my ground, I said, "I'm not peeing on this thing with you standing there."

He let out a frustrated sigh. "Fine. But the windows are nailed shut, so don't even think you can get out." With that, Bradford finally shut the door.

I spun around, taking everything in. There was nothing in the bathroom I could use as a weapon. Not even a shower curtain to wrap around his neck and strangle his ass. "Shit!" I whispered.

I moved quietly around the bathroom, opening cabinets that revealed emptiness. No cleaning containers, no towels. Not a damn thing.

Think, Morgan! Think!

Looking at the pregnancy test box, I cursed. Why had I said I was pregnant?

"Are you peeing yet?" Bradford called from behind the door.

"I'm trying! I need to run the water to make myself pee." Once I turned on the water, I hurried over to the first of two large windows.

The second I looked outside, I pressed my hand to my mouth to stifle a gasp. Something was running along the edge of the dim light that illuminated part of the front yard.

It was a man.

Had they found me? Had *Ryan* found me?

Rushing over to the other window, all I saw was blackness. Despite that, a burst of hope filled me. *Ryan was here.* I wasn't sure how I knew it was him. I just felt it in the depths of my soul.

Quickly turning back to the faucet, I pulled out one of the tests and stuck it under the water. There was no way I was going to pee on a test, only for that sicko to handle it. I flushed the toilet and turned the water off. I needed to distract Bradford so whoever was outside could find a way in.

I set the test down on a piece of toilet paper and flushed the toilet again.

"Can I come in now?" Bradford asked.

Rolling my eyes, I walked over to the door and tried to open it. It was locked from the outside. "You can come in."

"Stand back from the door."

"What am I going to do, hit you with toilet paper?"

The door opened, and Bradford looked around before stepping in. He immediately walked to the counter and picked up the pregnancy test.

"I...I don't think it's ready yet," I said. "They take a few minutes."

He stared at it, frowned, then dropped it in the sink. Turning, he took me by the elbow and walked me back toward the bedroom. I surreptitiously looked around the cabin to get my bearings. Aside from the front door, there was a back door as well. My gut churned when I saw what must have been about six locks on the front door, all of them keyed.

I glanced at the large picture window at the front of the cabin. It was pitch dark outside, which meant there was no moon tonight.

What if I pulled out of his grip, ran, and jumped through the window? How badly would I be hurt?

Pushing me into the bedroom, Bradford pointed to the box he'd brought me earlier. "Put it on. Right now."

Shaking my head, I said, "No."

His expression was a mixture of bemused and pissed off. "No?"

"*No.* I'm not going to let this happen. I don't want to sleep with you. I don't want you touching me. I swear, I'll fight you the entire damn time."

He slowly tilted his head, looking like he was thinking. Finally, he glared at me, eyes glittering. "Then I'll knock you out and fuck you while you're sleeping."

I sucked in a harsh breath. "You really are a sick motherfucker."

That was apparently the straw that broke the camel's back. He lunged toward me so fast, I barely managed to grab one of the chairs at the table. He leapt back as I swung it at him.

"Don't make me hurt you, Morgan. You've been blinded by Ryan. You know you want me. I've seen the way you look at me."

"Stay away from me, Rich or Bradford or whoever the hell you are! I don't want you! I've *never* wanted you. There is only one man I love, and I'll love him forever! You can rape me a million times, and *I will never want you!*"

Rage filled his face, and now I prayed to God I hadn't imagined that there was someone outside the house.

"You did this to yourself," he growled. "Remember that. We could have had a romantic first night together—but you ruined it with your filthy mouth!"

He tried to grab me, and I swung the chair again. No matter what happened, I was going to put up the fight of my life.

The front door burst open, and the startling sound of gunshots rang through the cabin. I dropped to the ground on instinct, screaming as I covered my head.

Bradford cursed violently, mumbling a question about how anyone had found him so soon. Then he ran out of the bedroom.

Mind racing, I knew I could either stay in the room, away from the gunshots—or I could run toward them.

I jumped to my feet, my decision made.

Men shouted, more shots were fired, and I immediately dropped back to the floor. I crawled toward the bedroom door, praying I didn't get hit by a stray bullet. I needed to get to a window and break it.

As soon as I had that thought, another occurred to me. What if I couldn't break the glass?

Then I froze in place and covered my head as I heard Bradford screaming.

"You won't take either of us alive! I'll kill her before I let you take her away from me!"

Change of plans. I needed to hide.

The sound of wood splintering into a million pieces caused me to scream again. Looking into the living room, I saw that the front door was missing, though I couldn't see Bradford or anyone else. If I ran out there now, it was very likely I would be shot in the crossfire.

Suddenly, I saw Bradford dive behind a chair. He had a handgun and kept swinging both the gun and his head back and forth, pointing the weapon at the front door, then the back. A loud thud made him turn toward the back door, where he aimed his gun.

The wailing of sirens in the distance told me the police were on their way. Bradford's gaze shot straight toward me.

I scrambled backward as he raced toward the bedroom. Before I could even get to my feet, he grabbed my hair and pulled. I screamed and started to struggle, but the more I thrashed, the more my scalp hurt.

He put the gun to the side of my head. "Stand up."

His cold, hard voice sent chills throughout my body. I stood, and he slowly walked us back into the living room, using my body to cover his own.

"Is this who you want?" he shouted. "Your whore? Your lying little *whore*?!"

"Bradford—I mean, *Rich*, please don't do this!" I begged.

"Shut up!" he yelled, pushing the barrel of the gun harder into my temple. Clamping my mouth shut, I frantically glanced at both doors.

"Ryan!" I screamed. Bradford swung me around by my hair and hit me so hard across the face, I literally saw stars.

Then I heard a furious scream that sounded like the devil himself was rising out of the ground.

I looked at the front door to see Ryan rushing in, a gun pointed toward us.

Bradford tried to turn me again to shield himself, and I bit down on his arm as hard as I could, tasting blood.

When he howled and pushed me away, I dove toward the floor—and the deafening sound of gunshots filled the air once more.

Then there was silence.

It was a strange, peaceful kind of silence…and I wondered for a moment if I'd been shot.

I was afraid to look. With my arms over my head, all I could hear was my own breathing. Then hands were on me, and for a moment I struggled…until I recognized that touch.

Looking up, I saw Ryan standing there.

I scrambled to my knees and threw myself toward him. He wrapped me in a tight embrace. The sirens grew louder, but all I cared about was being in Ryan's arms…and that feeling of immense safety. I buried my face in his chest, my entire body shaking.

Ryan stroked my hair gently, trying to calm me. "He's not going to touch you ever again."

I wanted to cry. I wanted to scream. Hell, I wanted to run out of that cabin, but I knew Ryan had me and I was going to be okay.

A sudden burst of loud voices in the cabin caused me to jump. Ryan helped me stand, tucking me close to his body. When I tried to look behind me, he grasped my chin, keeping my focus on him.

"Where is he?" I asked.

He placed his hand on the side of my face and brushed his thumb softly over my cheek. "The bastard hit you."

"I'll be fine. Where is he, Ryan?"

"He's gone, Morgan. It's over." Holding me even tighter, he started to walk us out of the cabin.

Everything inside of me screamed not to look…but I had to see for myself that he truly couldn't hurt me anymore. I quickly glanced over my shoulder.

Bradford lay on the floor face down, a pool of blood slowly seeping out from under his body.

I sucked in a shaky breath and looked straight ahead. The feel of the fresh night air hit my lungs, burning in a glorious way.

"I'm so tired," I said quietly as Ryan walked me toward the ambulance that had pulled up. "But I'm okay. I'm not hurt."

"Your body's cold, and I want someone to look you over."

I didn't have the energy to argue, so I let him lead me toward a paramedic. After a few minutes of repeating that I was okay, that Bradford hadn't touched me, I heard my mother shouting my name.

My head shot up, then I bolted toward her and my father. They both engulfed me.

"Oh, my sweet girl!" my mother cried as she wrapped her arms around me. My father kissed my forehead, holding both of us tightly before giving me a once-over.

"You're okay?" he asked anxiously.

I nodded. "I'm okay. Ryan got here just in time."

"Bradford didn't touch you, did he?" Dad asked.

I shook my head. "No, he didn't."

Night soon turned into morning, and I was beyond exhausted. I had to give a statement to both the police and the FBI, and so did Ryan and Nox. It was Nox who'd been the one to deliver the fatal gunshot to Bradford. When Ryan had seen me jump out of the way, he'd run toward me. According to Nox, Bradford's pistol had been aimed at Ryan, but Nox had shot him from behind first, killing him instantly.

I also learned Ryan had texted the cabin's address to Detective Billings right before he and Nox had arrived. They hadn't wanted any police sirens to tip off Bradford before they could gain entrance into the cabin.

"I don't want to go back to the apartment," I said softly.

Ryan nodded his head and looked at my parents. "Can we stay in the guest house for a couple of days?"

Taking my hands in hers, my mother said, "Of course you can. As long as you want."

"Come on, we'll drive you there," Dad said. "Hunter can get your truck, Ryan, and bring it over later today. I think we're all going to need a bit of sleep."

Once we got to the guest house, my mom fussed over changing the sheets on the bed. I was practically falling asleep on my feet. It was clear Mom was still running on adrenaline at that point, but my body was drained.

"Lincoln, our daughter is literally falling asleep against Ryan," Dad said. "Let's get out of here and let them get some rest."

After kissing them both goodbye, I crawled under the covers and Ryan wrapped himself around me. I was asleep the moment I closed my eyes.

Chapter Twenty-Six

RYAN

When I opened my eyes, the bedroom was dark and I was lying in the exact position I'd been in when Morgan and I had fallen asleep. The poor thing had been out as soon as she'd hit the pillow.

Kissing the back of her head, I carefully slipped out of bed. I stretched my aching body then headed to the bathroom to splash water on my face. The cold felt good on my skin and instantly had me wide awake. I felt like I'd slept for days.

After I dried my face and glanced up, I saw Morgan in the mirror, standing in the doorway of the bathroom.

"Did I wake you?"

She shook her head. "No, I don't think so."

Turning, I leaned against the counter. "Do you want to talk about it?"

"He was watching us, Ryan," she said quietly.

I met her tear-filled gaze. "I know. The cameras are all gone."

She slowly shook her head. "I don't want to stay there."

Pushing off the counter, I took the few steps toward her and opened my arms. She walked into them, burying her face in my chest.

"Can we move somewhere else?" she asked.

Stroking my hand up and down her back, I said, "Of course we can. Are you going to be okay in the design studio and the store?"

Morgan drew her head back and sighed. "Yes. I think I'll be fine there. It's just, knowing he was watching us in the most private areas of our home… I feel so violated. I know I won't be comfortable in that bedroom or bathroom anymore."

"Then we'll find somewhere else to live."

She let out a humorless chuckle. "The beginning of this relationship sure has been a journey."

"It sure has."

The look she gave me about broke my heart. "Thank you for not leaving."

Lowering my head to look her directly in the eyes, I cupped her face. "I will *never* leave you, Morgan Shaw. You are it for me. You're the one woman, the *only* woman, I've ever dreamed of having a future with. I'm so sorry I didn't see through Bradford."

"None of us did. It's not your fault."

"It still pisses me off he fooled us all."

"I'm sorry about the bar."

"I'm not. As much as I love tinkering around with brewing beer, it's not my future. I love what I do at the horse ranch, and I love standing by your side and watching your dreams come true."

"But what about *your* dreams, Ryan?"

Smiling, I pressed my mouth to her forehead and whispered, "You *are* my dream, Morgan. You are my past, my present, and my future. There's nothing I want more than to simply exist in your world."

Tears slowly trailed down her face, and I moved my mouth to her cheeks, kissing them away. She gripped my T-shirt in her fist and mumbled something I couldn't understand.

"What was that?" I asked.

With her face buried in my chest once more, she mumbled something again.

"I…so…never…life."

Stepping back, I laughed. "I can't understand a thing you're saying."

Sucking in a few breaths between sobs, she attempted to breathe normally before she closed her eyes and slowly said, "I am so in love with you, and I never in my life thought I could feel this way."

"I will love you until the day I take my last breath, Morgan Shaw. And even past that."

She gave me her first genuine smile since she'd been abducted. "That's so beautiful. I don't think I could even say anything to top that."

"I know something you can say."

Raising a brow, she asked, "What?"

"Tell me you love me."

Her eyes went dark with passion. "I love you, Ryan Marshall, more than I've ever loved anyone."

Pressing my mouth to hers, I kissed her tenderly, praying she could feel the love I had for her. When we finally drew apart, Morgan lifted her hand and ran her fingers through my hair. "Make love to me, Ryan. Please."

Scooping her up in my arms, I carried her back to the bed and proceeded to do exactly what she'd asked.

◆ ◆ ◆

Morgan and I walked up the steps of the white, one-story house for rent. I could see the excitement in her eyes as she took in its ranch-style design.

It had been three weeks since Bradford had kidnapped her, and I'd never in my life met a woman so damn strong. She was seeing a counselor whom her Aunt Kaylee had recommended, and I could tell it was doing her a world of good to talk to a professional.

"The porch wraps around both sides of the house and would make a wonderful place to sit in the evenings," Bailey, our real estate agent, commented.

"What a charming house," Morgan said as we walked into the front foyer.

Bailey nodded. "Lots of wood in this one, so I hope you like it!"

"Oh, definitely. It's so warm and welcoming!" Morgan laced her fingers with mine and we walked from the open foyer to the large living room.

Bailey walked ahead of us, pointing out its features. "It's big enough for a sectional sofa, as you can see. The living and dining rooms are all one open space, but you could make this another sitting area if you wanted to, since the kitchen is big enough for a small dining table."

"I like the idea of doing a separate little sitting area," Morgan said as we walked farther into the house.

Large, plank-wood floors ran throughout. The crown molding was also wood, adding to the warm feeling of the house.

"Now," Bailey said, "the kitchen is my favorite part. Knotty alder wood for all the cabinets and a farm-style sink. Look at all this room!"

I nodded. "It's a big kitchen, for sure."

"The cabinets are stunning," Morgan agreed. "And the granite's just as beautiful."

We toured the rest of the house with its three bedrooms and two-and-a-half baths. Everything about the place was stunning, and I could tell Morgan really liked it.

"It's a three-minute drive to the boutique for you, Morgan, and about fifteen minutes to Ryan's horse farm."

Morgan and I had been staying at my place over the barn at my parents' ranch. The only time she'd gone back into the apartment over the boutique was to pack up all her things. Rose mentioned that once she was out of school, she'd be interested in renting it. I think Lincoln was honestly hoping we would stay in the guest house for good, but my folks' ranch was closer to town than the Shaw's place.

"And they're open to going month to month after the first year's lease is up?" I asked.

Bailey nodded. "Yes. I told the homeowners you were in the process of looking for land and were going to have a house built at some point. They are more than happy to accommodate that. And if you want to get a dog, they're fine with that as well. The lawn is a great size for it. And I don't have to mention the view of the valley and the Bitterroot Mountains."

Morgan looked at me and smiled. "Do you like it?"

I nodded. "I do. I like it a lot. It's a lot of room, but I'd rather have more than we need than not enough."

Bouncing on her toes, Morgan asked, "So it's a yes?"

I grinned at how excited she was. "It's a yes."

Morgan threw her arms around my neck and squealed in delight. I couldn't help but laugh. I loved seeing my carefree girl back again. I'd missed her.

Bailey smiled. "I assume I can tell the owners you want to take the house?"

"Yes!" we said in unison.

"Wonderful! Let's get back to the office and draw up the lease. Once everything is all set, you can move in anytime."

Morgan spun around and gave me the biggest grin I'd ever seen. If I could put that same look on her face every day for the rest of our lives, I would be the happiest man in the world.

Chapter Twenty-Seven

MORGAN

Everyone in the design studio was buzzing with excitement. We were T-minus three weeks until Georgiana and Blayze's wedding, and today was the last day of fittings for the bridesmaids' dresses that I'd designed.

Rose, Lily, Avery, and Lady Mary—or simply Mary, as we called her—were all busy getting changed.

"We're coming out!" Avery, the youngest of the group, shouted.

My mother, Kaylee, Timberlynn, and Merit all sat on the sofa and chairs as they waited for their daughters. Since I'd asked them to send Lily out first, Timberlynn stood and came to stand next to me.

"I'm so excited to see these dresses!" she exclaimed as she hugged me—then gasped at the sight of her daughter. Lily went to school at Montana State and had been gone all summer for a study abroad program in Europe, so it was nice having her back home. At least until she headed back to Bozeman for school at the end of summer.

"Oh my goodness," Timberlynn whispered as a chorus of oohhs and ahhhs came from behind me.

"Lily Hope, you look breathtaking," Grams said from the doorway, and everyone turned to see her walking into the room.

"Stella! You made it," Lincoln said, standing to hug my grandmother.

"I'm sorry I was late. Did I miss anyone?"

"Nope," I said as I turned Lily so she could look at herself in the mirrors.

Smiling, she said, "It makes me look like I have boobs!"

Laughter erupted while I adjusted the cutout maxi dress. Georgiana had picked out a blush chiffon fabric with a tiny sage green and pink flower pattern. It wasn't overbearing at all with the pattern only adding to the beauty of the dress. When I'd suggested making one of the dresses with an exposed midriff, Georgiana had loved the idea. The bodice of Lily's dress had spaghetti straps, with the front middle attached to the full-length shirred skirt, allowing a bit of her midriff to show. Her lower back was exposed, giving the dress a bit of a sexy vibe.

"It fits you perfectly," I said, making sure the top didn't need to be taken in anywhere.

"Do you think Georgiana will like it?" Lily asked.

I rested my chin on her shoulder and stared at my beautiful younger cousin in the mirror. "She's going to love it. Trust me."

"I still can't believe she wants to be surprised with the dresses," Merit said.

"Me too, but she trusts me for some reason." I studied the top of the dress. "I'm going to make one small adjustment," I said, grabbing my notebook and then glancing at Lily. "I hope you don't mind if your boobs get pushed up a bit more?"

Her eyes sparkled. "If you can make these babies pop, I'm all for it."

Aunt Timberlynn groaned while everyone else laughed.

"You can go change," I said. "Hang it back up and leave it in there."

Next up was Avery. I'd designed her dress to be a bit less sexy. "Avery? You ready?" I called out.

It was Merit's turn to stand. When her daughter walked out, I saw her wipe away a tear.

"Sweetheart, you're growing up so fast."

"Isn't it beautiful, Mom?" Avery asked as she did a spin.

The group of women let out another round of compliments.

I smoothed down the skirt of Avery's dress. "So, for Avery's dress, I went with something a bit more simple since she's the baby of the group."

"Hey, don't call me a baby," Avery muttered, crossing her arms over her chest.

Pulling them down to her sides, I went on. "The delicate spaghetti straps and V-neckline still give it a romantic feel, but it's age appropriate. I love the crisscross in the back with the ruffles. It's so playful!"

"It's beautiful, Morgan," my mother assured me and Merit nodded.

"Thank you, Morgan. My daughter looks beautiful," she said, giving me a kiss on the cheek.

Rose was up next. Her dress was the same chiffon fabric but the design was a ruffled cold-shoulder cut with a deep V in the back.

Aunt Kaylee hugged her and whispered something in her ear that made Rose's cheeks turn a shade darker than her blush-colored dress.

"Now we have Mary's dress, the maid of honor!" I announced.

Mary and Georgiana had grown very close since Georgiana had first interviewed her last fall, and then remained with her and her brother for an extended stay. I had gotten to visit for a week right before Christmas, and Mary and I had instantly hit it off, becoming fast friends as well. She'd flown to Montana a couple of times to visit over the last several months, and now would be in town until after the wedding. She was staying with Georgiana and Blayze while she was here.

Slipping out of the dressing room, Mary smiled when everyone gasped at the sight of her. She wore the same material as the rest of us, but her dress was a figure-flattering drape with off-the-shoulder straps that gave the entire dress a romantic silhouette. The back was a draped cowl that cascaded in layers from the delicate straps, giving it a sexy, soft look. The full-length circle skirt showed off her hourglass shape to perfection.

I had to admit, I'd knocked it out of the park with these dresses.

"It fits you like a glove," I said as I admired her image in the mirror.

Speaking in her beautiful British accent, she replied, "Well, the designer clearly knows what she's doing."

I gave her a hug and then turned to the rest of the group. "Okay, Mary will change and help me with my dress now."

My mother beamed with happiness.

I slipped out of my clothes and donned the dress, a simple and charming seamed bodice with a flowing, full-length skirt. To add a touch of sexy, there was a center split and a flattering V neckline. The crisscross spaghetti straps added that classic romantic feel I was going for with all of the dresses.

Kelly Elliott

"It was smart to make each dress zip up in the back," Mary stated as she zipped me into mine. Placing her hands on my shoulders, she turned me to face her. "You know, if you ever want to expand your line, I would love to feature these gowns in my new bridal collection. And I saw the dress you designed for Georgiana. I want you to know...I offered to design her a gown, but she insisted on having you do it."

Tears instantly pricked at the back of my eyes, and I attempted to blink them away. I couldn't *believe* Georgiana had passed up Mary's offer to design her dress. My heart felt like it was going to explode in my chest. Mary was now one of Europe's top designers. She'd recently taken part in the Paris spring show and had gained even more popularity since. She was also making a name for herself here in the States.

"Georgiana picked *me* over you for her wedding gown? Is she insane?"

Mary dropped her head back as she laughed. When she looked at me again, she shook her head. "Did you hear the part where I asked to carry your gowns under my label, love? And I would love for you to design me a wedding gown or two for an exclusive line."

I opened my mouth, snapped it shut, opened it, then closed it again.

She smiled. "Take some time to think about it."

"Yes! Oh my gosh, Mary, yes! I'd be so honored. I...I don't know what to say. Thank you so much for believing in me."

"I believe in you because I can see your talent firsthand. I'll have a photographer here at the wedding, taking pictures. Your name will be splashed everywhere, along with A La Chic Boutique."

I quickly wiped away a tear. "That means so much to me. You have no idea. Thank you so much for helping us."

She waved me off. "I'm merely using my platform to promote two women whom I think are at the top of their game. Now, let's go show everyone your dress."

We walked out, and my mother instantly started to cry. I laughed and wiped my own tears away as she walked up and took my hands. "You better start designing your own wedding gown soon, darling."

Drawing my head back, I asked, "Why?"

She swept her eyes over me and motioned for me to do a spin. When I faced her again, she put her fingers to her mouth and let out a small sob. "When Ryan sees you in this dress, he's going to fall to his knees and beg you to marry him."

All the women let out a loud eruption of cheers as I laughed and hugged my mother tightly.

She moved her mouth to my ear and whispered, "I'm so, so proud of you, Morgan Elizabeth Shaw."

Holding her tighter, I replied, "I have you and Daddy to thank. I love you, Mom."

She held me back at arm's length and smiled. "Oh, I love you too, Morgan."

It was the day of the wedding, and the only way to describe the atmosphere appropriately was with one word—chaos.

The wedding was being held in one of the barns on our family ranch. My mother had hired someone to decorate it, and beautiful wasn't nearly a strong enough word to describe it. It looked like we'd stepped into a fairy-land barn. Delicate swaths of blush and white tulle were draped across the ceiling, and tin-kling white lights sparkled everywhere.

Rows of white chairs had been lined up with a beautiful white runner that ran between them and spanned the length of the barn. It ended at an arbor that my uncles and father had built for the wedding. It was covered in gardenias, freesias, irises, dahlias…all of Georgiana's favorite flowers.

Placed on the ground at the end of every row of chairs was a stunning assortment of cosmos and greenery.

The bridesmaids carried bouquets of cornflowers, which I thought was so sweet and simple and screamed Georgiana. The bride's bouquet was made with white freesias mixed with greenery. I could smell the flowers the moment I stepped foot in my parents' house, where we were all gathered before the ceremony.

My mom had transformed her bedroom into a dressing room for everyone to get ready. Lily was doing everyone's hair, while Rose insisted on doing our makeup. We all had our hair pulled up with little wisps hanging down in some form or fash-ion. Georgiana had her hair pulled back in the most elegant po-nytail I'd ever seen.

When she stepped out of the room while the other girls got changed, I slipped out to talk to her.

I found her sitting in my father's office. It had a view of the back pastures, where horses and cows were dotting the fields.

"How are you holding up?" I asked as I walked over and leaned against the desk. Georgiana was in a robe with her legs tucked up and her chin resting on her knees.

"I'm already exhausted." We both laughed. She turned to look up at me. "May I give you a piece of advice regarding weddings."

"Hit me with it."

"Elope."

I laughed harder and shook my head as I turned my attention to the view. "Thank you for letting me talk you into the two dresses."

"Mary is going to shit her pants when she sees them both."

I smiled. "I just thought that you should be comfortable during the reception."

She nodded. "I will be, in that dress."

"You helped design it, you know."

"I made the flowers and that was it."

"Please." I nudged her shoulder. "They're the most beautiful part of the dress."

Georgiana sighed.

"What's wrong?" I asked, frowning.

"I'm so happy, Morgan...and a part of me wonders if the rug is going to be pulled out from under me. I've loved your brother for so long, and the idea that I'm going to be his wife in a matter of hours seems like it's too good to be true."

I pushed off the desk and bent down over her. With my hand on hers, I said, "You deserve all the happiness in the world, Georgiana. And I know my brother deserves it as well, and the two of you complete one another. A love like the one you share is rare. Take a few deep breaths. I know a lot is going on, but remember, this is going to be one of the best days of your life—so enjoy it. And if anything goes wrong, that doesn't change your love for Blayze, nor does it change his love for you."

A tear slipped free and traveled down her beautiful face. I wiped it away softly. "Rose will kill you if you mess up your makeup."

Georgiana chuckled. "I'm okay. Go get ready. I'm dying to see the dresses."

"Okay! I'm off. Come back in ten minutes."

I stood, and Georgiana reached for my hand. "Thank you, Morgan. I've always wanted a sister."

I swallowed hard. "I'm leaving before you make *me* cry."

Chapter Twenty-Eight

Morgan

We all stood in a line with our bouquets, making last-minute adjustments on each other. There was a light knock on the door before Georgiana stepped inside.

Her eyes widened as she looked down the line. She covered her mouth with her hands, and I heard Rose whisper, "Shit, she's going to ruin her makeup."

"You all look so...so beautiful!"

Callie, Georgiana's mother, rushed over to her daughter with a Kleenex. "No, sweetie, don't cry!"

Dabbing her eyes, Georgiana walked over and hugged and kissed each one of us. She made sure to compliment each bridesmaid.

I was at the end of the line, and she pulled me into a fierce hug. "You are so damn talented."

"Georgiana, we need to get you into your dress," my mother said softly.

"I'll help," I said as I handed Rose my flowers.

Walking into the bathroom, I unzipped the bag that held both wedding gowns.

The gown for the ceremony was a lighter shade of blush than the bridesmaids' dresses. Carefully putting the gown on, Georgiana fidgeted anxiously while Callie and I helped fasten the buttons. A photographer—two, actually—took pictures of the moment. One of the photographers was with Mary, as promised.

"This is the most beautiful dress I've ever seen," Callie gushed and my mother winked at me. "The pattern of the appliquéd flowers looks so familiar to me."

"That's because I took a picture of the stained-glass window in our family room," Georgiana said. "The one that you saved from the old church they were tearing down? I always loved that window. I sent the picture to Morgan so she could incorporate it into the dress."

I had to hold back tears as I watched Callie blink rapidly, trying to do the same.

"Oh, Georgiana," she said. "My heart can't possibly take much more. That is such a beautiful gesture."

Smiling, Georgiana kissed her mother on the cheek. "I love you, Mom."

"And I love you."

My mother broke the soft and tender moment. "Can we please see the other dress now? Please!"

Callie clapped. "Oh yes! Let the mothers see it."

I chuckled and looked at Georgiana, who nodded.

"Fine. Here's the other dress."

I pulled the second dress out and held it up. My mother and Callie stared, their eyes widening. It was a stunning white ball-gown with a cropped top. I had hand appliqued sage green and deep blush flowers onto the bodice of the gown, which added to the fairytale theme Georgiana was going for with the wedding.

"Oh my goodness," Callie whispered as my mother continued to stare at the dress.

"Do you like it, Mom?" I asked nervously.

Her eyes met mine. "Like it? Morgan, I knew you were damn talented, but this is the most stunning dress I've ever seen."

Georgiana grinned and nodded. "It is, isn't it?"

There was a light knock on the door and the wedding planner poked her head in. "Ladies, we're running behind!"

Facing Georgiana once again, I asked, "Ready?"

"I'm ready."

"I'll go out first. Mom, come with me?"

"Oh, of course!" my mother said, and we left Callie and Georgiana alone for a moment.

As I shut the door, I saw my mother fighting to hold back tears. "Mom, don't bother holding back. They're happy tears, and happy tears should never be held back."

She pulled me into a hug and let the tears fall.

The wedding planner Georgiana had hired was on top of things. The woman walked around with an earpiece and snapping her fingers, getting things done. The bridesmaids were lined up outside the barn, waiting to start walking down the aisle. Georgiana wanted us to enter by age, with Mary, the maid of honor, walking in right before her.

Ryan was Blayze's best man. The groomsmen were Hunter, Bradly, Joshua, and Nathan, and they were all standing in the barn already, waiting for us to enter. When I walked through the door of the barn, my gaze immediately went to Ryan. He looked so sexy my knees shook, and I had to concentrate on walking. He wore a black tux with a blush-colored vest and a black tie.

Sweeping my eyes over to Blayze, I took in his traditional black and white tux. He looked so damn handsome. He was a miniature of my father, no doubt about it.

As I drew closer, I looked at Hunter and smiled as I mouthed "wow." He rolled his eyes, but then winked at me and mouthed that I looked beautiful. He favored our gorgeous mother, but for sure had plenty of our father in him. I could see his blue eyes sparkling as I walked down the aisle.

Bradly, Joshua, and Nathan also looked way too handsome for their own good. Lord, we had good genes in our family. Even if Bradly and Avery weren't technically blood cousins.

As the ceremony commenced and I listened to Georgiana and Blayze exchange their wedding vows, I couldn't help but glance at Ryan for the hundredth time. I knew exactly how Georgiana had felt earlier, when she'd said she was waiting for the rug to be pulled out from under her.

No. I put that thought out of my head. Ryan and I might have had a rough start, but it had nothing to do with our actual relationship. I knew that no matter what life threw at us, we would be able to face it together. And something about that caused my chest to warm and an overwhelming feeling of love to fill my heart.

Ryan's eyes met mine, and he smiled. He didn't have to mouth anything. I knew from his smile that he was telling me he loved me. I returned the smile, then focused on the bride and groom kissing for the first time as Mr. and Mrs. Shaw.

Chapter Twenty-Nine

RYAN

"You're next," Hunter said as he slapped me on the back.

"For?" I asked before taking a sip of my beer.

"Marriage. Morgan caught the bouquet, so doesn't that mean she's going to be the next one who gets married?"

Grinning, I set my beer down. "How do you know *you* won't be next?"

His face drained of all color. "Me? I hardly think I'm ready to get married. Shit, I just turned twenty-one and have my whole life ahead of me. Marriage is the last damn thing on my mind."

"Touché to that!" Bradly said as he pulled out a chair, spun it around, and sat down. Rose and Lily joined us at the table.

"Touché to what?" Lily asked.

"To Hunter being the next one to get married."

Rose and Lily both laughed—hard.

"Why is that so funny?" Hunter asked.

Rose set her wine glass down. "For one, you're only twenty-one. And you're at the top of your game with team roping."

Lily reached for Rose's wine and stole a drink. Then she said, "Not to mention you're always on the road with buckle bunnies throwing themselves at you. No woman wants to deal with any of that."

"My mother did," Hunter said. "She trusted my father when he was riding."

"That's because Aunt Lincoln would have kicked Uncle Brock's ass if he'd cheated," Rose stated matter-of-factly.

"That's true," Bradly said with a laugh.

"Have you made a decision about the reality show?" I asked.

Hunter closed his eyes as his cousins turned and stared at him with shocked expressions.

"What reality show?" Rose asked.

"Dude, are you going to be the next bachelor?" Bradly let out a hearty laugh.

Hunter shot him a dirty look. "Don't you have a bull or something to go ride?"

"What's going on?" Morgan slid into the seat next to me and reached for my beer.

"Did you know Hunter was going to be the next bachelor?" Lily stated with barely contained excitement in her voice.

"I am not!" Hunter nearly shouted. "For your information—and this is *not* to spread any farther than this table, do we all understand?"

Everyone nodded.

"I was asked to participate in a stupid social dating experiment."

"That sounds interesting. What's it called?" Rose asked.

"I don't have all the details, and to be honest, I told them no when they first approached my agent. Then they offered to donate a ridiculous amount of money to the foundation my dad set up. I mean, we could build a whole new arena with the amount of money they'd be shelling out, plus what they want to pay me to do it."

"So your pay would also be donated to the charity?" Lily asked.

Hunter nodded. "Basically. It's a new show they're using to try and kick off some new streaming network."

"How does it work?" Rose pressed.

"I think there'd be something like twenty women, and each week I'd have to read two different profiles. I swipe on the one I want to take on a date. If we hit it off, she stays. If either of us goes into some bullshit booth thing and says we didn't connect, then she leaves."

"Where will it be filmed?" Lily asked, still all excited. Morgan and I both chuckled.

"That's where it gets interesting. They want to film on the ranch over winter break."

Rose rubbed her hands together and flashed Hunter an evil smile. "Oh, this is so juicy! Please tell me we get to be on TV!"

"Yes! I totally want to be on TV too!" Lily added.

Hunter rolled his eyes. "I already said no to my family being involved. I mean, I guess if you really wanted to be on it, that would be up to the producers."

Morgan cleared her throat as Rose and Lily started going off about becoming famous. "When do you have to give them your answer?"

Hunter sighed. "In a couple of weeks."

"Have you talked to Dad about it?"

Hunter looked at Morgan and slowly shook his head. "Blayze thinks Dad won't have a problem with it as long as we stay away from the main barn."

"Where would everyone stay?" I asked.

"They said something about renting some mansion outside of Hamilton."

Bradly jumped in. "Wait—so all those hot girls won't be staying on the ranch?"

"You don't even live on the ranch, Bradly!" Rose said with a laugh.

"Yeah, but I'm there damn near every day when I'm in town."

"What are you going to do, hit on the girls when they're at the ranch?" Lily asked.

Bradly shrugged. "Hey, just because Hunter isn't looking for love, who says I'm not?"

Morgan huffed. "You're still a teenager, in case you forgot."

"Not to mention shy as all get out," Rose added.

Hunter held up his hands. "Why are we arguing about this? I'm not even sure I'm going to do it."

"Would you have some kind of celebrity host?" I asked.

With a one-shoulder shrug, he replied, "I don't know. They mentioned someone by the name of Kipton Howse."

Lily nearly choked on Rose's wine. "*Kipton Howse*! Are you freaking kidding me?"

Morgan and Rose both frowned, and Morgan asked, "Who's that?"

Lily's eyes went wide. "She was Miss Montana last year! They crowned a new one last month, but she was the one before that. How do you guys not know this?"

"Who's Miss Montana?" Bradly asked.

Lily shook her head in disbelief. "As in Miss USA. The most famous beauty pageant in the country?"

Bradly and Hunter both had blank expressions on their faces.

"Really?" Morgan said. "The two of you need to stop spending so much time with horses and bulls."

"This!" Lily shouted. "*This* is Kipton Howse!"

She passed her phone to all of us at the table. I thought Bradly and Hunter were going to fall out of their seats.

"Wow," Morgan and Rose said at the same time.

Rose took the phone and studied the young woman. "She's beautiful."

"I know!" Lily agreed. "She goes to Montana State. I've seen her on campus and at a few parties. If you think she's pretty there, you should see her in person. Somehow she looks even better with less makeup."

Hunter was studying the picture on Lily's phone. Morgan turned and looked at me, one brow raised.

Leaning toward her, I asked, "Does he seem smitten to you?"

She nodded, then looked at her younger brother. "Um, Hunter…I don't think you'll be swiping on Kipton."

He looked up and shot her a scowl. "I know that."

"Dude, did you need a moment or two alone with her photo?" Bradly teased.

Lily snatched her phone out of Hunter's hand. "Eww, gross!"

I let my head fall back as I enjoyed the heat of the sun. I was on my parents' ranch, sitting atop a new mare by the name of Tea. It was the first week of October and the days were starting to cool off, so I wanted to relish the warm sun while I still could.

Tea bounced her head and brought me back to the moment. Laughing, I rubbed her neck. "I know, girl. You worked hard this morning and want some playtime. Just a few more minutes, and she'll be here."

Tea snorted, and I laughed again. She was a spitfire, and I could see why my mother had decided to barrel train her. She would probably excel at the sport. Mom had a way of seeing things in the horses long before anyone else could.

"I can't tell what you're enjoying more: sitting on the horse or the sun on your face."

Looking down, I smiled at the sight of the love of my life walking toward me. Morgan in jeans, a long-sleeve T-shirt, and a baseball hat was one of the sexiest things I'd ever laid eyes on.

"Hey, what are you doing here?" I asked, hoping I sounded like I was surprised to see her.

Morgan slid between the wood planks of the pen and closed the distance between us. She moved her hands gently down Tea's neck, then she kissed the horse's cheek before looking up at me.

"Georgiana talked me into taking the rest of the day off and suggested I come out and ride Titan. It's been forever, so I thought it sounded like a great idea. Rex is getting him saddled up for me."

"Perfect timing. Tea's in the mood for going on a trail ride. Want to join us?"

Morgan chuckled. "Tea? As in the kind you drink?"

"Yep. I have a feeling she's a gossip in the pasture and knows all the good stuff."

The sound of a horse whinnying caused us both to turn.

Rex strolled over with Titan. "All set, Ms. Shaw."

I guided Tea to the gate while Morgan held it open for us to walk out before closing it behind us. "Rex, how many times do I have to tell you to call me Morgan?"

He blushed and looked down at the ground. "I'm sorry."

She took the reins from him. "Thank you."

"Thanks, Rex," I added as I smiled at the poor bastard. I knew exactly how it felt to admire the woman from afar. But now I was lucky enough to call her mine.

I watched Morgan easily mount her horse. She turned him around, then we walked side by side out of the barn area, and to one of the many trails on my parents' ranch.

"How has it been not having Avery there to help you at the store?" I asked.

"I miss seeing her every day. I definitely got used to it. She has such an eye for color, I swear. Georgiana thinks so as well. I wish she'd look into art classes."

"You think she could be a painter?"

Morgan shrugged. "Maybe. But…Avery was offered a modeling job."

"She was?"

"Yes!" she said with a happy laugh. "I mean, the girl is stunningly beautiful, and those deep sapphire eyes of hers are mesmerizing."

"Is she going to do it?"

Morgan's smile faded. "I don't think so. It's in Paris."

"Holy shit! Paris?"

"I know. Merit and Dirk are *not* thrilled. I think Avery wants to do it, though."

"Really?" I asked, surprised. "She'd want to leave her family and move to Paris?"

Morgan gave me a look. "You didn't see her face when Merit and Dirk told her she couldn't go."

"You were there?"

She nodded. "Avery asked me to be there when she talked to them about it. Do you know who Eden Briggs is?"

I shook my head. "No clue."

"I'm not surprised," she laughed. "She's a big-time model. Does all the large fashion shows and models a number of Mary's designs. That's how Avery met her. She came to the boutique, took one look at Avery, and said she needed to be in Paris modeling."

"Wow."

"Yeah, I know. Eden even called Merit and Dirk, said she'd make sure Avery still went to school. And she could stay with Eden over there, as well."

"I can see why they wouldn't want her to go. I mean, she's their little girl."

Morgan chewed on her lower lip. "I know she's only sixteen, but...I think they should let her try. If they don't, then Avery is going to spend the rest of her life wondering what could've happened if she'd been able to go."

"Then tell Merit and Dirk that."

"You think?"

I smiled, reached for her hand, and squeezed it. "I think."

We rode in silence for a bit.

"I saw Savannah this morning."

I snapped my head over to look at her. After Bradford was killed and the truth came out about everything he'd done, Savannah had left town. She never said goodbye or anything, just quit her job and took off. Her parents had been devastated, and I knew they were still worried about her.

"Is she back?" I asked. "How is she?"

Morgan gave me a sympathetic smile. "Ryan…God, it was so sad. She walked into the boutique and took one look at me and started to sob. I quickly walked her back to the office and shut the door. She practically tackled me as she hugged me, and then cried some more. It took her about ten minutes to finally calm down and be able to speak. She said she was so ashamed that she didn't realize what Bradford was up to that she couldn't face me—or anyone else. She's been in Boise, working for a news station there, and going to therapy."

"Good. I'm glad she's getting help."

"I am too," Morgan said softly. "She apologized, but I told her she had nothing to apologize for. She asked me if I'd talked to anyone professional, and I told her I've been seeing a therapist and that things are honestly going really well for me. She was glad to hear it, but I'm not sure the same goes for her. There was so much sadness in her eyes. It broke my heart."

"I can't imagine what it was like for her to know she was with a crazy lunatic."

"A monster, more like it. I think what messed with her the most was the same thing that bothered *me*."

"The cameras?"

She nodded. "Yeah. The fact that he was watching us. I hope she's able to find peace and happiness."

"Me too."

Letting out a huge sigh, Morgan raised her face to the sun. "Enough of that bullshit. Can we find an open pasture and let these two run for a bit? I want to feel the wind on my face."

"I think we can do that." I gave Tea a squeeze with my thighs, and she picked up her walk into a trot. A few minutes later, we were galloping free in a field. The smile on Morgan's face was like a gift from God. She looked so happy and care-free. I loved moments like this with her.

We stopped by the side of a small lake to let the horses take a break and graze for a bit. Morgan stood at the shore-line and stared at the mountain range in the distance. The sky was a beautiful deep blue with puffs of clouds that looked like someone had painted them on. The lake had a reflection of the sky and the mountains, and it was so calm it almost looked like glass.

"It's so beautiful," Morgan whispered. "It'll be snowing before we know it. It already is up in the mountains. Look at how white the snow seems from here."

I wrapped my arms around her, and she leaned back against my body. We stood there in silence as we took in the beauty that was Montana.

Morgan let out a long, deep sigh. "I don't ever want to leave here."

"Me neither. Bailey called me earlier."

She spun around in my arms and looked up at me. "Tell me she found some land."

"She found some land."

Morgan's eyes lit up. "Where? Is it close to Hamilton?"

I nodded.

"Close to your parents' ranch?"

"Oh yeah…pretty darn close."

She playfully hit me on the chest. "Tell me where, Ryan!"

Smiling, I said, "It's a fifty-acre ranch a mile west of here. So, it's closer to the mountain range."

Her eyes went wide. "The price?"

"The owner happens to be a good friend of my parents."

"Okay, did he say how much he wanted to sell it for?"

"Eight-hundred fifty-thousand."

Morgan's mouth dropped open. "For fifty acres? It's worth so much more."

"Do you want to go see it right now? I already told Bailey we might want to go look at it this afternoon."

She jumped into my arms and wrapped her legs around me. "Hell yes, I want to go see it!"

Chapter Thirty

Morgan

I had never been so excited in my life. Okay, that wasn't true. I was excited when Georgiana asked me to be partners with her at the boutique. And when Mary asked me to design wedding gowns for her new line. But owning land with Ryan, knowing we were taking a step toward our future, was a high I would never get again. I was positive of that.

Mr. Owens asked if we wanted to drive around the property in his side-by-side utility vehicle. Bailey sat up front with him while Ryan and I sat in the back. I nearly died when we came upon a herd of bighorn sheep. It wasn't like I had never seen them before, but there they were, grazing on our future land.

"It has an amazing view of the Bitterroot and Sapphire mountains," Ryan said as he laced his fingers with mine.

"It's stunning."

Mr. Owens craned his neck to talk to us. "There's a bridge up here that my grandfather built for my grandmother. This part of the land was her favorite. It goes over Lone Man's Creek, which runs right through the property. It really flows with the spring melt."

He came to a stop, and I got out of the vehicle and stared at the picture in front of me. A crystal-clear creek flowed at a decent clip—and standing at the edge, drinking water, was a herd of wild mustangs.

I hit Ryan in the chest. "Oh my God. Oh my God! Aunt Timberlynn would freak out right now!"

Ryan chuckled softly. "She would."

My aunt owned a horse rescue business, and wild mustangs were her favorite. I couldn't wait to show her this property. "Are they always on the land?" I asked Mr. Owens.

He nodded. "For as long as I can remember, and I grew up on this ranch. Getting too old to take care of it, though. I've also seen them with my horses in the pasture over by the ridge."

I slowly shook my head in disbelief.

"We can drive over the bridge," he said, "but I thought the two of you would like to take a stroll."

"That's a wonderful idea. Why don't you guys go walk for a bit? We'll be right here," Bailey said.

"I'd love to walk around," I said. "Thank you!"

Ryan and I started toward the bridge. As promised, it was wide enough for a truck to drive over, but I honestly wasn't so sure I'd want to attempt it. The thing looked pretty old.

"Not sure I'd want to drive over this bridge."

Laughing, I squeezed Ryan's hand. "I was thinking the same thing."

We walked along the creek in silence as we took in the views.

"I've been on this property plenty of times," Ryan said. "Up that hill right there is where I shot my first mule deer."

I stopped walking and looked at him. "Are you serious?"

He smiled as if recalling the memory. "I was so excited. I was exhausted from hiking through the snow and kept telling my father we were wasting our time. We came up over that ridge and bam! A herd of mule deer was standing there. Two huge bucks fighting. It was a sight I'll never forget."

"So the property already has memories for you?"

He nodded. "Yeah, it does."

I stopped walking and looked at the rolling foothills that led to the mountains beyond. "It doesn't even look real, it's so beautiful. The deep green mixed with the light green. Even in the beginning of fall, it still looks breathtaking. Can you imagine what the sunsets must look like?"

"I can," he replied. "There's something about that big sky and sunsets. No matter where you are in Montana, they're beautiful."

"So true," I whispered as I dropped Ryan's hand and stared out over the raw land. "Ryan, we have to get this place. It feels right. Like we were meant to be here. To live here and build our life here. Can you imagine raising our kids on this property?"

When I turned around to look at him, I sucked in a breath and stumbled back a few steps. Ryan was down on one knee—with an open ring box in his hands.

"I can imagine it. And if you'll do me the honor of becoming my wife, Morgan Elizabeth Shaw, I will try every day for the rest of my life to make you the happiest woman alive."

Falling to my knees in front of him, I cupped his face and tried to speak, but all that came out were sobs. Nodding my head, I whispered, "Yes. Ryan, yes!"

Ryan crushed his mouth to mine and kissed me with so much love, I swore I felt it coursing through my body.

When we broke apart, he leaned his forehead on mine. "I'm so glad you like this place...because I already own it."

I drew back and looked at him in shock. "What?"

He scrunched his nose and asked, "Are you mad? Please don't be mad! I had already asked Mr. Owens about buying it before we were...well, before we were serious. I've always loved this piece of land. The sale went through last month, but I was scared to death to tell you."

I felt a sobbing laugh escape, and I shook my head. "Ryan Marshall, why on earth would you be scared to tell me?"

"Well, it's a pretty big step, and you weren't part of the decision."

"If you already built a house, I'm going to be pissed."

He laughed. "No, no, I haven't built a house."

I placed my hand on the side of his face and felt such a sense of contentment. I wasn't the least bit upset because I knew in my heart of hearts that we were meant to own this land. "We're home."

He took my hand, placed it over his heart, and then put his hand on top of mine. "We're home."

"Put the ring on her finger already, so I can take the picture!" Georgiana shouted.

I whipped my head to the side to see Georgiana, Blayze, my parents, and Ryan's parents all standing there. "You all knew?"

They erupted in a chorus of laughter before my father shouted, "Yes! Now put the ring on her finger!"

Turning back to Ryan, I looked down at the beautiful cushion-cut diamond on a twisted band of white gold with strands of Pavé diamonds intertwined along each side.

"Ryan," I whispered. "It's beautiful."

"I hope you like the platinum band."

I smiled. "I thought it was white gold."

He shook his head. "You mentioned once that you like platinum."

Frowning, I asked, "When?"

A blush crept over his cheeks as he looked down at the ring on my hand. "I don't know…a few years ago. I was hoping you still liked it."

I sucked in a breath. "You remembered that?"

His eyes lifted and met mine. "There isn't anything about you, Morgan, that I've ever forgotten."

Tears rolled down my face as I wrapped my arms around his neck and buried my face in his neck. "I love you so much," I said softly.

Ryan held me tighter. "Not as much as I love you."

Drawing back, I smiled and let out a small laugh. "I want to do something crazy."

Glancing at our families, now standing a few yards away, Ryan looked back at me and lowered his voice. "I don't think your dad would appreciate us sneaking off and…you know." He wiggled his brows.

I shook my head, laughing. "No. I want to get married here, on our land."

"Okay, I love that idea."

"As soon as possible."

His eyes went wide while his mouth opened and closed. He stared at me like I'd lost my mind.

"Did I hear you say you wanted to get married as soon as possible?" my mother asked, rushing over to us.

Ryan managed to stand and help me up, but he still hadn't said anything.

"Yep. The sooner the better. Nothing fancy—just us, our families, a few friends, and this," I said as I threw out my arms and spun around.

"Wait. Morgan, you really don't want a big wedding?" Ryan asked.

I shook my head. "Nope. I want it to only be us and our loved ones. I want to be married to you as quickly as possible."

A wide grin broke out on Ryan's face. "I'm game if you are."

I jumped and clapped and then threw myself back into his arms. Putting my mouth to his ear, I whispered, "And by 'us,' I mean you, me, and the baby."

Ryan froze, and I had to bury my face into his neck to keep from giggling. He walked us farther away from our families, who were already busy making plans for an impromptu wedding.

He stopped several yards away and held both of my hands as he lowered his voice. "We're going to be parents?"

Nodding, I smiled so hard my cheeks hurt. "I know we didn't talk about it or plan it, but we're not always in control of certain things."

"Holy shit! I want to grab you and spin you around and yell out to the mountains and cry like a goddamn baby—but I'm guessing you don't want anyone to know yet?"

"Not yet. I'm barely over five weeks. I found out yesterday, when I went to the doctor to be tested. I didn't want to take a home test for…silly reasons."

He placed his hand on the side of my face. "They're not silly. And I love you so damn much."

"I love you too. Now, can you go back over there and pretend I didn't just drop a bomb on you?"

After kissing me quickly on the lips, Ryan nodded. "I can."

Holding hands, we walked back toward our families, both of us wearing smiles that probably gave away the bomb I had, in fact, just dropped. If they noticed, no one said anything.

Except for Georgiana, who looked at me and tilted her head slightly, wearing a smile that mirrored my own. My eyes went wide, and before I could say a word, she winked.

"Oh, this is going to be so much fun!" I whispered as I let out a happy laugh.

Epilogue

HUNTER

My father and mother stared at me as they let what I'd told them sink in.

When I couldn't take the silence any longer, I asked, "Are you both in shock, or should I be worried or something?"

"A reality dating show?" my father asked.

Mom scrunched her nose. "Called...*Swipe Right*?"

I nodded. "*The challenges of dating in the real world...* that's the tagline."

"But...it's reality TV...how is that the *real world*?" Dad asked.

Running my fingers through my hair, I sighed. "It's not, really...but Dad, they're offering to donate a crazy amount of money to your foundation. It could build a new outdoor arena *and* the toddler water park we talked about."

"Is this something you *want* to do, Hunter?" Dad asked.

My mind drifted back to that image of Kipton Howse, but I quickly shoved it away. "I wasn't on board at first, but if we get something good out of it, then what harm could it do? They want to film a lot of it on the ranch, though, and I won't agree to do it if you say no. Plus, they mentioned filming during my winter break, but their filming schedule is for two months. I'd have to take the spring semester off or work it out with the school to do remote classes in January. It's only a few weeks, so I'm sure they'd be on board. That way I can still compete in the circuit this spring."

My father looked at my mom, then turned back to me and smiled. It wasn't the kind of smile that gave me a feel-good vibe. No, it was the kind of smile that made me shudder.

Then I looked over at my mother. And she had an evil glint in her eye.

"I don't like the way you're looking at me," I said, glancing between them.

"I say do it!" Dad announced. "This should be one hell of a ride."

Mom covered her mouth with her hand in a sad attempt to hide the tiny burst of laughter that slipped free.

"You…you *want* me to do it?" I wouldn't lie, I had actually been hoping they'd say no. "And you're okay with them filming on the ranch?"

They both nodded. "But only if the school will let you take remote classes," Mom warned. "You know how we feel about you finishing college."

I blinked, looking back and forth between them.

"What's the matter, son? You look a little pale," Dad smirked as he reached over and hit me on the side of the arm. "Who knows? We may even get a new daughter-in-law out of this."

My mouth dropped open, and I stared as they both stood, joined hands, and walked out of the room…laughing their asses off.

Look for *Brave Enough*, book 3
in the Love in Montana series on August 29, 2023.

ABOUT THE AUTHOR

Kelly Elliott is a *New York Times* and *USA Today* bestselling contemporary romance author. Since finishing her bestelling Wanted series, Kelly has continued to spread her wings while remaining true to her roots with stories of hot men, strong women, and beautiful surroundings. Her bestselling works included *Wanted, Broken, Without You,* and *Lost Love.* Elliott has been passionate about writing since she was fifteen. After years of filling journals with stories, she finally followed her dream and published her first novel, Wanted, in November 2012.

Elliott lives in Central Texas with her husband, daughter, and two pups. When she's not writing, she enjoys reading and spending time with her family. She is down to earth and very in touch with her readers, both on social media and at signings. To learn more about Kelly and her books, you can find her through her website, www.kellyelliottauthor.com.

CONNECT WITH KELLY ELLIOTT

Kelly's Facebook Page
www.facebook.com/kellyelliottauthor

Kelly's Amazon Author Page
https://goo.gl/RGVXqv

Follow Kelly on Instagram
www.instagram.com/authorkellyelliott

Follow Kelly on BookBub
www.bookbub.com/profile/kelly-elliott

Kelly's Pinterest Page
www.pinterest.com/authorkellyelliott

Kelly's Author Website
www.kellyelliottauthor.com

Made in the USA
Monee, IL
20 June 2023

36438566R00163